A Deal With God

The Power of One

Michael Haden

A Deal With God is a work of fiction. Names, characters, places, and incidents either are the product of the author's imagination or are used fictitiously. Any resemblance to actual persons, living or dead, events, or locales is entirely coincidental.

PUBLISHED BY DENCO MEDIA

Copyright © 2011 Dean M. Polizzi
All rights reserved.
ISBN-10: 0984747400
ISBN-13: 978-0-9847474-0-5

DEDICATION

This book is dedicated to all the young girls who overcame great obstacles to become great women.

ACKNOWLEDGMENTS

A very special thanks to God, my wife Doreen, Adam Camuti, Dean Hutchison, Tony Miller, Dr. Clark Hersey, Kelly Hersey, Dr. Gilbert, Donna Brazelton, and Jackie Logemann.

A thank you so much to Mom and Dad, Haden, Jenna, and Alexandrea; Mike and Mary Morris. James Stauber, Emily Evans, Amy DeWitt, Edna Dunston, Suzanne Beauchaine, Marianne Screnock, Mr. Regan Upshaw, all of my in-laws and out-laws, The Rumores, The Arroyos, everyone at FC Tampa Soccer Club, M.A.D.D., and all friends and acquaintances that offered help, guidance, and inspiration along the way.

CONTENTS

PREFACE

In 1976 Elton Johns' lyricist Bernie Taupin wrote the chorus for a song on the Blue Moves album asking the question "If there's a God in Heaven what's He waiting for? If He can't hear the children, then He must see the war, but it seems to me that He leads his lambs to the slaughter house not the Promised Land."

I always equated what you hear about God outside of the church and outside of the Bible to what you hear on the evening news. You basically hear about the bad things and rarely about the good just like you hear a lot of the bad things being blamed on God. Maybe the reason you don't hear about the good things he does is because it's part of the deal.

CHAPTER 1
REBECCAH SAMUELS

Rebeccah Johnson met Leon Samuels her junior year when they were both in college. They were at a big party and were very much attracted to each other, which soon led to a steady dating relationship. One fateful summer night as the young couple celebrated Rebeccah's 21st birthday, too much wine temporarily clouded their judgment. Three weeks later, a home pregnancy test confirmed what Rebeccah suspected; she was pregnant.

Leon and Rebeccah were both Christians. So, not having the baby was never considered. However, as far as Rebeccah was concerned, the timing could not have been worse.

Leon asked Rebeccah to marry him and the hastily arranged wedding went smoothly. But, in the remaining 7 months of her pregnancy she could only complete 30 of the 48 credit hours she needed to graduate. With 18 credit hours still required, Matthew was born. She vowed to finish college within the next couple of years. But, only 5 months after the birth of Matthew she was pregnant again with baby Mark.

Rebeccah was from Macon Georgia. Leon was from Athens Georgia. When they married, they decided to move to the middle to Morrison Georgia. Leon could commute to the beverage distributorship that he drove a truck for in less than half an hour. Rebeccah could get to her parents house in 55 minutes.

Due to their youth and Leon being relatively new at his job they could not qualify for the house Rebeccah liked in Morrison. Leon found a great deal on a house they could qualify for in neighboring Dothan, but Dothan never really grew on Rebeccah.

Soon, Matthew started 1st grade and Mark started Kindergarten. Rebeccah re-enrolled in college. She decided to start with 9 credit hours - 3 classes worth 3 credit hours each. If she made good grades, she could go back for the spring semester and finish the last 9 hours and graduate.

It was a solid plan. Unfortunately, college is easier when you're single and without children. She received two passing grades which earned her 6 more credit hours. However, she had to drop the third class because it was a core class that was very difficult and time consuming. She was frustrated things were not going the way she wanted.

Rebeccah finished the semester in December needing 12 more credit hours to graduate. That January, she signed up for two classes, both core. She hoped reducing her course load would make things easier. Then, lightning struck a third time. As she was gearing up for the new semester, she missed her period, found out she was pregnant, and struggled with the worst morning sickness of her three pregnancies.

By the time she started feeling better and was able to focus on her class work and studies, she was far behind. If she dropped these two classes it would be nearly impossible to add them at a later date. She was running out of drop/adds and her grade point average was falling.

Rebeccah was depressed and starting to resign herself to being a non-college graduate. She was heartbroken. Unfairly, she blamed Leon for her predicament. She hated being a "housewife."

On August 23rd, Luke was born. At first, she tried to make the best of the situation. Rebeccah occupied herself running the household. She paid the bills, made the domestic purchases, and handled all the decisions about the boys.

She also started lashing out at Leon more and more. Leon didn't understand why, but he didn't complain. Rebeccah showed him less affection and attention than ever. She yelled at the boys frequently and habitually reminded Leon their house was too small, especially for five people.

Unfortunately, having more dependants doesn't raise your credit score.

Rebeccah had grown to appreciate the peace and quiet she enjoyed during the day when Matthew and Mark were at school. Now, she felt she was back at square one with a baby demanding all her time. She became more depressed and her relationships with Leon, Matthew and Mark suffered.

As Luke's second birthday approached, Rebeccah became even more withdrawn. On weekends, she would take Leon's truck to her parents' home leaving the boys with Leon. Sometimes she would leave Saturday morning and not come home until Sunday night. Sunday mornings, Leon would carry Luke and walk the half mile to church with Matthew and Mark walking by his side. Still, Leon never grumbled.

After about a month of this, Rebeccah's parents told her to get her head together and start being a better wife and mother. She realized her mindset was not where it needed to be and she started putting things into perspective. She began cooking and cleaning for the boys like she used to. As her mood improved she was easier to get along with.

Even though she felt she didn't have the temperament or patience, Rebeccah was trying to become a more loving, nurturing mother. Things were slowly but surely improving in the Samuels' household.

Luke was almost three years old now. He was easier to care for compared to when he was an infant. He could entertain himself by playing with toys or watching TV. He could get his own snacks and took regular naps.

Rebeccah was now thirty-two years old. She had been a very healthy child and a relatively healthy adult. But, on a hot August 21st night, she went to bed early and never woke up. She suffered a brain aneurysm in her sleep.

It was a strange sensation. Rebeccah felt her body floating thru an immense tunnel and could see a brilliant yellow light in the distance. At first, she was drawn to the light. Then she had a premonition. It was a chilling vision about her son Mark.

Mark was Rebeccah's middle son who was now nine years old. But, in her vision she saw Mark as a teenager roaming the high school grounds with another boy shooting and killing classmates at random. Mark still had a gun in his hand when the policeman shot him.

Rebeccah was horrified realizing her son's tragic future. Overcome with emotion she collapsed to the tunnel's floor.

Motionless, she began to pray.

Rebeccah was horrified, realizing her family's tragic fate. She completely shut down. She remained on to the tunnels' floor and did not move. No matter how strong the force was Rebeccah still did not move.

God saw what had happened and it was a mistake. No one leaving this realm should have to see their family's fate, especially a fate this terrible. God took mercy on Rebeccah. She did not deserve to be a tortured soul. God reached out to Rebeccah.

"Rebeccah your life has ended and this will not be changed. But, if you will proceed to the light, I will send someone to watch over your family. And, what you saw in your vision will not happen. I need an immediate response if you desire my help."

Rebeccah, filled with gratitude, immediately agreed and entered the light.

"Bring me Deana Murphy," God demanded, "the young woman in the coma from Tampa."

CHAPTER 2
DEANA MURPHY

Deana Murphy is an extraordinary young woman. The first thirteen years of her life were absolutely horrific, sad and brutal. I cried the first time I wrote the beginning of this chapter because it was difficult to write the words to describe what Deana had to endure. Her resiliency is beyond belief.

She was born August 22nd, 1987. Her biological father was never in her life. He left Deana's mother before she was born. Jamie Murphy, Deana's mom, moved forward the best she could with all of the challenges of being a single mother.

In 1990, due to complications from an illness and not enough money for proper medical attention, Jamie passed away.

Jamie's parents had died years earlier and there were no suitable family members to care for Deana.

Deana became a ward to the state of Florida. A family in Tampa with a biological 4 year old daughter provided foster care for Deana. Deana would soon celebrate her 3rd birthday. The household was middle class. In the beginning the mother and father were attentive and nurturing.

Even though Deana had no surviving biological parents, she led a pretty normal life. She did very well in school and seemed to prosper in her foster home. Everything was fine and ordinary thru 5th grade.

Tragically, in the summer before 6th grade, one of the worst things that could happen to a child took place. To this day no one really understands what drove Deana's foster father to sexually assault her. In an effort to cover his crime, after he got Deana pregnant he forced her to have an abortion.

The procedure went horribly wrong. The combination of an inept doctor and a rushed job left Deana with complications. Imagine being twelve years old and receiving the news that you'll be sterile for life.

The foster father was found out; his own wife turned him in. He was arrested and prosecuted by the State. He was sentenced to eight years in a tough Federal penitentiary. Three years into his sentence he got into an altercation with another prisoner. He was beaten and left to die on the cold prison cement floor. Child predators don't do well in prison.

Deana had been the lead witness and required to testify frequently. The court appearances physically made her sick to her stomach and depressed her. She spent her junior high school years in courtrooms with her school books desperately trying not to get behind. Her focus on her schoolwork was steadfast and helped keep her mind off the trial.

Even in the midst of her tragedy God was working. A Tampa attorney, who wished to remain anonymous, heard about Deana. He was well off and a man of faith. He paid a very reputable Christian orphanage to take Deana in.

Alfred and Myra Wilson had six boys with ages ranging from 4 to 11 at their foster home. There was an autistic ten year old girl named Tammy that the Wilsons were told would be almost impossible to place. The Wilsons were willing to foster parent the girl, but putting her in with six boys created a problem. The attorney brought Deana to the Wilsons and it was a good fit. They could foster Deana and Tammy by giving them their own room together and putting the boys together in other rooms.

The orphanage was designed for two adults and eight children. Deana was almost thirteen and would be the oldest. She liked being the oldest because the Wilsons treated her like a young adult and not a child.

The Wilsons almost felt guilty having Deana help cook, clean and assist with the younger children. But, they were both in their 60's and having Deana was a blessing.

While at the orphanage, Deana got to go to church on Wednesday nights and Sundays. This is when she first learned about Jesus; accepted Him as her Savior and was baptized. It was important to Deana to get her life back on the right track, especially with the beginning of high school approaching.

Deana loved to play soccer. She did not have a true athlete's body. She was only of average height, on the heavy side and not real fast. She was, however, smart, tenacious and an extremely hard worker.

Her coaches stressed teamwork, discipline and the willingness to give extra effort. Even if you think you can't, you can if you have faith.

At first, the team was not very good. They lost a lot of games, sometimes badly. The coaches never got mad or yelled at the team. Instead, the coaches and girls arrived at practice earlier and stayed later. Their training was very intense.

The coaches emphasized taking the initiative and being a catalyst. The coaches did not believe in star players. When one player took the lead by forcing a turnover or making a big play to set up a goal by giving extra effort, the other girls were expected to do the same.

Instead of losing 5-1, the losses were becoming more like 4-3. As they learned to play better team defense the scores became 2-2 and 1-1. Teams that used to beat them badly now were struggling to beat them.

The following season, all of the hard work started paying dividends. What used to be close losses were now ties and close victories. Eight wins, two losses and four ties earned a division championship. Winning a division championship earned them the opportunity to play for the State Championship.

Properly named, the state championship tournament is called the "State Cup." The top teams play against each other. When it's down to the final sixteen teams it becomes a single elimination tournament.

Deana's Tampa team won its first four games and they were now in the final four. A fringe benefit for the girls was that the end of this tournament was played in Cocoa Beach. The girls enjoyed a nice little road trip. They knew they were long shots to win the championship, but just being there was exciting in its own right.

The first game was against Southside. One of the players on Southside was the daughter of a popular professional football player. There was actually a member of the national media at the game.

The Southside team was the fastest team in the

tournament. Southside was a team that could easily beat you 7-0 if you did not bring your best effort. Southside scored within the first four minutes. They scored again before the half. Tampa was down 2-0 and it was an intense talk at halftime.

The head coach told them they needed to play with even more heart and passion than they did in the first half. He led a prayer for the strength to dig down deep into their hearts. Every girl had to play to 100 percent of her potential.

In the second half, Southside's defense stole the ball from Tampa and chipped the ball high to their best midfielder. Deana played defensive midfield and had done a really nice job defending this girl so far. In the first half, the girl had tried to overpower Deana. At the time, Deana was almost 5'4, 155 pounds and solid as a rock. The Southside girl had been unsuccessful; Deana was too strong.

Deana figured this time the girl would try something different. Deana was afraid of the girl going wide on her and beating Deana with her speed. So Deana spread her cleats wide to take that away. Deana wanted to bait and dare the girl to try to go thru Deana's legs with the ball.

Dribbling the soccer ball between an opponent's legs is called a "meg." It helps an offensive player get from point "A" to point "B" as quick as possible. But, you have to execute it correctly.

Sure enough, the Southside player went for the "meg" and as she did Deana buckled her right leg making a literal bar out of it. This technique traps the ball to the defender as the dribbler runs past having lost possession.

Eighteen girls on the field went the direction of the girl they thought had the ball. The Tampa left winger Meghan went the other way as did Deana with the ball. Deana had a clear path to the goal on the right side as she dribbled around a lone Southside defender. The Southside goalie now had to challenge Deana because Deana was raising her leg to shoot. Deana stared at the right post and the goalie dove that way.

Instead of shooting, Deana passed the ball left. Meghan had stayed onside so she was in a trailing position. The pass was a bit out in front of Meghan but Deana had sold the fake so brilliantly, Meghan could have walked the ball into the goal. Meghan scored and the Southside lead was cut to 2-1.

Tampa now had the momentum and felt they could beat Southside if they could somehow score the next goal. You could see how motivated Tampa was by the increased tempo of the game. There were no more smiles on any players' faces, just serious and focused expressions. There were good shots by both teams and good saves by both goalies.

One of the shots by Tampa was really hard and fast and the Southside goalie did not think she could catch the ball cleanly.

She decided to punch the ball out into the field as hard as she could to clear the ball out of the defensive zone. The ball went past Tampa's offense and Southside's defense. The ball landed between the top of the eighteen yard box and the midfield line.

Tampa's smallest midfielder, Alexa, was also one of Tampa's fastest players. She was the anchor on her high school track team. She sped to the ball, which was still bouncing. She got her foot up under the ball and kicked it as hard as she could. The ball whizzed rapidly past a Southside player's ear. By the time the goalie tried to make a play on the ball it was already heading into the back of the net. Tampa 2, Southside 2.

The game ended tied 2-2. At that time they played "Golden Goal." Basically, the girls have an extra 30 minutes to play until someone scores. If no one scores they do a shootout.

The overtime seemed to last forever. Then, a Southside player made a hand ball infraction inside their own defensive eighteen yard box. Tampa was awarded a penalty kick and they scored off of it. Tampa 3, Southside 2.

Later that afternoon they had to play in the finals. They were going up against a team from Jacksonville. Jacksonville was ranked 7th in the country. Tampa lost 4-1, but finishing 2nd out of thirty-eight teams in Division One was outstanding. Each girl received a large trophy. Deana said it was the first time she'd ever received any kind of accolade other than Honor Roll at school.

She was now sixteen and good enough to make her high school Varsity team. Even though she was only a sophomore, she started every game and played every minute. The high school team lost most of their games, but Deana earned the respect of every team she played. She had the reputation for being a fierce competitor. Her coaches to this day remember the huge effort she always gave.

As Deana approached age seventeen, the Wilsons were now approaching their upper sixties. The orphanage was down to four boys, plus Tammy and Deana. Deana was afraid the Wilsons would have to close the orphanage if it got to be too much work for them to handle. Deana took on even more responsibilities to make things easier for the Wilsons.

With the help of Mrs. Wilson, Deana was becoming an above average cook. She also had a penchant for dealing with and mentoring her foster brothers. Mr. Wilson had an amazing ability to reconcile any differences that arose among the boys. He had a natural way with children, even ones with difficult personalities. Mr. Wilson was the master of using positive rewards and incentives to motivate the kids.

Deana also seemed to have natural parenting skills, much of which she learned from the Wilsons. Being an orphan herself, she wanted to one day adopt children of her own and be an excellent mother.

Deana earned very high grades in high school and qualified for a substantial amount of grant, aid and scholarship money for college. She figured if she could handle a job working twenty to thirty hours a week and still keep her grades up, she could get thru college with very little debt when she graduated.

Deana stayed in Tampa to go to college. She attended The University of South Florida. Her grant money covered most of her tuition, dorm expenses and the school food program.

She got a job waiting tables at a local full service Italian restaurant. She went to class from 9am to 3:30, and then worked from 4:30 to 9:30. Waiting tables wasn't exactly Deana's passion. She'd have to lug heavy trays and clean up big messes. Nonetheless, living at the orphanage had prepared her well for this job. She was, in her own right, a very good waitress.

Unfortunately for Deana, she seldom had the free time enjoyed by most teenage girls. When she was done with work or had a day off she would study to keep her grades high so the grant and aid money would keep coming in. Despite her difficult schedule, she never complained or felt sorry for herself.

Deana graduated college April, 2011. She got her Bachelor of Arts degree in Business Administration. She got a job at a finance company that made loans to families and small businesses. Her company also did mortgage loans. Handling the mortgage loans was her preference, but she would need more experience and training to advance in her career.

On June 4th 2012, a husband and wife were scheduled to come to the office where Deana worked to fill out an application for a small home improvement loan. They called to say they were running late. They didn't get to the office until 8:20 pm. By the time the loan was approved and the paperwork finished, it was well after 10 o'clock. Deana got in her Dodge Stratus intending to drive home to her apartment so she could enjoy a long overdue dinner.

She was driving north on Dale Mabry Highway, having just passed the Busch Boulevard overpass. A drunk driver going southbound jumped the median and went into Deana's car head on. Deana was knocked unconscious and into a coma that would last over eleven weeks.

Late in the evening of August 21st Deana was in the intensive care unit at a Tampa hospital. Over the weeks since she'd been brought in, she'd seemed to be improving.

It was shocking to the Intensive Care Unit nurse when the machine monitoring Deana's vital signs suddenly flat lined.

Deana felt her body floating thru a huge tunnel with a dazzling yellow light in the distance.

Deana was heartbroken, shaken and panic stricken. She screamed at the top of her lungs: "Lord please don't take me yet.

I have worked so hard to turn my life around. Please give me one more chance. I will do anything, I mean anything if you will send me back."

"Deana Murphy," God said, "I will send you back but there will be strict parameters."

"You will move permanently to Dothan, Georgia."

"A realty man named McGee will rent to you and watch out for you."

"His niece Delores will help you find work."

"You are to become the new matriarch of the Samuels' family. The father Leon is a good man."

"You are to meet the Samuels this November 4th, at Dothan Christian Church."

"On April 20, 2020, the middle son Mark will be harmed at his school. You must prevent this. Tell no one of this deal. Do your best, you have my blessing."

When Deana had flat lined the ICU nurse summoned the emergency room doctor and performed CPR. Within 20 seconds the doctor rushed to Deana's bed. Deana's vital signs returned to normal.

In a loud, firm voice Deana said the word: "DEAL!"

CHAPTER 3
LEAVING TAMPA

"Happy Birthday Miss Murphy," the emergency room doctor said to Deana, as he was reading her chart. "Well Happy Birthday in about six more minutes." It was 11:54pm.

"But doctor, it won't be my birthday for two and a half more months."

"Well, Miss Murphy, here's the story. The night you came in was June 4th. You've been in a coma for over eleven weeks. In a few minutes it will be August 22nd."

"You must be kidding." However, as Deana looked around the intensive care ward she realized it was no joke.

"How do you pronounce your first name Miss Murphy?" The doctor asked politely.

"DEE-nuh, with only two syllables. The first 'a' is silent." As Deana responded to the doctor she had been looking around for a mirror. She saw her reflection in a glass and something did not look right. "How bad and how permanent are my injuries? May I have a mirror to see my face?"

The doctor paused before replying. "Your head injuries are minor and you seem to have no brain trauma, so you should end up being fine. During your eleven week coma, your broken bones healed and our emergency room doctor and his ophthalmologist colleague Dr. Roberts did an amazing job saving your eyes. You're very lucky, Deana. The night you came in on June 4th, glass from your windshield was embedded in your eyes. Usually when patients come into the emergency room like you did, the main objective is to stabilize you only. But in your case the doctor was afraid of permanent blindness if the glass was not removed immediately. Your vision seems fine and your eyes look beautiful. Are you seeing everything clearly Deana?"

"As long as I keep from crying, my vision seems normal. But my nose and chin look strange."

The nurse had given Deana a mirror.

"Your chin and nose can be corrected with simple procedures. The damage to your chest can also be repaired. They do amazing things with cosmetic surgery after your kind of accident."

Deana reached down to her breasts and started to cry. There wasn't much left under the bandages.

"Honest Deana, the damage can be fixed. Look at it this way, the insurance company has a financial incentive to bring in the very best reconstructive specialists. If you take them to court and show permanent disfigurement to the jury, you'll receive hundreds of thousands of dollars in compensation. They don't want to pay that kind of money. By making you look good they can pay you a much smaller settlement. I can have someone help you find which insurance agent to deal with. The important thing now is getting you well."

The next day was one MRI after another. The hospital's doctors wanted to confirm there was no brain damage. She was even given a CT scan.

Deana appeared alert, coherent, and sharp. She was, however, having trouble walking. The healing process would require extensive physical therapy. Deana thought to herself, I have to regain my strength, get three surgeries and be in Dothan by November 4th. I'm understanding the gist of strict parameters.

She asked to talk to the doctor to figure out a game plan. Dr. James was the doctor from the previous night and Deana felt comfortable talking to him.

When Dr. James came to her bedside he sought to boost Deana's spirits, "Your dark brown hair has grown three or four inches since you first got here. It looks really flattering with your complexion and green eyes. Also, they've scheduled your cosmetic surgery for next Tuesday. Between now and then we need to get you walking, even if it's with crutches."

"Thank for the compliment, Dr. James. I'm grateful for all you've done for me. I've been doing some thinking and before we map out my rehab schedule I should let you know I'm moving to Georgia. I have to be there the 1st week of November, if not sooner. My entire future depends on this move."

"Deana, this accident was very serious. You are going to need months, if not years, of therapy. If you can walk without a limp or without crutches by November it will be a minor miracle. But if you're more comfortable rehabbing there, it's your call. Would you mind if I asked you why the quick move?"

"I want to live in a small town where the pace is slower and I don't have to drive so much. I also have someone to look out for me in Georgia. In addition, I've kind of been set up on a blind date." Deana laughed lightly.

"Oh, a love interest. Your date may go better if you can walk without braces or crutches."

"Yes sir, exactly. I'm open to any suggestions that will help me speed up my recovery. I'll work day and night as hard as I can."

"You have the right attitude, Deana. This next week will be critical. You need to get your muscles working before your surgeries because you'll need some down time to recover. Get a good night's sleep and get to the rehab center first thing in the morning. The insurance agent left a message saying he can come by tomorrow around lunchtime."

The next day Deana was up shortly after dawn. The physical therapist put her on a machine like a treadmill. The difference was there were bars on both sides to hold on to. The problem was her arms were as weak as her legs from being immobile so long. She was getting discouraged.

The physical therapist was quick to reassure Deana. "Why don't we do some exercises to build up your arms first? Then you can ride an exercise bike. In a few days we'll try the treadmill again."

By ten o'clock she was utterly exhausted. The physical therapist was amazed Deana made it through almost three hours of therapy.

Deana went back to her room. She had a friend go over to her apartment to retrieve her lap top computer. By pressing a few keys Deana quickly paid almost three months of bills. After checking her account balance online she felt a twinge of nervousness about how low she was getting on money.

She grabbed a snack, said a quick prayer and hoped everything would go well with the insurance agent.

Promptly at 12pm, a distinguished man in his late forties came to see Deana. He introduced himself and sat about ten feet away from her.

"I see you're going to get your three surgeries next Tuesday. Are you sure you don't want to do your nose and chin next week and your chest maybe a week or two later?"

"I have to be in Georgia by the end of October or the start of November. It's imperative I'm up there by then. It should speed up my physical therapy to have as little down time as possible."

"If the doctors are fine with that, we're more than happy to oblige you. We'll take care of anything medical you need. Also, if we can forego the attorneys, I can get you a quick cash settlement so you can have money for a new car and your moving expenses."

Deana, being a Finance major, had a quick reply. "I'm going to be looking for a little more than moving money. Besides the ten thousand for a replacement Dodge Stratus SXT I expect fifteen thousand for lost wages and an additional ten thousand for pain and suffering. If you write a check for thirty-five thousand dollars, I won't hire an attorney and I will sign off for you."

"That sounds fair. Let me talk to my manager and I'll let

you know. Tomorrow is Friday. I'll come back tomorrow afternoon and we can readdress this issue. Thank you Miss Murphy. It was a pleasure meeting you."

"Thank you," Deana replied. She said another prayer and took a nap. At 3:30pm she woke up and buzzed the nurse. "I'm ready to go back to the rehab center."

The nurse looked at Deana like she was crazy. "You worked out for three hours this morning. You need your rest. Tomorrow is another day."

"If I lay in bed all day, I'll never get better. I've been working out at a very slow tempo. I know I can do another half hour. Please?"

"Let me ask the doctor." Ten minutes later the nurse was back with a wheelchair. "He said all right if you agree to take it easy."

Deana nodded and was soon back at the rehab center. At six o'clock they asked her to leave. They could tell she had done enough for one day.

"You are going to be sore tomorrow young lady," the floor physical therapist said. Unfortunately, he was right.

At 7am the next morning Deana was practically unable to move. She was sore in parts of her body she didn't know she had. Nonetheless, she buzzed the nurse and asked to go back to the rehab center. She didn't care how uncomfortable she was, she wasn't going to lay around all day. She pushed herself hard to make progress, no matter how small the improvement.

Deana did three more hours of exercises. She went even slower than the previous day. She didn't care. She wanted to do the treadmill by Monday, before her surgeries.

After a three hour nap, she was still exhausted. She would have slept even longer but at two o'clock the insurance agent called to say he was on his way back to her room.

"I think I have good news for you Miss Murphy. I mean at least it's not bad news. You can replace your Stratus for about $8,500 dollars. They usually don't give more than $10,000 for lost wages without a lot of IRS return scrutiny, and it's tough to get $10,000 for pain and suffering because it's so hard to gauge. My manager wanted me to offer you $25,000, but I told him I didn't think you'd settle for less than $30,000. He okayed the $30,000. I have the check and the paperwork here in my briefcase."

"I'll accept the settlement, however, I think an attorney could have gotten me a lot more."

The agent smiled at Deana. "Yes and no. Maybe you'd get $75,000 or $100,000, but an attorney typically keeps 30-40% of the settlement. Also, you wouldn't see a dime for two to three years. Plus, think of all the time you'd spend in court. All things considered, this is better."

Deana halfheartedly agreed. She took the check and signed

the papers, realizing there was no way she could go thru a lengthy court process in Florida.

Three-thirty approached and Deana buzzed the nurse. "I have to do at least a little more, I can tell I'm getting stronger."

Deana suffered a setback. She tried the treadmill again but her right leg buckled and she fell forward onto her hands and knees. She wanted to cry. She gathered herself, asked to be moved to the stationary bike and did the easier exercise. She did leg presses and leg curls. She did the bench press. After two hours the therapists sent her back to her room. They were afraid of Deana going too hard and hurting herself.

Saturday morning at 7am, Deana was back for more. She was sore, tired, and in a bad mood. She was, however, motivated. She did the bench press, bicep curls, leg presses, and leg curls.

As she was doing her leg exercises Dr. James came into the hospital rehab center. It was his day off and Deana was happy, yet surprised to see him. An intern was following him with a big bag of equipment.

"I have something that may help you get over the hump, Deana. This is pretty cutting edge physical therapy. It's a generic version of an exercise they are doing at some of the Veteran Administration hospitals for the returning injured soldiers."

The first item from the bag was installed over the treadmill Deana was having trouble with. It looked like a canopy. Straps dropped down and offered far more support than when she tried to use it with just the handrails. There were four straps. Two of the straps went between her legs and were very uncomfortable and somewhat embarrassing.

Deana did not let that stop her. She did the exercise and walked for the first time in almost twelve weeks. Deana was probably only supporting 30% of her weight but she was thrilled and optimistic she would be walking on her own soon.

Deana worked out hard thru the weekend and on Monday. She made progress every day. Her Monday workout would be her last until Saturday.

Surgery was Tuesday morning and she'd need three additional days doing nothing but resting for recovery. The surgeries went well with no glitches. It was nice having a normal feeling chest again. Even more so, it was nice not having her nose and chin sitting sideways on her face.

Saturday morning Dr. James brought the treadmill apparatus for her again. It was a big help because it was an exercise that actually simulated walking. She worked hard all weekend and took Labor Day Monday off.

On Tuesday at 7am she was back for more rehab. When she returned to her room at ten she went online to look for her replacement Stratus. A Dodge dealer two towns north had a black 2005 Stratus SXT almost identical to Deana's white Stratus SXT.

Deana's had a few thousand less miles but that was the only difference.

The dealer was asking $9500 and Deana offered $9000. They split the difference. The dealership brought the car to the hospital, let her test drive it, finished the paperwork and Deana was back in the saddle again, so to say.

Driving a car the first time after a bad accident can be very traumatic. It was for Deana. She was scared to death. It was a very short test drive. She had no idea how she was going to drive six hours to Dothan in seven weeks.

As Deana's strength improved, her physical therapy was becoming more intense and diverse. There was lots of core training. Soon, Deana was doing sit-ups and bridges with a physio ball.

She was also doing proprioception exercises to help with her balance and agility. They had her wear a gait belt which was attached to a rolling four wheel walker. Progress was coming faster and faster. It looked like she'd be able to go home in two to three weeks. She'd have to walk with crutches or a cane but she would be self reliant.

Deana's boss from work came to visit her that evening. She brought Deana her sick pay and vacation allowance because she worried Deana would have trouble paying her bills. Deana was very grateful.

Deana did not know how to tell her boss about moving to Georgia. Her boss, however, made it easier by asking Deana when she would be back to work.

It was then Deana admitted she would not be staying in Tampa. She told her boss she needed a slower, quieter life and she was moving to Dothan, Georgia.

"Dothan sounds like a very small town. Where will you be working? Do you need a reference?"

Deana was stopped dead in her tracks. She hesitated, thought a minute, and then answered the best she could. "I'll be working with my friend Delores at her business." It was the best answer she could think of.

Her boss looked disappointed. "We'll miss you Deana. You're very bright with so much potential. If things don't work out in Georgia, please come back to Tampa and work for us again."

Deana thanked her and expressed her sincere gratitude. In the bottom of her heart though, she knew she was never coming back.

Deana rehabbed at the hospital thru Sept. 23rd. She'd made remarkable progress. Monday, September 24th, Deana was discharged from the hospital. She was glad to be back in her own apartment. She was walking on crutches, but for the first time since the accident, she was starting to feel stable on her feet.

Wednesday, she would start therapy at an outpatient physical therapy center. She was also given a list of exercises she could do at her apartment. She scheduled Monday, Wednesday and Friday rehab appointments thru Friday October 26th.

She had gone online and found Frank McGee in the Dothan real estate section. She called him on the phone and they worked out a rental agreement. She would be living in the second half of Mr. McGee's duplex and he would be her neighbor. As moving day approached, Deana was very nervous about relocating to Georgia. She prayed for strength and called the movers.

She scheduled the movers for the weekend of the 27th and 28th. She would be moving into her new place that weekend.

Before she moved to Dothan, there was one more thing she needed. Between the accident, coma, and hard rehab she had lost quite a bit of weight.

At the physical therapy center, she got on the scale. Before the accident she weighed between 150-155 pounds. Without shoes but fully dressed, she weighed in at 124 pounds. The physical therapist also wanted to check her height. Five foot three and one-eighth. Deana looked at her chart. "In high school I was over five foot four. How did I get shorter?"

"It says here in your file you waited tables in college. It's in your history because of the night when the glass at your restaurant broke and you needed stitches. That type of work usually involves heavy trays on your shoulders which can compact discs and vertebrae. You also may have compacted a few discs in your car accident. Plus, you are about ten years older now."

Deana laughed. "Thanks for reminding me."

At least, she now knew why her clothes fit so poorly. Truth be told though, her wardrobe wasn't very flattering even before the accident. Deana came to one simple conclusion. It was time to pay a visit to her favorite store at the mall and spend some of the money she now had.

She went early in the morning so it wouldn't be crowded. She was still on crutches and a little self-conscious. She would also be needing help from one of the attendants.

Deana met a store clerk named Gail in the woman's section. So far Deana was her only customer.

"This might sound strange to you, but I'm moving to Georgia in two weeks. I have something similar to a blind date with a man who is supposedly very nice. I know he's a Christian and I'm assuming on the conservative side. I'm hoping you can help me pick something out that will make a good impression. I've always been something of a tomboy."

Gail could not help but smile at Deana. "You have a great figure. I don't think this will be too tough. At first you may want to shy away from pants and shorts. I'd suggest you go with skirts and dresses."

"Dresses are tough for me; I'm chesty up top, but thin in the waist, hips and legs. My top is at least two sizes bigger than my bottom. Unfortunately, they don't make dresses to accommodate my build. I do like the skirt idea. What do you suggest?"

"I think you'd look amazing in this blue, floral mid-length tiered skirt. It's what they used to call a peasant skirt. It will flare nicely over your curves and fall neatly just below your knee. It will look so cute on you."

Deana tried it on and it fit perfect. It was so comfortable and feminine. In addition to the blue floral she just tried on, the store had similar skirts in brown, pink, green, yellow and lavender. She bought all six along with light blue and dark blue denim button up knee length skirts.

"Now comes the hard part," said Deana. "I've always had trouble finding tops I like.'

"I have an idea, why don't you try some dark colored tank tops? You can try a style that comes up a little closer to the neck with wide shoulder bands. If you stay away from the light colors the tank tops won't be too revealing. Also, you have three additional cover up options. You can wear a short sleeve sweater over your tank top to be more formal. You can wear a short sleeve shrug to be less formal or my favorite; this short sleeve jacket that ties at the waist would be perfect for church."

Deana bought the jacket which looked amazing on her. She also bought three shrugs, two sweaters and a variety of tank tops. When she took off the jacket and was left in just the skirt and tank top something didn't seem right.

Gail excused herself and said she would be right back. "This happens all the time to women that gain or lose a lot of weight. This is called a T- Shirt Bra. It's a 34C. This is the size you are now."

Deana looked surprised. "I've been a 36C since I was thirteen." Deana went into the fitting room and came out absolutely amazed. "This is so comfortable and fits perfect. You can't even see any lines under the tank top. Thank you so much!"

"Glad to help." Next, Gail sent Deana down to the cosmetologist. "Jenny is amazing. She'll put make-up on you and it won't even look like you have any on."

Deana thanked Gail and spent an hour with Jenny learning make-up tricks. She bought a few items and headed for the shoe department.

Deana found a pair of beige sandals with clear straps she thought were really cute and quickly added them to her new wardrobe.

As she left the mall she had very little idea how beautiful she looked.

Two weeks later it was October 27th. The crutches and cane were gone and so was Deana.

Michael Haden

CHAPTER 4
DOTHAN GEORGIA

Mr. McGee had a very good idea. Deana had called him that Thursday to confirm she'd be arriving at the duplex late Sunday afternoon. He said that would be fine. He suggested she have the movers drive up with her in tandem. She could drive a little ahead of the moving van and if something were to happen she'd have help.

Deana liked the plan. She asked the movers if they would be okay with the idea and they said it would be no problem. They spent all day Saturday at Deana's Tampa apartment loading all her belongings.

Deana went to church Sunday morning. It was a very

tearful and emotional good-bye for her. She had spent her entire twenty-five years in Tampa and had many friends and special relationships. She would miss the Wilsons, her old coaches, the other people at her church and a lifetime of acquaintances.

Deana met the moving van at 12pm at Bruce B. Downs and I75 North. They jumped on the highway and in just three hours she saw the signs for Valdosta Georgia. Valdosta is the first city in Georgia you go thru when you leave Florida and enter Georgia if you are driving north on I75. Good-bye Florida.

Just over three hours later Deana and the moving van pulled up to Mr. McGee's duplex. He was there waiting for her. Deana appreciated his kindness. Georgia in late October was colder than she expected. There were vast mountains and hills. The terrain was very rough and spread out. She was used to the flatlands of Tampa. This was definitely different.

Deana had not been eating or sleeping well the past three weeks. There were times when she had started shaking as she was driving earlier in the day. Her nerves were frazzled. She had spent most of the day trying not to cry and being as strong as she could.

It took the movers over six hours to unpack her belongings. They helped her set her things where they needed to be. Her new place was almost the same size as her Tampa apartment so everything was a good fit. The movers were finished and left just after 1am.

Mr. McGee had stayed up to make sure Deana was all right. Despite her best efforts, Deana broke down and cried. Mr. McGee was compassionate and understanding. He did his best to console Deana and assure her everything would be all right.

"Tomorrow we can go to the restaurant and meet Delores and Mr. Vito."

"Why are we meeting Delores at a restaurant and who is Mr. Vito?" Deana asked.

"Mr. Vito owns the restaurant where Delores waits tables. Vito's is where you can work. You are a waitress aren't you?"

Tears welled up in Deana's eyes but she refused to cry again. "Yes Sir", I'm a waitress," she reluctantly replied. "I have four years experience being a waitress. Obviously this is what God wants from me."

Deana thanked Mr. McGee and excused herself. She went into her new kitchen and fixed a small snack before heading into the new bathroom and then into her new bedroom. She sat on her bed. She stared into space. I went to school for seventeen years. I can put my diploma in the break room of the restaurant where I wait tables.

Deana was very unhappy.

Late the next morning Mr. McGee took Deana to Vito's. It was bigger than she expected but not huge. Mr. Vito had intended it to be an Italian restaurant. But, to keep the customers happy in Dothan he was forced to put some barbecue and other southern specialties on the menu.

Deana read the menu and had to laugh. What a hodge-podge of different foods. Not too many menus have scungilli marinara and deep fried pickles on the same page.

Everybody at the restaurant was very pleasant. She liked Mr. Vito. Delores was nice and closer to Deana's age than Peggy, the other waitress. Delores was in her early thirties and Peggy was in her mid forties. Robert was the cook; he looked young. Delores later told Deana he was twenty-two. He gave Deana a wink when they were introduced and she did not know if that was good or bad. Delores said he was nice and he did seem like he'd be okay to work with.

Dothan was small with a population just over one thousand people. The restaurant was only a few blocks away from her duplex. The church and downtown were both within walking distance. Only a couple of miles away, there was a beautiful national park with a beach.

Deana was starting to feel better about her move to Dothan. She would start work Wednesday night at 4:55pm. She would be working the dinner shift. She would have most of the day to work out, rehab and train. She would also have time to do whatever it was going to take to be the next Mrs. Samuels.

Dothan did not offer much in the way of stores. The

bigger stores were in the next town over called Morrison. For the first time in her life Deana bought a scale. She knew she had lost more weight and was curious to see how much. She weighed in at just under 121 pounds. She knew she was thin. Her old yellow sweatpants were falling off of her. She really had to tighten the drawstring.

Wednesday night was pretty slow, but it gave her time to acclimate to her new job. She was told week nights usually were that way. Toward the end of her shift a mother with a boy in his early teens sat in Deana's station. They were very polite, but the boy kept staring at Deana. When they were finished eating Deana put together their bill. As she dropped it off, she heard the mother tell the boy, "It's all right if you tell her."

Deana was expecting the worst. The butterscotch colored polyester uniform dress she was required to wear at work was ugly and didn't fit very well.

"I think you are very beautiful," the boy said as if it were the most obvious thing in the world.

"Well bless your heart," Deana replied. She was enjoying how polite and warm everyone had been to her since she'd moved to Georgia. She just wasn't used to getting compliments on her appearance.

Thursday night was slow which gave Deana a chance to get to know Delores.

Delores was thirty-three years old with a fourteen year old son. Her husband joined the military just after they'd married and had been deployed a good portion of their marriage. He'd recently left the military and taken a job in the private sector near Atlanta. Delores was enjoying a second honeymoon of sorts because it was the first time in a long while they'd been able to spend much time together.

Friday morning Deana woke up with butterflies in her stomach. It was November 2nd. In two days, she'd be meeting the Samuels at church. She had wanted to speak briefly with Delores about Leon Samuels the previous night at work, but Deana was afraid of revealing too much. Deana ended up saying nothing at all.

Intent on continuing her rehabilitation, Deana had gotten in the habit of jogging to the park, all the way to the beach. Today, however, she decided to take a leisurely walk to the front of the park and back home. Deep in thought, she realized her life would soon be completely changed. She felt like she was on a fast moving ride she couldn't get off. She prayed it would be more like a carnival ride and not a train wreck.

When she got back to her place she watched a few country videos on TV then flipped on the contemporary Christian radio station. She went online and got the chords and lyrics to some songs she liked and practiced them on her guitar. The guitar was a gift from her soccer coach when she was living at the orphanage. Feeling better, she got ready for work.

Friday night would be the first real test of Deana's table waiting skills. Before Wednesday she hadn't waited tables in over a year and a half. It never got really busy, but stayed steady. All three waitresses were working the floor and helping each other as much as they could.

Late in the evening, one of Peggy's dinner orders came up in the window. Deana brought the food out for her to a table of three high school guys.

Deana and the first two boys exchanged pleasantries as she gave them their food. The third boy just stared at her. "Whoa" was all he said.

"I hope 'whoa' means this food looks great and you want to eat here every night," Deana joked.

"'Whoa' means you are DDG."

"Why am I afraid to ask you what 'DDG' means?"

"DDG is like LOL or BFF. It means drop dead gorgeous. I can't believe I'm the first guy to ever say that to you. You're not from here are you?"

"Actually I'm not; this is my first week here. I just moved up from Tampa Florida."

"Well you need to tell all your cute girl friends to move up here with you."

"I'll send them a text," Deana said, walking back to her station. She had seen Peggy coming over to make sure the boys were all set.

Deana cleared her last round of tables, and then headed home for bed. She realized how close it was getting to Sunday morning November 4th.

Deana was too tired to think or worry anymore. Her head hit the pillow and she enjoyed the best night of sleep she'd had in weeks. Saturday morning she got in a brisk jog then drove to Morrison to shop for a few things.

At 4:55pm she was back at Vito's ready for another busy weekend shift. Patrons came in steadily but it was slower than what she was used to in Tampa. Thank God for the settlement money and what her old boss had given her because she wasn't making much money at Vito's.

Deana was home by eleven so she watched the music video countdown on TV. She wasn't that tired and knew it would be hard getting to sleep. She was right. By 7:30am she was up. She was too nervous to eat breakfast. The church service started at ten. She didn't want to arrive too early because if the Samuels got there after her it would look strange if she moved to sit close to them. If they got there first, she could casually come in, sit near them and introduce herself after the service, before they left.

She slowly and deliberately prepared the new Deana. First,

she put on her make-up just like Jenny had shown her. Next, she put on the outfit Gail had picked out for her along with her cute beige sandals. She finished off her look by styling her hair. Her hair had grown to a length of a few inches below her shoulders. Starting from her right temple she created a thick braid which she wrapped four times, creating a quadruple braid.

Deana hoped the quadruple braid would set her apart. The new Deana wanted to be unique and make an impression.

It was now 9:40am. She put a soccer ball, a football and a Frisbee in the trunk of her car. She loaded some hamburger, a big block of mozzarella cheese and a jar of spaghetti sauce in a large cooler filled with ice on her back seat. In a bag she had two pounds of uncooked ziti, olive oil and grated cheese.

Deana jumped in the Stratus and went to church. She parked the car at 9:50am and walked slowly towards the sanctuary. She was polite and said hello to everyone she could. To those that seemed interested, she introduced herself.

Deana had already met a few of the people during the week at Vito's. She would try to meet a few more after the service.

When Deana walked thru the door at 9:55am she looked for any clue that would lead her to identifying the Samuels. After several minutes of scanning the church, she shook her head in utter bewilderment. All she could do was take a seat in the back and hope God would send her a sign.

At 10:05am, God sent her a sign all right. Four of the most unkempt looking individuals Deana had ever seen walked into the church, creating a ruckus. The nine and ten year olds were fighting with each other. The father looked despondent. His hair was long and uncombed; his beard was straggly and he was heavy set. He almost looked like a hillbilly. He was followed by a little boy who looked like something the cat had dragged in.

The father, Leon Samuels, picked up the little boy and walked into the only empty pew in the church. Leon entered from the left and put his youngest to his right. The nine and ten year old stayed to their dad's left.

During the commotion, Deana moved to the far right of the Samuels' pew hoping not to draw attention to herself. The little boy soon noticed Deana twelve feet away and immediately scooted next to her. She gave him a friendly hug. He smelt awful but was really cute at the same time.

Leon did not look happy. Deana with the young boy in her arms, shifted left about eight feet so the boy would be close to both his father and Deana. Hopefully this would make the boy happy enough to sit still.

It was a good idea that yielded mixed results. The little boy remained still only when Deana let him sit on her lap. Deana did not want to seem too presumptuous, but did not say a word. The oldest boy looked over and seemed intrigued by his little brother's new friend. The middle brother, Mark, stared out the window as if his mind was elsewhere.

When the service finished, Leon looked over to Deana and said, "I'm sorry ma'am." He opened his large arms and Deana handed the boy to the very big man.

Deana smiled at Leon. "I'm Deana, I just moved into town." As Deana spoke she looked down at the little boy. "I enjoyed making a new friend today."

The little boy could neither stop smiling or looking at Deana. The oldest boy asked Deana where she was from.

"I just moved here from Tampa, Florida. I'm the new waitress at Vito's. Are you going to stay for the luncheon they are about to have now?" Deana had heard the pastor mention the luncheon before his sermon.

"It's the main reason we're here," the boy joked.

Leon gave Matthew a stern look and sent him to get some bottled waters.

While he was gone, Deana asked Mark if they played sports in the courtyard of their church like they did back at her old church in Tampa.

Mark's eyes lit up. "We used to play football here all the time, but I guess someone lost the ball so we stopped. You wouldn't happen to have a football, would you?"

"I think my foster brother left one in the trunk of my car. I'll go look." When Deana finished speaking, Matthew handed her a water.

Deana went to the trunk and got the brand new leather football she bought yesterday.

"This is a pretty nice one, I think. My foster brother spared no expense when he was getting sports equipment."

"What's a foster brother?" Mark asked.

Deana was hoping he would ask this. "My mother died when I was little. My father left before she died, so I grew up in an orphanage. The other children I grew up with at the orphanage are my foster brothers and sisters."

Matthew overheard Deana's explanation. "Our mother died not too long ago. I guess we have something in common."

Mark back-pedaled about twenty yards away. Deana had left her jacket in the car, so it would be easy to throw the football. She threw a perfect spiral with a lot of velocity. Mark put his hands up to catch the ball and it went right thru his hands.

"Holy crap," Mark said. "Where did you learn to throw like that?"

"I told you, I grew up in an orphanage with a lot of foster brothers. Also, having this doesn't hurt." Deana curled her right arm showing off her bicep. Deana was a little more muscular than your average twenty-five year old woman. Throw in the intense rehab she just went thru and the tank top she was wearing, and Deana looked pretty impressive.

Deana, Matthew, Mark and a 23 year old guy who introduced himself as Jerod, played football, ate lunch and played more football. They had a great time.

The boys knew 1pm was approaching. Their dad wanted to watch the big football game on TV, so he'd want to leave soon.

Deana had prepared for this moment all week. She walked up to Leon who had been tending to Luke while she was playing football with Matthew and Mark in the courtyard.

Leon had not told Deana his name yet. Leon had called her 'ma'am' earlier, so, in an effort to be as safe as possible she called him 'sir.'

"Sir, I know this is going to sound strange, but the stove at my new place does not work. I have not been able to cook a hot meal for myself all week. I just went shopping and have lots of ziti, if I could use your oven I would be glad to share."

Before Leon could respond, Matthew answered for him, "We'd love to have you over. We live at the end of the next street. Just follow us." Deana got to her car as quickly as possible, not wanting to give Leon a chance to object.

She saw the four of them get into a large Dodge extended cab truck and drive in the direction Matthew said. Deana went slow and kept her distance. She was praying Leon would not be upset.

The front door was left open for her, which she took as a good sign. She collected her ingredients and headed into the kitchen. The boys went straight for the TV.

The kitchen was a disaster. Dishes, glasses, utensils and mail were scattered everywhere, except where they should be. Deana was going to have to clean for at least half an hour just to make a path to the stove. Not to mention the time it would take her to scrub the pans, plates and silverware she would need.

She had to work tonight, so she had less than four hours. She started the water boiling and the pasta cooking while she was cleaning. She knew the best time to serve the food would be at half time, which should be around 2:30pm.

As the second quarter of the football game ended, Deana was filling plates in a clean dining room that bore little resemblance to how she'd found it.

Leon did not say a word but it was obvious he was impressed. He had three helpings. Deana was quite a cook. She knew the secret to making ziti is the mozzarella cheese. She used a two pound block plus grated parmesan cheese. She also knew food presentation; not only did her food taste good, it looked good too.

The four Samuels and Deana, mostly the four Samuels, devoured the entire pan. Over four pounds of food was gone.

One thing surprised Deana though. Luke and Mark picked out most of the hamburger. She had never met boys that didn't like hamburger.

It was killing her. She had to ask. "Y'all don't like hamburger?"

"We used to" Mark explained. "But pretty much all we've eaten the last two months is take out burgers. We're just kinda getting tired of it."

"I understand," Deana replied.

With that said the boys expressed their thanks and went back into the living room to watch the end of the game. Deana just stared at the big empty pan in disbelief.

While she was cleaning the dining room, she found an old Nintendo video game system. It must have been close to twenty years old. She knew most boys loved video games. She plugged it in to see if it still worked, but she couldn't get it to power up.

Matthew and Mark must have heard her trying to get the player to work. They both came into the dining room.

"It's dead," Matthew said. "We played it so much it finally stopped working."

Deana turned towards Matthew as she unplugged the Nintendo system. "I have a practically new Sony PlayStation at my place. My foster brother got it for me when I was in the hospital. He felt bad for me because I can't play competitive soccer anymore because of my accident."

The boys' eyes lit up. "Is there any way we can use your PlayStation?" Mark asked. "We love video games."

"The only game I have is soccer; I would love it if you could teach me to play it. I'm off from work tomorrow. What time do you get done with school?"

"We don't go to school anymore," Matthew answered. "Since my mom died last August our dad says we are being home schooled. We have to stay home to watch Luke."

"Oh, I have to run into town in the morning, but I can be back here by twelve. We can have lunch together and play the soccer game if your dad says it's all right. By the way, what is your father's favorite meal for dinner?"

"Fried chicken and corn bread is his favorite, "Mark answered. "Do you think we can have dinner again here tomorrow?"

"There's only one way to find out." Deana went into the living room. There were only three minutes left in the game. She very quietly sat down in a chair. Luke immediately came over and sat on her knee. She intended to wait for the game to end, then talk to Leon.

Mark and Matthew beat her to the punch. Before Deana could say anything the boys blurted out, "Deana is bringing her PlayStation over tomorrow. She's going to make fried chicken and corn bread for us."

"Is that all right sir?" Deana leaned closer to Leon. He nodded his head in agreement.

"I apologize for not formally introducing myself, Deana. My name is Leon Samuels. Thank you for dinner. It was very nice."

"I enjoyed it too. Thank you for lending me your stove."

Deana handed him Luke and shook his hand just like they had at church.

"Well I work Wednesday thru Sunday night. It's time for me to head home and change. Thanks again." Deana headed for the door. She got in her car quickly, trying not to show any emotion. She recalled her agreement with God, but knew there was no way she'd ever fall in love with this man.

To make matters worse, Jerod from church came to the restaurant to see Deana. He was quite taken with her and asked Deana to go out with him on a date.

Jerod was very much Deana's type. He was tan and athletic, almost six feet tall, with blonde hair, blue eyes and a great smile. Deana wanted to say 'yes' in the worst way, but said 'no.'

"I have a dinner date tomorrow night with someone and I don't think it's right to be dating two guys at the same time. I really am sorry," Deana said.

She quickly retreated to the ladies' room. She tried her best to hold back the tears. Delores saw her go in and knew something was wrong.

Deana refused to let on how upset she was. "I hated saying 'no' to Jerod. However, I'm kind of seeing someone."

"Is that someone Leon Samuels?" Delores asked.

Deana gulped. "Yes, please don't tell anyone yet; we are just friends."

"If you're only friends with Leon, why won't you go out with Jerod?"

"I'm not able to have biological children," Deana explained. "Leon being older and having children of his own makes things far less complicated. Me with a twenty-three year old wouldn't work. I've got way too much baggage for Jerod to deal with."

Deana was doing her best sales job. She didn't know if she believed it herself or if Delores would either. "Please trust me, Delores; it's complicated. Can we keep what I just told you between us?"

"I won't say anything Deana" Delores said. "But, there is something you should know. Two local policemen who come in here all the time sat at my station last night. I overheard them talking. The store owners in town are complaining about Leon's boys loitering outside their stores during the day while Leon is working. They're going to crack down on Leon because he's not properly home schooling his kids."

Deana thanked Delores but said nothing more. She finished her shift, cleaned her station and went home. Still in her uniform, Deana laid face down on her bed and cried into her pillow until she drifted off to sleep.

CHAPTER 5
BIG CHANGES FOR THE SAMUELS' BOYS

Deana awoke just after 8am. She got in a quick workout, showered and went online to find the closest gaming store. The cheapest PlayStation system was almost three hundred dollars. Even the soccer game was over sixty dollars.

To save money, Deana decided not to buy a television for the boys to hook the PlayStation to. Instead, she took the 27" television out of her bedroom. In Tampa, her apartment was cable ready in the living room and bedroom. Her duplex only had cable in the living room, so the bedroom television wasn't going to get used much anyway.

Deana went grocery shopping and barely made it to the

Samuels by noon, like she promised.

The boys were eagerly awaiting her arrival. "Did you bring your PlayStation?"

"Of course. Let's have a quick lunch and then we can put everything together."

Deana bought sandwich fixings and potato chips for lunch. She also had picked up the ingredients to make fried chicken, corn bread, and green beans for dinner. She cleaned a few plates and put the lunch food out so the boys could make their sandwiches.

Deana made sandwiches for Luke and herself, as Matthew and Mark watched. Then Matthew and Mark made their own sandwiches following Deana's lead. She had the older boys assemble their own; she wanted them to start learning to be self-sufficient. Lunch did not last long. The boys were ready to hook up the television and game console.

"Like I said yesterday, I'm more than happy to lend you my PlayStation, game and television. But there are a couple of important rules I need you to follow and I need a favor in return."

"Anything," Mark said. "Whatever you want," Matthew added.

"For the next two hours I'm going to do laundry, clean up the kitchen and take care of Luke. You both can play all two hours. At 3pm, I'm going to start dinner. Let Luke play the game while you clean your room and put away the clothes I'm washing. Sound fair?"

"Yes, absolutely," the boys agreed.

"If you can follow my rules, you can play again after dinner while I talk to your father."

Matthew was curious. "What are the rules?"

"The PlayStation is only for the five of us. I will leave it here, but it's only for us to use. Also, absolutely no trash talking or swearing of any kind. I'm very strict about that."

"No problem," Matthew said.

Next, Deana turned on the radio and started to clean. Deana would dance to the music while cleaning and Luke laughed hysterically.

The boys had the game set up and were playing within a matter of minutes. The Samuels' household was already benefiting from Deana's feminine touch.

Just after 3 pm, two large loads of laundry were done and the kitchen was clean. Deana gave Luke a bath and clean clothes. He wasn't a smelly little boy anymore. Matthew and Mark let Luke play the video game as they cleaned their bedroom and put away their laundry.

Deana got the largest frying pan the Samuels had and went to work. She knew a trick to make her fried chicken extra special.

She butter basted the fried bread crumbs. As the chicken was done frying she quickly got it out of the oil and onto a plate. Immediately, she coated it with lots of butter using a cooking brush.

She also used lots of butter on the corn bread and green beans. She needed Leon to love tonight's meal. She had something important to ask him and she wanted him in a good mood.

Leon got home just after 5 pm and looked around in amazement. Luke and Deana were having fun playing the video game. Mark and Matthew were cleaning their room. The kitchen and dining rooms were clean and the delightful aroma of freshly fried chicken filled the home.

Deana had fried over six pounds of chicken. She baked a big loaf of corn bread and made plenty of green beans. The dinner table was set and ready. Everything looked perfect. Thirty minutes later, everyone was stuffed.

Deana was thinking she might have to start working overtime at the restaurant to cover the expense of feeding the Samuels' family.

"Dinner was absolutely amazing," Leon said. "You definitely know your way around a kitchen."

Deana appreciated the compliment. "Thank you, I'm going to do the dishes and clean up. Why don't you go relax in the living room? There is something I'd like to discuss with you when I'm done."

"I'll help you with the dishes, and the boys can help clear the table."

"I promised the boys they could play the video game after dinner. You worked hard all day. Go relax. Me and Luke can knock this out pretty quick. She turned the radio back on. Luke and Deana laughed and danced, as she cleaned. Half an hour later, Deana asked Matthew and Mark to let Luke play too so she could talk to Leon in private.

Matthew and Mark wanted to know what she was going to ask Leon.

"If your father agrees to my suggestion, I'll buy the Sony baseball and football games and spend more time here with you. Please let me talk to your dad in private. I promise I'll explain everything to you before I leave tonight."

Apparently the boys were okay with this. They let Luke into the game and Deana walked into the living room. It was just her and Leon. She sat down next to him on the couch. "Leon, I've been praying you won't hate me for what I'm about to suggest. At my restaurant, policemen come in all the time. Delores overheard them saying the other night that you are headed for trouble because the boys aren't in school. Sometimes they go into town during the day and there have been complaints from the store owners."

Deana paused before continuing. "Will you let me watch Luke during the day? You wouldn't have to give me anything in return, except to let Matthew and Mark go back to school. Tomorrow, I can get all the paperwork, take the boys to the doctor for their check-ups and bring home the papers you need to sign. I can have everything pretty much done by the time you get home tomorrow night."

"I'd welcome your help" Leon said. "Rebeccah, my deceased wife, always did this every fall. When she died this past August it all overwhelmed me."

"Another thing," Deana added. "The boys will be a little behind in their schoolwork. I would like to tutor them. At the orphanage I grew up in, I used to tutor many of my foster brothers. I just graduated college a year and a half ago so most of the subjects are still pretty fresh in my mind."

Leon did not know what to say other than 'thank you' to Deana.

That was the answer Deana was looking for. Now she had to tell the boys.

"How did your talk go with my dad?" Matthew asked. "Are you really going to buy the baseball and football games?" Mark added.

"My talk with your father went well. We are on the same

page. Yes, I will buy the baseball and football games, but you are going to have to earn your playing time."

"What does that mean?" Mark asked.

"It's early November and you two should be back in school, I'll help tutor you with your classes until you're both caught up. I'll watch Luke during the day and help with your meals the best I can. If you go to all your classes and do well, you'll be rewarded with playing time."

The boys weren't thrilled about going back to school, but they did not complain. Luke, however, started to cry when he heard that he would no longer be with his brothers during the day.

Deana asked Luke to go with her to his bedroom so they could speak in private.

"Luke, when children are a certain age they have to go to school. Your brothers are that age. You will be that age soon. For now, I'd like to pay you 25 cents a day to be my helper. When I go for my jog, you'll ride in the stroller so I can push you. We'll go to the park and the beach every morning. You'll hang out with me and kick the soccer ball with me."

Luke's face brightened as Deana spoke. He liked what he was hearing. It sounded like fun.

Deana told the boys she would be back tomorrow at 9am to pick them up for a trip to Morrison. The school and their doctor's office were both in Morrison. She bought a car seat for Luke that morning so the four of them would fit perfect in the Stratus.

The following morning they drove to the boys' school first. Deana filled out forms, grabbed the school bus schedule and picked up the paperwork Leon would need to sign.

Next, they swung by the doctors' office and got more forms for Leon to sign. They'd have to come back tomorrow for the boys to get their school physicals.

Deana took the boys out to lunch, followed by haircuts. They went to the video game store and bought the baseball and football games. They couldn't start school until Thursday, so hopefully the games would keep them in the house and occupied until then.

They stopped by the grocery store to pick up items for tonight's dinner. She decided to do Mexican food. She had a unique version of quesadillas she liked to make.

They got back just before Leon returned home from work. The meal was quick to prepare. Deana made 20 quesadillas. Thirty minutes later the food was gone. Once again, Leon seemed more than pleased with Deana's cooking.

"The way you guys eat is definitely a compliment to my cooking." As she started to clean the table there was a knock at the front door. The two policemen that frequented Vito's were talking to Leon. Deana went to her purse and got all the paperwork from earlier.

She knew why they were there and she was prepared. "The boys start school on Thursday. We spent most of the day at the school dealing with paperwork and it's all either started or finished," Deana replied.

The officers were surprised to see Deana there. They knew she had moved in next to Mr. McGee, but weren't aware she was friends with Leon.

"Feel free to call the school on Thursday morning, Matthew and Mark will both be in attendance," Deana said.

Relieved, the policemen thanked Deana and Leon for resolving the issue.

As they drove away Leon went to the mailbox. He brought back a large handful of mail. Deana got the impression he did this only once or twice a week, not every day. He set the mail inside on a ledge without looking at it.

Deana had set a big pile of his mail in a basket next to the table during her cleaning the previous day. "Leon, do you want me to help you sort through the mail? I can throw out some of the junk mail and give you what looks important."

"I feel guilty making you do all this work," Leon said. "If you could just help me figure out what Rebeccah used to do, and show me how to organize everything, I'd be very grateful."

"If you promise not to laugh too hard, I'll tell you what my major was in college. I'm a finance major. I specialized in personal finance so I'm pretty sure I can help you."

Two-thirds of the mail was junk, which Deana quickly tossed out. "Leon, you have several urgent looking statements from Georgia Mortgage. Have you been paying them every month?"

Leon was embarrassed to admit the truth to Deana. The mortgage had not been paid since August when Rebeccah mailed them a check. In October, the electricity and cable had been shut off. He had to find out from a neighbor where to go so he could pay in cash. He immediately went down and had them turned back on.

"I'm going to take your silence as a 'no'," Deana said. "May I open some of these statements so I can figure out where you're at?"

"Please," Leon replied.

Deana opened a few of the envelopes from Georgia Mortgage and found out August 15th was the Samuels' last received payment. Leon was only a few days away from being 90 days past due.

"Leon, you need to make three payments of seven-hundred and twelve dollars. Do you have that in your checking account?"

"I have about six hundred dollars. I get paid this Friday."

Deana went to her purse and got one hundred and fifty dollars out. "Leon, take this cash and invoice to your bank. Have your bank manager direct wire the money into the Georgia Mortgage account I circled. You may have to pay a small wire service fee, but you need to do this tomorrow. You can pay me back next week. When you get paid again on the twenty-third, you need to make another payment."

"That shouldn't be a problem. I'm saving quite a bit of money not having to buy takeout food two or three times a day. But now I have a new problem."

"What is it?" Deana asked.

"Including this one hundred and fifty dollars, which I'll pay you back on Friday, I'm running up quite a bit of debt to you. Why are you doing all this for me?"

Deana answered quickly. "It's something God laid on my heart." She didn't say another word. Leon nodded in the affirmative, but remained quiet.

There was an awkward silence.

Finally Deana elaborated. "Other than Delores, you guys are my only friends in Georgia. I just feel real comfortable with you."

Leon gave her a look that said he didn't quite believe her.

After another long pause Deana continued, "Fine, Leon,

here's the truth. I'd like us to eventually become more than friends. And, I've been hoping and praying that you might feel the same way about me."

Embarrassed, she quickly ran into Leon's bathroom and closed the door. If God wanted her to marry this man, he needed to believe she had strong feelings for him.

She went back into the living room and apologized to Leon. "I'm sorry for acting so immature. I just wasn't quite ready to express my feelings for you yet."

"It's my fault," Leon replied "I didn't mean to press you."

Deana did her best to give a little half smile, half laugh. Leon did the same; his smile filled with genuine warmth.

Deana excused herself and hugged the boys goodbye. "I'll be back tomorrow morning, Leon, please don't forget to sign the papers I brought you."

CHAPTER 6
SEASON'S CHANGE, HEARTS CHANGE

Deana woke up early so she had time to work out before picking up the boys for their physicals. Dothan was much colder than Tampa, which made it challenging for Deana to breathe while jogging. After finishing her run and getting in some push-ups and sit-ups, she took a hot shower. If the weather was this cold in early November, what would it be like in January?

Deana arrived at the Samuels' house just after 9am and waited for the boys to get dressed. Leon had all the paperwork signed.

As she looked around the living room, she made a mental note that it really needed a good cleaning. What a mess. There were stacks of old photographs by the television; most were of the boys. One picture, however, stood out. It was a picture of Leon, Rebeccah, Matthew and Mark. Leon and Rebeccah appeared to be in their mid twenties.

Deana had never seen Leon look so happy. His hair was cut and groomed; his beard was trimmed. He was thinner. In fact, Leon looked surprisingly handsome; Deana was both shocked and pleased. He reminded Deana of the lead singer in the country group Alabama back in their early days.

The boys were now ready. They wanted to get the physicals over with so they could get back home to play the new video games.

Both physicals were done in less than 40 minutes. On the way home, they swung by the grocery store and picked up supplies for dinner.

They got back just after 1pm and had lunch. Deana set out the sandwich fixings and made a sandwich for herself and Luke. Like last time, the boys assembled their own.

After lunch, Matthew and Mark played video football. Luke stayed close to Deana as she cleaned the living room and did more laundry; they were quickly forming a strong bond.

As it was getting close to 4pm, Deana was only three-quarters finished. Nonetheless, she needed to start dinner. She had an idea for a lasagna dish that should please all of the

Samuels.

From what she'd observed Sunday, Mark and Luke preferred the macaroni and cheese. Matthew and Leon liked the meat and sauce. So, on the left side of the pan it was almost all macaroni and cheese with very little sauce and no meat. On the right side she mixed sausage and hamburger with extra sauce.

Deana was about to call Matthew to explain what she was doing. She was working that night so she would not be eating with them.

It was at that moment she overheard Mark gloating. "I KICKED YOUR ASS AGAIN MATTHEW, YOU SUCK!!!"

"Mark, I thought we had an agreement." Deana gave Mark a stern look. She walked over to the console, disconnected the system and took the set and controllers out to her car.

She went back into the house to explain her lasagna dish to Matthew, but Mark was waiting for her.

"You can't do that, it isn't fair." Mark clenched his hands in anger. "We aren't finished playing."

"Mark, I explained to you there were rules involving the games. I brought you the games for two reasons. Reason 1 was to have something to reward you with when you do well. Reason 2 was to teach you good sportsmanship. Do you think what you said to Matthew shows good sportsmanship?"

"No ma'am," Mark answered.

"If you do well tomorrow in school and come home and study while I cook dinner, your video game privileges will be restored. But, I expect you to follow my rules even if I'm not here to enforce them. Do you understand?"

"Yes ma'am."

Deana had her uniform with her. She changed in Leon's bathroom as dinner cooked. When it was almost done, she explained the lasagna dish to Matthew. "When your dad gets home it should be ready to serve." She gave Matthew and Mark a goodbye kiss on their foreheads. She had never kissed the older boys before.

Deana was becoming more of a parent figure. The boys had mixed feelings about this. Regardless, they knew their quality of life was much better with Deana around.

That night at work Deana's thoughts kept drifting to the boys first day of school. Not too many students start their school year on November 8th. But better late than never Deana thought as she and Luke walked the boys to the bus stop. She said a quick prayer for Matthew and Mark as they hopped on the bus that would drive them to school.

Back at the house, Deana put Luke in his car seat and said, "It's time for us to go to work."

They drove over to Deana's and went inside. First came the sit-ups. She was teaching Luke to count as she trained. Next were her push-ups. For her next exercise, she laced up her running shoes and brought out the jogging stroller. She put Luke in the three wheel stroller and gave him a soccer ball to carry on her jog thru the park to the beach.

Deana and Luke played soccer on the beach. It was too cold to swim but the water was pretty. They ran around in the sand and had a blast. By the time they got back to Deana's place, Luke was exhausted. While Luke enjoyed a much needed nap, Deana practiced her guitar.

Deana had borrowed a few children's books from Delores. Luke's diction and word annunciation were poor for a 3 year old. Deana read to Luke and had Luke read to her. Deana could tell it would be a slow process, but one that she'd enjoy.

It was time to head back to Leon's. The boys would be home soon and she needed to start dinner. Tonight's meal would include pork chops, baked apples, yellow rice and peas.

Deana was thankful the meal was easy to prepare. She wanted to help Matthew and Mark with their homework; both boys had quite a bit. Deana showed them how to organize their assignments; this would help them focus on the task at hand.

She called Mr. Vito to see if she could come in a little late. He gave her an extra half an hour.

Both boys seemed very bright. They did their work without asking too many questions.

Leon was surprised to see Deana still at his house. She explained how important it was for the boys to get caught up as quickly as possible.

"Speaking of getting caught up," Leon said. "I went to the bank and did as you said. I'll have your one hundred and fifty dollars back to you tomorrow and I'll make another mortgage payment on the 23rd. But how do I repay you for all of this food?"

"Don't worry about it, Leon. I would have had to buy most of it for myself anyway and much of it would've been wasted. I'm glad food doesn't get wasted here; it makes me feel good that someone enjoys my cooking."

Deana changed into her work uniform in Leon's bathroom. She then took the PlayStation and controllers from her car, and reconnected the system. "Leon, if the boys study and work hard until 8pm it's all right with me if they play video games until they go to bed. Is that all right with you?"

"Sounds good. I know tomorrow night you don't get off work until after 10pm, but since it's Friday night do you think you might be able to come back over after work?"

"I'd really like that." Deana replied with a smile.

She kissed the boys goodbye and drove to Vito's. Deana was flattered Leon wanted to see her tomorrow; but, she was still unsure about his feelings toward her.

On Friday, Deana's routine was similar to the day before. She and Luke walked Matthew and Mark to their bus. Luke earned another quarter. She helped the boys with their studies as she prepared pot roast, potatoes, and carrots for dinner.

When she left at 4:35pm for work she told the boys they could play video games tonight if they agreed to let her tutor them tomorrow morning. The boys were happy with that.

For the first time since she started working at Vito's, it was actually busy. Time flew by and before Deana knew it, it was ten o'clock. She cleaned her station and sped home to shower and change.

She got to Leon's by 10:50pm.

"I didn't think you were going to make it," Leon said. "I have something for you."

Leon handed her an envelope and a lovely bouquet of flowers. "The envelope has the money I owe you.. The flowers are my way of saying thank you for all your help. I really appreciate everything you've done."

Deana almost cried. But, she kept her composure and told Leon she was glad to help out. She thanked him for making her feel so comfortable and welcome.

Deana said she'd be back tomorrow morning around 10am to tutor the boys some more. She asked Leon if they could watch a college football game together in the afternoon. Leon smiled and nodded 'yes.'

Just before midnight, Deana drove home and put her flowers in a clear glass vase with water. It felt nice to receive flowers.

While Deana was tutoring the boys on Saturday, they asked her if she would come over early Sunday morning before church so they could have breakfast together. Deana realized they were getting tired of cereal every morning.

On Sunday morning, Deana arrived at 7:45am and fixed the Samuels a real Southern breakfast with eggs, biscuits, grits and country sausage. Instead of driving separate vehicles to church, Deana rode in the truck with Leon and the boys. The five of them entered the church together with Luke in Deana's arms. Leon was clean shaven and the boys looked picture perfect. Members of the congregation could see they really were a beautiful family together.

Monday morning, Deana made the Samuels her chocolate chip pancakes for breakfast. Leon left first for work; then Matthew and Mark headed for the bus stop. Luke and Deana did their workout then went to the grocery store. This was usually Luke's nap time so he was cranky.

While they were in the check-out line Luke grabbed a bag of Craddles. Craddles are candy coated sugar tarts. When Deana told him 'No,' Luke threw a fit.

People in the store were waiting for Deana to scold or spank Luke. She did neither. Instead, she took out her cell phone, pressed a button and pointed it at Luke as he yelled and screamed. When Luke finally stopped, Deana apologized to everyone around her and promised it would never happen again.

She paid her bill, carried Luke and her groceries to her car and drove home. She did not look at Luke or say one word to him; it was silent the entire way home.

When they got back to Deana's, she got out her lap top computer which had an eighteen inch screen. She connected her cell phone to the computer and pressed a button to play the video of Luke's tantrum on the computer screen.

Luke was horrified. Deana took full advantage of this.

"When I show this video to your brothers, what do you think they will say about this?" Deana asked.

"When I show this video to your father, what do you think he will say and do? Your father told you to cooperate for me. Do you think this is appropriate behavior?"

"No Ma'am," Luke said fighting back his tears. "Please don't show this to them. I will do gooder next time."

Deana did not want to laugh. "Tell me you will do 'better' next time. I also expect you to do better every time. If you ever do this again, I will tape your next tantrum and edit it with this tantrum to make one long video. I will then show it to everyone on the big screen television."

Luke never challenged Deana again.

Around 2pm, Deana sent Leon a text message: *If I may use your stove again tonight, I will make my fried chicken you guys liked. I'm off work again tomorrow so I can stay up late. I would love to have someone to watch the football game with.*

She did not need to wait long for Leon's response: *That would be great.*

Luke was already asleep in her bed. Since she'd be staying up late tonight, a nap seemed like a great idea. She set her phone alarm for 3:30 and dozed on the couch.

Luke, Deana, Matthew and Mark all got to the Samuels' house at the same time. Deana cooked fried chicken and the boys studied and did their schoolwork. After dinner, Deana cleaned up and then played Luke in soccer on the PlayStation. Later, she helped Matthew and Mark finish their assignments.

At 8pm Matthew and Mark were allowed to play the video games. Deana read a book to Luke and put him to bed. Just after 8:30 the football game came on. At 9:00 she kissed Matthew and Mark good-night.

Deana walked into the living room. "Well it's just the two of us." She took a seat in a chair next to the couch Leon was on.

Every time Leon watched football with Deana it never ceased to amaze him how well she understood the game. She recognized many of the players and appreciated the strategy. Plus, it was pretty cool to watch football with someone that could give the cheerleaders a run for their money in the looks department.

Late in the fourth quarter, the game was out of hand. With about four minutes left, Leon got up which Deana took as a cue to head for home. Leon went to kiss her good-night but she was exhausted and missed his signal. She walked right past him and out the door.

It wasn't until she was sitting in her car that she realized what had just happened. She thought to herself: I hope I didn't hurt his feelings. It might be a good idea if I show him at least some affection. I'll have to see what I can come up with tomorrow.

The next morning Deana picked up Luke and they did their usual routine. For dinner, she'd fix hot dogs for the boys and a rib eye steak for Leon. She wanted him to be in a good mood.

At 9:30pm all three boys were in bed. Deana and Leon watched TV together until eleven. As Deana was getting ready to head home, she took the initiative to kiss Leon good-bye. Leon was sitting on the couch and looked pleasantly surprised when Deana approached him.

Deana put her left leg in between Leon's legs and leaned over to give him a very small kiss on the lips. Deana completely lost her balance and realized there was no way for Leon to keep her from tumbling onto him without having to grab her in a very private part of her body.

She knew it was all her fault and she was preparing to be completely humiliated. Deana had no idea how Leon did what he did. He somehow got his right arm all the way around the small of her back. His large strong hand caught her in between the top of her hip and bottom of her lowest right rib. Deana's mouth was now three inches from Leon's.

Deana was so grateful. Instead of a one second kiss, she gave Leon a ten second kiss. It was Deana's way of rewarding the most chivalrous act any man had ever shown her.

With most twenty-five year old women the above incident would not have been a big deal. With Deana things are different. Because of what had happened to her in her past she had trust issues with men.

By treating her with respect, what Leon had just done went a long way to alleviate those trust issues.

CHAPTER 7
MEET THE IN-LAWS

It was 4:55pm, Wednesday night. Deana was back at Vito's. Thanksgiving was only eight days away. In previous years the Friday, Saturday and Sunday after Thanksgiving were particularly slow. Mr. Vito said he'd only need two waitresses on those nights. Besides getting Thanksgiving off, each waitress would get a bonus day off.

Peggy had the most seniority and wanted Sunday off. Delores chose Saturday. That left Deana with Friday off. With two days off in a row, she would have time to drive back to Tampa early Thursday morning, have dinner and spend Friday with the Wilsons like she usually did. She could drive back

Saturday morning and be home in time for work Saturday night.

But, something was telling Deana to stay in Georgia. The six hour drive really made her nervous. Recalling the drive up three weeks ago still gave her the shakes.

Also, Deana was hoping Leon would invite her to spend Thanksgiving with the Samuels. It also wouldn't be a bad idea to stay home, catch up on her sleep and practice some new songs on her guitar.

Saturday morning would be the next time she would have time to talk to Leon. Due to their work schedules, Leon and Deana did not get to see each other that much Wednesday through Friday.

At the restaurant, Mr. Vito had been noticing a change in his customer base. The number of families and couples was about the same. But a lot more single people were stopping in. It wasn't just young single guys either. It was a mix of men and women; young and old.

When Deana first started working at Vito's three weeks ago, she did something he had mixed emotions about. If the restaurant was slow and a single person came in Deana would make an extra effort to talk with them. Perhaps, more importantly she would listen to them; kind of like a bartender for people that didn't go to bars.

One day Mr. Vito asked her about it; he wasn't sure he

liked one of his servers chatting so much with the customers.

Deana explained, "No matter how good our food or service may be, there are only so many times a family can afford to eat out. Single people, however, can afford to dine out more frequently. As a matter of fact, sometimes they can even save money because they aren't buying food at the grocery store that ends up getting wasted. Being single, I can empathize with anyone who would prefer not to eat alone. It's nice to have a place to go and have a friend who will listen to you and your problems. With the holidays coming up, single people may be our best customers."

After hearing her reasoning, Mr. Vito nodded his approval.

On Saturday morning, Deana arrived at the Samuels at 9am. She had not seen Leon since Tuesday night. Leon had gotten a haircut. He was starting to look more like the attractive man in the photograph that had caught her eye.

She made breakfast and helped the boys with their schoolwork. For three solid hours they studied. Deana focused on math and how to construct sentences. She also gave them some pointers on how to take good notes.

By 1pm, major strides had been made. Deana let Matthew and Mark play video games while Luke took a nap. Deana peeked into the living room and noticed Leon was watching football on

TV. "Could you stand a little company?"

"Absolutely" Leon replied. "By the way, have you decided what you're doing for Thanksgiving? Are you going home to Tampa or staying here?"

"I haven't decided yet. Next week is going to be strange. I'm off Monday and Tuesday. I work Wednesday and I'm off again on Thursday and Friday; but I have to work all weekend."

Leon nodded. "I have a favor to ask you. We always go to my parents' house for Thanksgiving. My folks are in their early seventies and my mom doesn't really cook much anymore. Claire, my sister- in-law, and Rebeccah always cooked turkeys and sides at home so we could bring all of the food prepared to my parents house."

Leon continued, "You're so great in the kitchen; I was hoping you might be up for handling the cooking and spending the day with us. I understand how much work it is and I understand if you say no, but you are such a great cook and I would love to spend Thanksgiving with you. The boys feel the same way. I know it's a lot of work, but I promise to make it up to you."

"I'm pretty sure I can put together a decent Thanksgiving dinner for you. You do have my curiosity going though. What did you have in mind when you said you'd make it up to me?"

"Every Thanksgiving night, Rebeccah's parents take the

boys for the long weekend," Leon said. "I was hoping Friday night you'd let me take you out to dinner; just the two of us."

"So you are finally ready to make all your friends jealous by showing off your hot new girlfriend?" Deana joked. "I guess this has become a little more than a girl needing a good stove."

The game ended at 3:30 and Deana excused herself so she could go home and get ready for work. Leon got up to walk her to her car. This time there was no missed signal; Leon kissed Deana with warmth and passion. She had never been kissed like that before.

Out of the corner of her eye she saw the boys looking at her and Leon through the window. She wasn't sure how they'd react to her and Leon becoming a couple.

Sunday morning, 8:30am found Deana in the Samuels' kitchen making breakfast. Leon, Mark and Luke appeared to be in good spirits but Matthew seemed a little down. Deana planned to talk to him alone after the church service.

When church ended, many stayed after to mingle in the courtyard. Mark had been keeping Deana's football in Leon's truck so they could play on Sundays. Mark wanted Deana to teach him how to throw tight spirals.

"Mark, there are two things to remember" Deana explained. "If you have small hands like I do, only put your pinky on the laces when you grip the ball. Also, the power and velocity is created by flicking your wrist." Deana set up Mark's hand on the ball. Matthew was about twenty yards away. Mark threw a great spiral and put the ball right in Matthew's hands.

Before they left to get home in time to watch the 1pm NFL game on TV, Deana was able to get Matthew alone for a minute.

"I know you saw your father kiss me yesterday," Deana said. "I've been praying this did not upset you. Leon and I are becoming closer and I hope this will be a positive for all of you and not a negative."

"When I first met you three weeks ago I thought you were really cute," Matthew explained. "I knew I liked you and I thought you liked me. That is why I wanted you to come to our house for dinner."

"Thank you Matthew," Deana replied. "I am really cute and you are too. I do really like you. But, I can like you only in a certain way because I am twenty-five and you are ten. It is wrong for an adult to have romantic feelings for someone your age. These feelings are for adults, like your father and I. I hope you are not mad at me."

At that minute Leon called out he was ready to go home. The five of them jumped in the truck and headed back to Leon's. Deana made corned beef and cabbage. Being at least half Irish, she considered it one of her specialties.

Monday was very cold. She did not want Luke to get sick so they worked out inside her half of the duplex. She did her sit-ups and push-ups but instead of running outside, she skipped rope inside. Luke was able to count faster now and he was able to keep her count. She was very proud of him.

At 3:30pm they met Matthew and Mark back at Leon's house. She cooked her fried chicken dish and helped the boys with their homework.

At 8:30pm the football game was starting and she wanted to watch it with Leon. But it was cold now even inside the house. Deana usually sat in a chair next to the couch Leon sat on. Tonight would be different.

Deana went and got a blanket. She then sat down next to Leon on the couch. She pulled her legs up onto the couch and tucked the flair of her skirt between them so the material would be pinned in by her knees. She lifted Leon's left arm so her head and body leaned against the left side of Leon's torso. Her knees and body faced the television. Her feet were up against the back of the couch. Leon put the blanket and his left arm around her. She took her right hand and held his dangling left hand. They looked absolutely perfect together.

6am Thursday morning Deana arrived at the Leon's house with a fourteen pound turkey, bread, onions and celery for stuffing, real potatoes and a block of yellow American cheese. For the vegetable she had bought three pounds of green beans which she would smother in butter.

Deana mixed the bread, the celery, the onions and the seasonings to make Mrs. Wilson styled stuffing. She then got the turkey in the oven fully seasoned and stuffed before seven. Every hour she took the turkey out of the oven and basted it with its own juices and butter. She did this four times. Having worked in restaurants for so many years, she knew how the food looks is almost as important as how it tastes. The continual basting gave the turkey flavor, but it also gave it a nice light brown coating which made it look absolutely delicious.

While the turkey was cooking she peeled the potatoes, boiled them and then mashed them. She took thin slices of the yellow American cheese and baked the cheese into the potatoes. She boiled the green beans then drenched them in real butter.

At 11:15am, Deana, Matthew, Mark, Luke and Leon loaded up the Dodge Ram and headed to Leon's parents house in south Athens. Deana was very nervous about meeting Leon's parents, brother, sister-in-law, and niece.

On the way Leon did his best to describe to Deana the five new people she would be meeting.

"You will love my mother Gracie," Leon started. "She is a sweet, easy going Christian woman. She gets along with just about everyone. I think her secret is she is on the quiet side and keeps her opinions to herself."

"My father is the opposite," Leon explained. "He is very outspoken. He likes to be called Colonel. He was in the military in the late 1950's. He served between The Korean War and The Viet Nam conflict. He never really saw heavy action, but don't tell him that. He is in a wheel chair. He had a stroke a few years ago. He likes people to believe it is from a combat injury. He has a problem keeping his hands to himself. The first time he met Rebeccah he grabbed her inappropriately and she never forgave him. It caused a lot of hard feelings. If you want to ignore him and stay away from him I would understand."

"My brother Lester is four years older than me," Leon continued. "He is thirty-six. He was a Parade All-American award winning football player. He's even taller than me. I'm 6'1, he is 6'3. He played Division 1 college football for The University of Georgia. He hurt his knee his junior year. By the time his knee was completely better, he was close to graduation. In his day he was a phenom. He played tight end. There was no pass he could not catch. He married his wife Claire fourteen years ago. They have a daughter Julie, who is eleven."

"Claire is thirty-three years-old. Claire has been the 'it' girl since she was like four years old. She has won beauty contests, Little Miss Georgia pageants and State Fair pageants. She was the Homecoming Queen in high school. She has done modeling. She was the girl the parade sponsors wanted riding on their floats during parades. She's never been a big fan of mine, but she got along real well with Rebeccah. I hope she is nice to you also."

"Julie can be a pain in the butt. I guess many eleven year old girls are. She also is very beautiful but I've never liked her attitude. I've never really liked the way she carries herself either. She would be easier to deal with if she were more respectful."

"So that is what you have to look forward to today. I hope I didn't scare you off."

"You gave me quite a bit of information to process," Deana replied. "I just hope everyone likes me. I said a little prayer last night. I hope it helps."

There was one thing Leon did not tell Deana. He had told Lester and his parents how pretty she was. Lester told Claire the rumor was Leon's new girlfriend was very attractive. This did not sit well with Claire at all. She wasn't nineteen anymore. On top of that, she and Lester were trying to get pregnant again. So it wasn't like she could go to the gym and get into great shape like Deana. The weight gain from the pregnancy would make it hard for her to compete.

What really hurt Claire was the way Lester responded the first time he met Deana at the elder Samuels'.

When Leon, Deana, Matthew, Mark, and Luke got to the elder Samuel's home, Leon brought in the huge pan with the turkey and the stuffing. Matthew carried in the cheese mashed potatoes and Mark had the green beans. Deana, carrying Luke, walked in last.

As she entered the foyer a large man said loudly, "My Lord, what a firecracker! If that girl was seven or eight inches taller she would be completely unstoppable. Put the baby down and let me get a good look at you."

Deana was not completely sure what Lester meant and she was very uncomfortable. She was wearing church clothes. She had on the long tiered skirt and the full jacket. She was carrying a three-year-old. It wasn't a response she was expecting.

Deana asked Mark if he would go get the football out of the truck. That way she could be outside with the boys for a little bit. She wasn't quite ready for more Lester. She needed time to figure out Lester's statements and how she wanted to proceed.

As they threw the football, Gracie came outside and walked toward them. Deana stopped playing and walked over to her meeting her half way.

"I am so sorry for seeming disrespectful," Deana said. "When Lester called me a firecracker, I looked at his wife's face and I could see how badly what he said hurt her. I did not know how to react. I was hoping maybe Leon could sort this out before dinner."

"You did nothing wrong honey," Gracie said. "That was

just Lester being Lester. Trust me, Claire is used to it by now. Lester obviously thinks you are hot."

"As a Christian woman," Deana replied, "I put the onus on myself to be humble and demure. The meek shall inherit the earth."

"I work as a waitress," Deana continued. "Everyone tells me if I work at the chicken restaurant in the next town wearing shorty-shorts and a too tight white T-shirt I could make double the money. But that's just not me. Yes, we make jokes about how ugly our conservative uniforms are. Because we parade around men all day, sometimes I thank the Lord for the ugly uniform."

Gracie was very much impressed with Deana's candor. When Deana spoke Gracie could feel Deana's emotion and sense her honesty. Deana offered, "I will come in and help you put everything together for dinner if you want me to, Gracie."

"Thank you, Deana, that's a good idea. Claire doesn't exactly have the reputation of being a wiz in the kitchen."

This time Deana entered the home from the side into the kitchen with Gracie and away from the men. Claire and Julie were assembling the plates and pans of food to take into the dining room. Deana's turkey looked so much better than Claire's, Deana hoped no one would notice or at least not say anything.

Deana outstretched her hand and shook hands with Claire. "I'm Deana," I apologize about earlier. I was a little caught off guard. I didn't mean to be disrespectful."

"I'm glad you didn't engage Lester," Claire replied. "You had every right to be put off by what he said." Julie gave her mom a strange look but did not say a word.

Deana introduced herself to Julie. "I'm Deana, you must be Julie," she said extending her hand. Julie halfheartedly shook it. "I'm friends with your Uncle."

"He said you are his girlfriend," Julie replied. "Is that true?"

"Tomorrow is our first formal date other than us going to church together," Deana qualified. "So technically we are dating. So yes, I am your Uncle Leon's girlfriend."

"You look a lot younger than my Uncle. What if someone thinks you are his daughter?"

"Julie, enough!" Claire intervened. "Let's not tell Deana who she should or should not date."

Deana was thinking to herself, maybe I should have gone back to Tampa for a couple of days.

The boys were coming in from outside, the ladies were bringing the food into the dining room for dinner. The men were in the living room watching football.

Deana walked over to Lester. She looked him right in the eyes. "I apologize if I came off as disrespectful to you earlier. It was not my intention."

Lester really didn't even listen to what Deana said."What you have done with the boys, Leon included, is really amazing," Lester stated. "They look great. You've made a big difference. You are a very interesting young woman."

"If I am to take interesting as a compliment," Deana responded, "Thank you."

Lester chuckled and shook his head.

Deana went over to the Colonel. "I'm Deana, she said. "It is a pleasure to meet you." When she extended her hand he seemed to have trouble extending his. When she went in closer, she could swear he tried to smack her on the butt. She remembered what Leon had said earlier. She quickly spun away. The Colonel got a little of her skirt but no body parts. She got behind his wheelchair and rubbed his shoulders and told him he must have been a really strong man.

Rubbing a strange man's shoulders was not a natural occurrence for Deana. However, she realized getting Leon's parents to like her would be vital for her to have a successful relationship with Leon.

"What do you mean used to be strong, young lady? I still am," the Colonel boasted.

"Dinner is served," Gracie said.

Deana went to help the boys get cleaned up for dinner. "Make sure you eat Aunt Claire's turkey also, I don't want to offend her."

"Her turkey looked terrible, Deana," Mark replied. "Aunt Claire is just not a good cook."

"Please keep that to yourself Mark, we don't want anyone with hurt feelings."

Deana's plan did not work. Everyone, Julie and Lester included, went right for the Deana turkey. Deana's turkey looked better, tasted better and her stuffing was incredible.

You'll never guess who the first one was to bring this to Claire's attention. Yes, it was Lester.

"Claire, I know what I'm getting you for Christmas," Lester joked, "cooking lessons from Deana."

Deana was absolutely mortified. She wished in the worst way she had her Stratus with her. She wanted to get in and drive a long, long, way away.

Deana kept her head down the rest of the meal. She didn't even want to look up. To make matters worse, she had taken three slices of Claire's turkey. She was trying to be nice. It had to be the worst turkey she'd ever tasted.

After dinner, Deana and Claire cleaned up. Not a word was spoken. Deana felt so bad for Claire, but she didn't want to say anything to make things even worse.

When the kitchen was clean, Deana and Claire joined everyone else in the living room. All of the chairs were taken.

Leon, however, had left about a three and a half foot space between himself and the end of the couch. Deana was exhausted. She sat next to him on his left, like she did on Monday night. She put her sandals in front of the couch below her. She tucked her legs up and in with the flare of her skirt pinned between her knees. She put Leon's arm around her. She took his left hand in her right hand. She kissed the back of his hand and went to sleep in the safety of his embrace.

Sometimes body language is stronger than the written word. They belonged together. You could just tell. It was the way they fit.

CHAPTER 8
GETTING READY FOR CHRISTMAS

Deana slept the whole ride from Athens to Macon. After working Wednesday night, then getting up at 5am to cook the Thanksgiving dinner, Deana was wiped out. She wanted to make a good impression on the Johnsons, but was sound asleep when they arrived. She stayed in the truck the whole time as Leon unloaded the boys. She awoke in time to catch what sounded like the end of a conversation between Mrs. Johnson and Leon.

"She's very beautiful, Leon, but she looks so young."

Leon shrugged his shoulders. "Deana is twenty-five Mrs. Johnson and the truth is she's more responsible and mature than I am."

"You already sound quite taken with her."

"Yes ma'am, she's wonderful." Leon's voice reflected his admiration for Deana. "I don't know how I would've gotten by without her."

As Leon got back in the truck and drove towards Dothan, Deana pretended to still be asleep. Up until she heard what Leon said about her, she thought she was having a bad day. Leon's kind words he had just said to Mrs. Johnson made Deana's Thanksgiving a whole lot better.

As they approached Dothan, Deana heard a song on the radio she liked and started singing along. She hoped Leon would like her voice.

"Your singing is really beautiful Deana. Where did you learn to sing like that?"

"At church. Back in Tampa my church had quite a bit more music and singing than here in Dothan. I kind of miss it."

Leon was now entering Dothan. They were close to his house. "If you are too tired to drive home, you are more than welcome to spend the night with me."

"I would love to spend the night with you, Leon," Deana replied. "But I can't. I have to get up early tomorrow. Remember, I have a big date tomorrow night. Please pick me up at six. Thanks again for including me in your Thanksgiving."

She leaned over and kissed Leon. Leon held her tightly

and kissed her back, not wanting to let her go. But, he knew he had to. She jumped out of his truck and into her Stratus. He watched her tail lights get smaller as she headed to her duplex.

I don't know how long it's been since I've been out on a date, Deana thought to herself. She wanted to make the best of it. Last night alone with Leon in his truck was fun. She enjoyed the singing, kissing and talking; boyfriend and girlfriend stuff. She hoped the momentum would carry over into tonight.

She went into town and got her hair done. She had removed the quad braid earlier that morning and went back to the center part.

Deana found a really cute pair of ankle boots with a big heel. She liked that they made her look taller. She was unhappy when Lester insinuated she was short.

Around four o'clock she started to get ready. She wore more make-up than usual. Combined with her new hair style, it made her look more mature. For the first time since she moved to Georgia, she wore her dark denim jean skirt along with a green sweater top and the new boots. She wore a special perfume.

It was 5:40pm, Deana was ahead of schedule. She got out her guitar and played two songs. She was about to start a third song as she heard Leon's truck pull up; he was early. Deana didn't mind. She grabbed her purse, locked the door and went out to greet him.

"I guess I was a little over anxious," Leon apologized. "The house was starting to creep me out. I haven't been alone in a long time."

Leon had to do everything in his power not to gawk or overreact to how Deana looked and smelled. She was intoxicating.

"It's all right if you throw me at least a little compliment," Deana coaxed. I thought you'd like seeing a little different look from me."

"Oh my God, Deana, you really do look beautiful. I just didn't want to sound like my brother did yesterday. I felt really bad about what he said."

Leon reached into the back seat and pulled out a Teddy Bear. "I know it's not much, but I didn't want to come empty handed."

Deana hugged the bear. "It's so cute, Leon, thank you."

Leon had made reservations at the nicest restaurant in Athens. The sun was going down. Dusk was beautiful this time of year in Georgia.

They shared an incredible meal and a bottle of wine. Deana liked that she got to be waited on for a change. Conversing with Leon was easy and never forced. They seemed to have a natural chemistry. Leon was a good listener and Deana felt comfortable talking to him.

After dinner, Leon told Deana there was a unique place he'd like to take her. She was curious and quickly agreed. He took her beyond where the paved road ended; into a clearing in the woods. He parked in a spot that overlooked the most beautiful lake she'd ever seen.

It was very cold. Leon put on the heat and her favorite radio station. When a slow, romantic song came on they kissed. He held her close and kept her warm. It was a wonderful night.

"I know you have to work tomorrow night," Leon said, as he dropped Deana off at her place. "Could we do something together during the day?"

"I haven't been to the movies in over six months, if you want to pick me up around eleven, we can catch the first matinee. As long as I'm back here by 4:30, I'll have plenty of time to get ready for work and be on time."

"Is there any way you can do that braid thing you do with your hair?" Leon asked. "It looks so good on you."

"You actually liked the quad braid?"

Leon nodded yes.

"Your niece told me I looked too much like your daughter; I did every trick I knew of to look older for you tonight."

"Don't get me wrong," Leon said. "You looked amazing tonight. I just think the coolest part about you is how unique you are. The braid is part of your mystique. Whatever you decide is fine. I'll be back here at eleven. Thank you so much for going out with me. I had a great time."

"Thank you. Leon." Deana gathered her purse and Teddy Bear. "I'll redo my hair and look forward to seeing you tomorrow."

Deana was ecstatic. She couldn't believe what a good time she had with Leon. It was hard to believe they had only known each other about three weeks. Talking to Leon was like talking to an old friend. It was disappointing their date had to end; she wished she was still with him.

The next morning she re-did the quad braid and got ready for the movies. She had only one outfit left she had never worn in front of Leon. It was the 19" faded denim skirt with the frayed bottom that buttoned waist to knee.

Deana wore the orange tank top, which she did not tuck in. It made her look longer-waisted. She put on the short sleeved shrug over the tank top and wore her new boots.

She heard Leon's truck come up the driveway. With purse and keys in hand, she jumped into the passenger seat next to Leon. Leon's eyes lit up when he saw Deana. She knew he would like this look.

When they got back later that afternoon, Leon said, "I'll be back here tomorrow at 9am. I'll bring breakfast and we can go to church together."

"Thanks Leon." Deana wanted to call in sick to work in the worst way. She'd rather be back in Leon's truck, finding somewhere picturesque like last night. But she knew Delores was already off, and it would be unfair to leave Peggy alone.

She got to Vito's a couple of minutes late, but she punched in before five, so it was okay.

"Deana Murphy, what has gotten into you?" Peggy asked. "I've never seen you smile like that or look so happy."

"I've been on a dating spree. I had a Thanksgiving day date, a Friday night dinner date, a movie date this afternoon and I have a church date tomorrow morning,"

"I guess you and Leon have been really hitting it off. I kind of thought y'all were an unlikely couple, but Delores kept telling me I was wrong."

"Why do you see me and Leon as unlikely?"

"Leon looks so much older than thirty-two and you barely look twenty-five. But I do have to admit, when I saw y'all walk into church last Sunday together, all five of you; it looked very natural and meant to be."

Just after 8:30 the dinner rush subsided. Deana had only one couple in her entire station. When no one was looking, she sent Leon a text. It read: *I miss you. Please come to Vito's for dinner or dessert. Your choice, I'll buy. D.*

Leon texted her back, it read: *Miss u 2, b there in 20. L.* And he was there in twenty minutes. Deana got Leon his food. When he was done Peggy said it was all right if Deana left a little early.

Deana asked Leon if he had any more special spots like last night. Leon said he knew of a place she might enjoy.

They found another scenic clearing in the woods. It was very remote. They turned the radio up loud. They laughed and danced. Deana sang her favorite song to Leon. Leon put the tailgate down. He had brought a blanket; he wrapped Deana in the blanket and in his arms. Then he kissed her for a very long time.

Nine o'clock the next morning Leon brought coffee and donuts to Deana's. She thought it was sweet of him.

After service, Deana and Leon had lunch together and then watched the football game. Just after four o'clock Deana went home to get ready for work and Leon headed to Macon to pick up the boys.

Monday night, after dinner once the boys were in bed, Deana and Leon were on the couch watching football. During half time, Leon asked her why she made it sound like she didn't date much back in Tampa.

"Because I didn't date much back in Tampa," she answered. "My circumstance can make long term relationships complicated. You realize I'm about to drop a bomb on you right now don't you Leon?"

Leon looked befuddled. He was not sure what Deana meant.

"When I was in college I dated guys between eighteen and twenty-five." Deana explained. "We would go out on our first date and it would go great. The guy would say he never met anyone like me and how special I was. I always got a second date. On the second date the guy would start talking like he wanted a long term relationship with me. Before things went too far, I would tell him my situation. Then I never heard from him again."

"I don't understand, Deana,' Leon responded. "What is your situation?"

"I can't have biological children. When I want to have a family I'll have to adopt. I'm fine with that, but finding the right guy is complicated."

"Maybe someone that already has children would be a good match for you. I just might happen to know the right guy."

"Well Leon, now that you bring it up, it is one of the things that drew me to you three weeks ago in church. You were cute. You were also patient in the way you handled the boys. I like the fact you're older. I was hoping you'd have the maturity to deal with someone like me."

"To be honest, finding a woman that can't have children takes a lot of pressure off of me. There were three times in my eleven year relationship with Rebeccah where she really got upset with me. It was the first time she got pregnant, the second time she got pregnant and the third time she really went off."

Deana was surprised when Leon said that.

"After Matthew was born, obviously Rebeccah got pregnant again quickly," Leon continued. "I really wanted a little girl. But when Mark was born he was healthy and so great. I was so happy. It was the same when we had Luke. Having the three boys the house was, literally, full."

This was the first serious heart to heart conversation she'd ever had with Leon. The talk was over and his arm was still around her. They were still holding hands. She took this as a good sign.

Wednesday night at Vito's Deana had an interesting customer. The restaurant was slow, and like she did with most single customers she spent time talking to him. His name was Paul.

"Where are you from?" Paul asked. "I can tell you're not from Georgia."

"I'm from Tampa, Florida. I moved up about a month ago."

Paul was in his late twenties, handsome and articulate. He said he worked for a large pharmaceutical company as a sales representative. He was well spoken and interesting. Deana, as usual, let the customer do most of the talking. She sat across from him listening intently. It was almost an hour before he was done talking and eating.

When he was finished, Deana said, "give me a quick second and I'll prepare your bill."

As she was getting up from the booth Paul looked her right in the eyes and said, "Deana will you marry me?"

Deana was hoping he was joking. She was so surprised. But what surprised Deana the most was the way she replied to his proposal.

"I already have a wonderful man in my life that I hope to marry." As soon as she blurted that out she hurried to the back to be alone for a second. Oh my gosh, she thought, I've known Leon less than a month. Even if it is what I believe, it is way too soon to talk about it. Maybe I need to slow things down; maybe things are going too fast.

Paul's bill came to $9.52. He gave Deana thirty dollars. "Please keep the change Deana."

"Thank you so much," Deana replied. "Please come back again."

On Saturday morning, Deana got to the Samuels' extra early. She hadn't seen Leon since Tuesday night. She made a big breakfast and she tutored the boys.

"Leon there is a fourteen year old girl named Jenny who is supposed to be a good sitter. If I can get her to stay with the boys tonight, maybe I can get off early and we can go for a drive in your truck."

Leon really liked the idea and agreed to have Jenny over. Deana was able to get off work at nine and brought Jenny to Leon's. Luke was about to go to sleep and the boys were playing video games. Deana and Leon headed toward the clearing by the lake.

As it got later, it got colder outside. But it was warm in Leon's truck. They had blankets, the radio, the heater and each other.

They got back to Leon's just after midnight. Jenny was asleep on the couch. Deana woke her up.

"I told my parents I was spending the night. Is that all right?" she asked.

Deana was surprised. This was not what she was expecting. If Jenny charged by the hour like she said she did, either Deana or Leon would be out quite a bit of money. Since it was her idea, she didn't want to saddle Leon with the tab.

Deana went into the bedroom and kissed and cuddled with Leon. He held her tight and kept her warm. An hour later they were both falling asleep. Deana grabbed a couple of blankets and went to sleep in the chair next to the living room couch. She couldn't believe she was spending the night. It was nice, though, not spending another night alone.

Jenny got up at 6 o'clock. Deana drove her home. Jenny reminded Deana she makes six dollars an hour for watching three children.

"Do you mean you want me to give you fifty-four dollars Jenny?" Deana asked. "That's close to everything I made working dinner shift last night."

"Fifty dollars would be enough if you pay cash," Jenny answered.

Deana realized Jenny was going to grow up to be one shrewd business woman.

It was already into December and soon the boys would be off from school for Christmas break. They would have their mid-term exams their first week back in school in January. Deana had promised the boys' teachers she would have them caught up by then. It was going to be a lot of work.

Vito's was continuing to do well with the single crowd. It didn't hurt that it was the Holiday season. One young woman that frequented Vito's often was named Tracy. She always sat in Deana's section. Sometimes she came with a friend; sometimes she came alone.

"When are you hitting the ATL with me," Tracy asked Deana. Tonight Tracy was alone. "We need to go clubbing together." Tracy knew Deana would be the perfect wingman. Deana would be pretty enough to attract the attention of many men but not aggressive enough to take any action away from Tracy.

"Waiting tables is a poor vocation if you want any semblance of a social life," Deana lamented. "We work all the good bar nights. I'm pretty much here until late every Thursday, Friday and Saturday nights. Add in an hour to get ready and the hour drive to Atlanta, it would be almost 1am before I got there. I would be falling asleep by then. I have a hard time dating my own boyfriend because of this. It's good being off all day to take care of the boys, but I don't get to go out much."

"Well if things ever change," Tracy said, "please let me know."

"I really will try," Deana said. "I do enjoy getting out with friends; sometimes it just takes a little creativity.

On Saturday night, Deana didn't get to Leon's until almost eleven o'clock. They had been surprisingly busy at the restaurant. Still in her uniform she sat on the couch with Leon. They started to kiss. As they became more comfortable with each other, the touching and kissing got more passionate. Deana did not want to go too fast. But she wasn't sure how to slow things down.

One thing that can slow romance down is the children. The boys were off from school for the next three weeks. Mark had been getting caught up in all his subjects except Math. Matthew was behind in Math and English.

Every day from 10am to 1pm, Deana worked with the boys. She told them if they made progress she'd get them a little something extra for Christmas. Mark wanted the new video basketball game and Matthew wanted the hockey game.

It was Tuesday, December 18, and it was Leon's payday this Friday. Deana had set it up for Leon to make another mortgage payment. If he made this payment he'd only be a couple days past 30 days late. He was getting close to catching up.

At 9:30pm Deana put Luke to bed, the boys played video games and Deana went to watch television with Leon.

"Deana, if I make this mortgage payment on Friday I'll have no money for Christmas" Leon sadly admitted. "I'll have less than fifty dollars. I wanted to get you and the boys something nice."

"It's all right," Deana replied. "We can postpone giving each other gifts. I'm buying the boys the hockey and basketball video games, if they keep doing so well. I'll wrap the games up and say they're from both of us. Just buy Luke a little Santa gift and I'll buy Luke a gift from both of us. It will work out perfect. The important thing is that you have to pay the mortgage."

Deana was not happy when she found out Christmas Eve was a Monday night and Christmas was a Tuesday. New Year's would be the same. Deana would get no extra days off.

Luke did not have a very good grasp of Christmas. Deana had fun finding books to read with him to get him excited about the birth of Jesus. Deana also taught him the story of Santa.

Luke was just starting to read and was improving. The books Deana brought him had lots of pictures to help him follow the storylines. It was cute seeing his enthusiasm as he counted down the days until Christmas.

Deana found a place where they had some bargain Christmas trees. She bought the least expensive one, but did not cut any corners decorating it with the boys. They had a lot of fun with the decorating process. It looked nice when they turned on the lights and it lit up the living room.

On Saturday, three days before Christmas, Leon and Deana game planned for the big day. Christmas morning the Johnson's go to church with us," Leon said. "After, we come home and open the gifts. Around 12:30pm, the five of us head to Athens and the Johnson's go back to Macon. I hate to do this to you again, and I'll understand if you want to back out, but it's a little like Thanksgiving."

"Claire makes a ham and brings that. She usually does a halfway decent job with it. Then Rebeccah only had to bring the sides. If you don't mind kicking out a couple of sides, I would be extremely grateful."

"I'll say yes," Deana answered, "but I want an incentive package like I got for Thanksgiving."

"I'm sure I can come up with something" Leon replied. "I may, however, need a week or two."

Monday morning, Christmas Eve, Deana started bright and early. She wanted to do the cooking today because she would be in church tomorrow morning. She baked a big pan of macaroni and cheese. She made a broccoli casserole. She baked a big loaf of cornbread and fried two and a half pounds of okra.

When the Johnson's arrived at Leon's house Christmas morning, they had very mixed emotions. They loved how well the boys were doing, Leon included. Matthew, Mark and Luke were cleaner, better dressed and more articulate than they had ever been. They were very respectful; looked well taken care of and seemed quite happy.

However, Rebeccah was their daughter and it was heartbreaking to see her replaced. To make things worse, Deana was better with the boys, the house was cleaner than ever and her sides were sitting on the counter looking absolutely amazing.

Deana was soft spoken, polite and respectful to the Johnson's. There was no way they could dislike her. Nonetheless, all this did little to alleviate their pain.

Deana, Leon, Matthew, Mark and Luke got to the elder Samuels' just before two o'clock. Each one carried one of the sides into the home except Luke. Luke was playing a little hand held game Santa had brought him.

Deana fired up Gracie's oven to warm up the food. Claire, Julie and Deana set the table and got everything ready for dinner. Claire's ham looked good and Deana's sides looked delicious. This should be smooth sailing.

All ten sat down to dinner and the Colonel said a prayer. Everyone was complimentary about how good the food looked and tasted.

"As you can see, Claire is becoming a much better cook," Lester remarked. "When we first got married she thought the smoke alarm going off meant the food was done."

CHAPTER 9
TAMPA GIRL SHAKE IT FOR ME

There was something interesting Deana found out about Georgia. Most big fireworks are illegal in the state. In Florida it was much different. Pyro shows and big fireworks were abundant. If you were anywhere near a populated area either New Year's Eve or 4th of July in Tampa, you were pretty likely to see something going off.

New Year's Eve would be Monday night this year. It was expected to be extremely cold. There was a chance it might even snow. Living in Tampa her whole life and never having traveled, she had never seen snow before.

Leon asked Deana to spend the entire day and night. He

wanted to watch the big college football game with her in the afternoon. After dinner he would build a big burn pit in the back yard. A burn pit was something else new to Deana. Leon dug a hole. He put firewood, regular wood and dead shrubs into the pit. He encased part of the pit with cinder blocks.

As late evening set in along with light snow flurries, Leon set the pit on fire. The burning embers and the lightly falling snow were absolutely beautiful. Leon had built little benches so everyone could sit around the fire and roast marshmallows. After dessert, Deana started getting the boys ready for bed. She read a little book to Luke as Mark beat Matthew in video game hockey. She was pleased when the game was over and Mark told Matthew "good game". It was almost eleven when Deana kissed Matthew, Mark and Luke good night. She grabbed a blanket and met Leon at the burn pit. They put the New Year's Eve countdown show on the television and listened to it as they sat in front of the fire.

They tightly embraced and kissed like they did down by the lake. This was Deana's favorite New Year's Eve's ever.

"I know it wasn't much," Leon said. "But I hope maybe it was a little compensation for Christmas."

"It was wonderful," Deana said laughing. At that second the ball started to drop on television. Leon gave her another kiss and when the kiss was over it was officially 2013.

"Please don't go home tonight," Leon abruptly stated.

"Even if you want me to sleep on the couch, I want you here with me tonight."

Deana was surprised. Leon was usually not that assertive.

"I would love to spend the night with you, Leon," Deana replied. "And we can sleep together in the same bed. We just can't …"

"I understand," Leon quickly answered "I don't want to ask you to do anything you are uncomfortable with."

Deana was happy how cool Leon was about everything. Not all men were as patient as he was. This was a quality of his she greatly admired.

In the morning the boys were surprised to see Deana and Leon together having coffee. Deana usually came later and would be wearing her own clothes. Deana was wearing one of Leon's old T-shirts.

"Your father and I had a couple of drinks last night," Deana explained. "It is wrong to drink and drive, so I slept here."

That was all she said. It was Tuesday, her other day off and she usually spent most of Tuesday there anyway. At eleven o'clock the Bowl game from Tampa was on, and Deana wanted to watch it with Leon. She told Matthew and Mark if they would let her tutor them after the game for a couple of hours, they could play outside or on the game console for the rest of the day.

Deana started spending more nights with Leon. The next

week they spent Saturday, Monday and Tuesday night together. The following Saturday night, when Deana came over after work, Leon made a surprising request of her.

"Next Saturday night is my friend Kenny's birthday. I would like to take him up to Athens and party a little bit. What if we get that Jenny girl from up the street until nine or ten? If you get off work early, you could get Jenny home so it won't be too much money. Then you can watch the boys until we get back home later.

Deana did her best to remain expressionless. Obviously she failed.

"Why are you upset?" Leon asked. "We won't be home too late and we can still spend the rest of the night together."

"It's like we talked about in November, Leon," Deana replied. "The local police eat at Vito's and we hear them talk. Every Friday and Saturday night they park up on the main highway and catch as many people as they can for drunk driving. They pull over just about everyone. They brag about how many people they nail. Once they get you in the system it's about six thousand dollars to get your license back and get clear."

Leon had a co-worker get busted on a DUI and he knew what Deana was saying was true. A DUI conviction can pretty much ruin your life if you don't have a lot of resources.

"Do you have a picture of your friend Kenny?" Deana

asked. "I may have a plan."

"Yes I do. Why do you ask?"

"May I see the picture?" Deana grinned. "I think I have an idea."

The picture Leon had of Kenny was a good one.

"Is Kenny single?" Deana asked.

Leon nodded his head.

"Let me keep this picture for a day or two. I think we can throw Kenny a birthday party here you'll both enjoy."

Deana sent a text to Tracy. It read: *I might have a way we can have some fun together next Saturday night. Please come to the restaurant tomorrow night so we can talk. D.*

Tracy was sitting in Deana's station when she got to work Sunday night.

"Tracy, I need a huge favor. The guy in this picture, what do you think of him?"

"He's cute."

Deana reached in her pocket and took out eighty dollars. She gave it to Tracy. "Next Saturday is this guy's birthday. His name is Kenny. He is Leon's best friend. I really don't want them clubbing together and getting into trouble. I want to throw a four person party at Leon's house. I know we can give them a memorable evening. The eighty dollars is for two hours of babysitting and any party supplies you can think of."

"This could be fun," Tracy said. "I like your style Deana."

The next night, Leon and Deana watched a hockey game together on television. The Monday Night Football games were over.

"Leon, I have good news about Saturday night." Deana stated. "My friend Tracy will come over at eight o'clock and watch the boys. Tracy is my age and very pretty. She really likes to party. Tracy and your friend should really hit it off. You and Kenny can stay local, shoot some pool and have a couple of beers but stay off of the main roads. Between ten o'clock and eleven we can all meet back here. I promise we will do everything in our power to give you the night of your lives."

How could Leon say no to that?

The next morning Deana and Luke went shopping. Matthew and Mark were back in school and Luke was happy to go anywhere with Deana. First they went to a big country store. She bought a brown velour skirt and vest with lots of tassels. She bought brown cowgirl boots with little tassels.

Then Deana and Luke went to the hardware store. Deana bought a six foot by four foot 1 inch thick piece of plywood. She bought 2 by 4's and nails to elevate and reinforce the platform.

She drove back to Leon's and put Luke to bed for his nap. She assembled the mini platform in Leon's driveway with a hammer and nails she found in the carport. When she was finished, she slid it under Leon's bed where it would stay hidden until Saturday night.

She went to her computer and burned half an hour of cool dance music onto a disc. She found two killer rap songs she liked, two fast pop songs and two up tempo country songs.

She got rid of the quad braid. Instead, she made eight small braids on both sides of her head, going back to a center part. Later, Leon saw the new hair style and absolutely loved it. She hoped she could keep the momentum going into Saturday night.

Saturday afternoon, before Deana got ready for work, she talked to Tracy on the phone. "Tonight is going to be a blast, I'm so excited." Deana wanted to get Tracy as pumped as possible for tonight.

"I bought a fifth of Jack Daniels and a fifth of Grey Goose vodka," Tracy said. "I also bought the ingredients for adult brownies."

Adult brownies are little chocolate cakes drenched with chocolate liqueur.

"It definitely sounds like a party." Deana laughed. "I'll be there just after ten; can you be there by eight?"

"Pretty close," Tracy replied.

"Matthew, Mark and Luke are pretty easy, I told them they have to behave for you. Just let them watch television or play video games. Put them to bed by ten and when I get there I'll kiss them good night. We can all party together by the burn pit. After about an hour, if you like Kenny, I'll take Leon inside and you guys can have some privacy."

"I might not need an entire hour," Tracy teased. "I'll just follow your lead."

Deana got out of the restaurant just after nine-thirty and hurried home. She took a quick shower and put on the faded denim light blue skirt Leon liked. She put on the new vest with the tassels and the new boots. Later, all she would have to do is change skirts.

She got to Leon's just after ten. Tracy was there but the boys were all awake. Deana went in and put all the boys to bed. She sent Leon a text. It read: *We are waiting. D.*

Leon texted back. It read: *B there in 10. L.*

The brownies were almost done baking. Matthew, Mark and Luke were upset they couldn't have any. Tracy explained they were for Kenny's birthday. She told them Deana would get them different brownies tomorrow. They cut the one big brownie into four pieces.

"We have to make sure everyone eats their entire brownie," Tracy joked.

The brownies came out of the oven as Leon and Kenny walked into the door. Tracy looked at Kenny. Kenny looked at

Tracy and they gave each other big smiles.

"Please tell me you are hungry," Deana said. "The boys have been staring these things down all night. If we don't eat them I'm afraid they will."

Tracy brought the brownies, plates and utensils to the burn pit. Deana brought the beverages. Leon struck a match and everything lit up. They turned on the radio, laughed and sang. They ate, drank and had a blast.

One hour later, Deana took Leon by the hand and into the bedroom. "Let's pretend it's your birthday, too," Deana teased.

"What I am about to do for you would cost you one hundred and fifty dollars uptown. It is so good I'm not sober right now."

Deana got Leon a folding chair. She pulled out her hand made platform from under the bed and put it in front of the now seated Leon. She spun around quickly and changed her skirt. She loaded her disk into her computer and put it on the bed. The music started playing. Deana stepped on the platform and she danced. She danced as if everything that mattered was on the line.

For thirty minutes she danced. She put her heart and soul into it. She used a dancers technique at the end that made men want to come back and pay another one hundred and fifty dollars the next night. It is amazing what you can learn to do on the internet. Leon was floored.

Deana did not take her clothes off or do anything improper. She was, however, miles and miles out of her comfort zone. She was a very modest woman. Yet, she had a strong commitment to Leon. There was very little she would not do for him.

Leon and Deana went to bed together. Although they didn't make love in the biblical sense, Deana showed Leon more love and affection than he'd ever known.

Later on, Leon went to check on Kenny and Tracy. They had a great time. As Kenny was leaving, he told Leon it was his best birthday ever. Kenny walked Tracy to her car and got her number.

As February approached, Deana looked at the calendar and got upset. Valentine's Day would be on a Thursday this year. I usually don't even get to see Leon at all on Thursdays, Deana thought to herself sadly. She had no idea how this was going to play out. One of the few Valentine's Days she actually had a boyfriend and they both had to work.

"Do you think Leon will take me out Tuesday night instead?" Deana asked Delores as they prepared their stations. "Valentine's Day is on a Thursday this year. We both work and Leon is short on money. I might be getting only a card."

"You never know with men," Delores warned.

"Sometimes they surprise you with something wonderful, sometimes they brutally disappoint you."

"You've known Leon a long time," Deana stated. "I really want your opinion on this."

"Expect the unexpected," Delores predicted. "I know it's a cliché, and probably not what you want to hear, but it's the best I can do."

It was Saturday afternoon, five days before Valentine's Day. Deana and Leon were in the living room together watching television. Deana tried dropping hints.

"It's going to be an interesting week coming up, Leon," Deana stated. "I think they have some day coming up where if you have someone real special in your life, you kind of celebrate it, I forget what they call it, but I think it's Thursday this year."

"Aw man," Leon said. "Thursday is the worst day of the week. We usually don't even see each other. Maybe next year it will be a better day of the week and I'll have a little more money."

Deana was crushed, but did not say a word. They went to church on Sunday; they spent most of Monday and Tuesday evenings together. There was no mention of Valentine's Day.

After work Wednesday night, Deana was home alone and feeling vulnerable. She had no real family. Her friends were distant. What if Leon was just using her as a cook, companion and babysitting service. Maybe his feelings for her were not that deep.

Early the next afternoon Leon called Mr. Vito at the restaurant. "I know it will be busy at the restaurant tonight," Leon told Mr. Vito. "But if there is any way you could let Deana off just half an hour early tonight, say maybe 9:30, I'd really appreciate it. I want to pick her up and do something special for her."

"I have to ask Peggy and Delores first," Mr. Vito replied. "If they are all right with Deana leaving early, it's all right with me. I'll call you back at five."

Mr. Vito called Leon back later and okayed his request after talking to his other two waitresses.

At 9:30pm, Leon walked in with a bouquet of red roses and a little heart shaped box of chocolates. Deana, who by this time had been feeling very melancholy, was ecstatic. She jumped into Leon's arms and started to cry.

Deana had her arms around the flowers and chocolate and Leon had his arms around her as they walked to his truck. They drove to the clearing by the lake she liked so much.

The radio played their favorite songs. Deana's shoulders were wrapped tightly in Leon's blanket and Leon's arms. At first they kissed with Deana sitting next to Leon. As things warmed up, Deana spun on top of Leon's lap. They were waist to waist, chest to chest. It was their most intimate, longest kiss ever.

Deana sucked on Leon's ear lobe and then circled his outer ear with her tongue. "I am so ready to take this to the next level Leon," Deana proclaimed. "Saturday afternoon, when I'm down off of this cloud, we need to talk."

She kissed Leon again. This time it was more than just passion. It was lust, desire, and two people falling in love.

CHAPTER 10
THE PROPOSAL

It was Saturday, February 16th, 2013. Deana was over early so she could make the boys their favorite chocolate chip pancakes. Matthew, Mark and Luke liked whipped cream on theirs. Leon preferred syrup. Deana knew food was a great way to put Leon in a good mood. Today was the day Deana and Leon would have their most important talk ever.

Deana cleaned up after breakfast and helped Matthew and Mark with their studies. When they were finished the boys played video games. Deana went into the living room to be with Leon. Leon was watching college basketball. When Deana walked into the living room he turned down the volume. He knew she had something to say, he just wasn't completely sure what.

"As we've discussed before," Deana started, "one of the reasons I moved to Dothan is because it's close to Atlanta and Dr. Rodriguez, a very respected internist practices there. One of my physicians in Tampa, Dr. James, set me up with Dr. Rodriguez. Two weeks from Monday, I go for my final check-up to make sure I'm completely recovered from my accident. I'll be checked and tested head to toe."

"As you know," Deana continued, "I suffered extensive internal injuries. Even some of my female parts were affected. The good news is I expect to get a clean bill of health. Physically, for the first time, I'd be able to be fully intimate with you."

"The bad news," Deana explained, "which I hope isn't too bad, is spiritually I'm not comfortable making love to a man that is not going to be my husband. If I was engaged and had a commitment, I'd feel so much more at ease."

"Leon, please understand, if you're not ready to make this big of a commitment, I understand," Deana concluded. "I'm perfectly happy the way things are. This is the most incredible relationship I've ever been in. I just wanted you to know I'm emotionally and soon physically ready to take our relationship to the next level."

"Are you saying you've never been with a man Deana," Leon asked carefully.

"This is something I never talk about," Deana replied. "However, I think you deserve an answer. When I was very young and in foster care, my first foster father forced himself on me against my will. I have never voluntarily given myself to anyone. The first and only man I want to give myself to and make love to will be the man that will be my husband."

Leon looked stunned but remained silent. Deana was mature beyond her years. The fact she'd dealt with so much in childhood shed quite a bit of light on Deana the adult.

Meanwhile, a couple of blocks away at Dothan Christian Church, Pastor Beckmann and church Deacon Simms were having a conversation.

"I'm concerned about our attendance," Pastor Beckmann said. "Even with the high price of gas people are driving over towards Morrison to go to the new church. I'm told they're doing some kind of guitar service. Is that what you're hearing?"

"Yes, Pastor," Simms said. "These two brothers, Eli and Edwin Jacobson are terrific guitar players. These guitar services are popular all over the country."

"Do any of our members play guitar?"

"The new girl, Deana, can play. Some days in the early afternoon I see her on her porch playing. She takes care of Leon Samuels' little boy, Luke. I guess when Luke takes his nap the Murphy girl goes outside to practice so she doesn't wake him."

"How good is she? Can she sing?"

"I don't know," Simms answered. "She's a waitress at Vito's. Why don't we have Italian for dinner and we can sit in her station and talk to her."

That night, they paid her a visit at work and requested her as their waitress.

"Miss Murphy we need your help," Pastor Beckmann began. "Attendance at our church is in decline. We think some of our former members are driving to a new church near Morrison because they like their style of praise and worship music."

"It's funny you mention it, Pastor," Deana said. "Leon and I have discussed this before. My former church in Tampa has amazing music during the service. Good music can really add so much to the worship experience. You should get a couple of good musicians to help Mrs. Jarvis."

"Actually Deana, we're thinking of replacing Mrs. Jarvis," Deacon Simms said. "She doesn't seem to resonate with the younger members. We're considering going in a different direction; getting someone younger. Also, everyone has grown tired of organ music."

"Sir," Deana said respectfully. "That would break Mrs. Jarvis' heart. Her music means so much to her. Wouldn't it be better to help her than replace her?"

Obviously, the two men were not interested in Deana's

opinion, just her talent.

"Deana, what kind of singing voice do you have?" Pastor Beckmann asked.

At that second, Peggy walked by. "Oh my, Pastor Beckmann," Peggy said. "Are you saying you've never heard Deana sing? She has a voice people would drive to listen to. Her singing is amazing."

"Is this true, Miss Murphy?" Pastor Beckmann asked.

"I'm a good singer, Pastor Beckmann," Deana replied. "But I'm not that good a guitar player. I definitely can't do it solo."

"You're such a pretty girl, no one will notice," Deacon Simms said. "We'll tell Mrs. Jarvis tomorrow will be her last Sunday."

"I can't do that, sir," Deana said, trying to be as respectful as possible.

Saying 'no' to the head of your church in rural Georgia could definitely cause problems for Deana. She had to think fast.

"Gentlemen, I think I have a solution that will solve all of our problems. Please don't talk to Mrs. Jarvis yet. I'm off from work on Monday. Please let me handle this."

"All right, Miss Murphy," Pastor Beckmann said. "You have one week to take care of this."

After service the following day, Deana sat down with Mrs.

Jarvis.

"You know how to read music, don't you, Mrs. Jarvis?"

"Yes, of course," Mrs. Jarvis answered. "Why do you ask?"

"I play guitar and I'm having a hard time learning to play a couple of songs I like. Could you meet me back here at three tomorrow and maybe help me for a bit."

"Yes, of course dear. I'd be glad to help."

"Thank you so much." Deana said gratefully.

Deana went to find Pastor Beckmann.

"I know I can make this work Pastor Beckmann," Deana stated, "but I need your cooperation. Please be here at three o'clock tomorrow and don't say anything to Mrs. Jarvis. I want you to listen to a song I'm working on. I think you'll be happy with what you hear."

Early Monday morning, Deana and Luke went to a big music store in Athens. Deana found a beautiful, used electric piano. It was not too expensive, so Deana bought it. She put it in the back of the Stratus and drove Luke home so he could take his nap. While he slept, Deana went online and found the chords, lyrics, and bass and treble lines to her favorite new Christian song. She printed out the song and took it with her to church.

She plugged in the electric piano, found a seat for Luke and set up the sheet music. She started to practice the song on her guitar. As she strummed a few chords Mrs. Jarvis walked in. Deana asked Mrs. Jarvis to join her.

"You play the lead off the treble and bass line and I'll play the rhythm on guitar. I'll sing the first song." Deana stated.

Deana nodded to Mrs. Jarvis to begin. The acoustic guitar provided the rhythm and the electric piano provided the lead. It sounded beautiful. Then Deana started to sing; and she sang like a professional. The sound was outstanding and fresh. Pastor Beckmann loved it and asked Deana and Mrs. Jarvis to play new songs together every Sunday.

Deana was pleased by Mrs. Jarvis' enthusiasm. In fact, she confided to Deana that she'd been ready for a change in the music at the church for a while; she just wasn't sure how to bring up the topic for discussion.

Later that evening after dinner, the boys did their homework and played video games. At bedtime, as Deana was putting the boys to sleep, Leon was in the kitchen getting a drink of water. What he heard coming from the boys' bedroom made him smile; the sound of laughter, singing and happy children.

Six months earlier Leon had stood in this same spot as Rebeccah was putting the boys to sleep. He heard bickering, fighting and feelings getting hurt. What an amazing difference one person can make.

He heard the boys and Deana tell each other "I love you."

There was a pause and Leon knew Deana was kissing the boys good night. Deana was the warmest, most affectionate woman he'd ever known.

The next day at work Leon was asked a question by a younger driver. He wasn't sure how to respond.

"Aren't you the dude that dates Deana, the real pretty waitress?" the young man asked.

Leon nodded yes.

"I don't know how you bagged her, but that is one rocking girl. I really admire you, you must have some game."

The truth was, Deana was a source of pride for Leon. He loved having her on his arm when he walked into the nice restaurant in Athens, when they went to the movies and even church.

Leon had a huge decision to make. He loved Deana, but he hated being married.

It was Tuesday and Deana had extra time to cook today. She prepared the butter basted fried chicken that Leon and the boys liked so much. It was becoming her favorite also. It was that good.

When Leon got home he was starving. Deana was just taking the food out of the oven as he walked in. She also had a pitcher of sweet tea ready for him. It was the perfect meal.

When dinner was over, Leon went into the living room to

watch television. Matthew and Mark did their homework. Luke stayed in the kitchen to be with Deana. He had a little toy truck he played with while he waited for Deana to finish. Later, Deana would read to him.

Leon heard Deana turn on the radio in the kitchen. She often listened to the radio as she cleaned. He overheard Luke laughing and knew Deana must be dancing for him. Deana would dance if she was in a good mood. Leon couldn't help but peek into the kitchen to see. Sure enough, a fast song Deana liked was playing. She would shake her butt to the beat and Luke would laugh hysterically.

Leon was torn. Deana was the most amazing woman he'd ever met. He knew he could date a different woman every day for the rest of his life and still never find one like Deana. She was the woman he wanted to spend the rest of his life with. Still, the thought of being married again petrified him.

The last four months with Deana had been the best four months of his life. Deana had brought him so much happiness. She lifted his spirit; took care of his home and his family. She'd given him everything except for one thing and she wanted to give him that. But Leon would have to be ready to take the next step. Again, it was marriage.

Deana came into the living room just after nine o'clock. They watched television together until almost eleven. They started to kiss. Leon loved the way she kissed him and gave him her affection. Half an hour later she got up to leave. He walked her to her car and hugged and kissed her. He did not want her to leave. They would not be seeing each other until Friday night this week. Leon hated the time apart. And yes, he knew the solution to his problem.

Leon decided it was time to invest in a diamond ring.

All day Saturday, Deana was nervous about performing at church the next morning. She had been practicing the song alone all week. She left Leon's a little earlier than usual to get in an extra twenty minutes of practice time.

Sunday morning, Matthew, Mark, Luke, Leon and Deana walked into church together. Instead of sitting with the boys as usual, Deana with guitar case in hand, walked to the front to sit with Mrs. Jarvis. They were going to play one song. It was the most popular song on that week's Christian music countdown. It was the song they had played Monday.

When the time came for Deana and Mrs. Jarvis to perform, Deana had butterflies. Her voice shook and her hands trembled as she played the chords. The first two minutes were rough. Deana struggled. Fortunately, they had decided in advance to play the long version of the song. She had five minutes to redeem herself. Soon, she caught her groove and let loose. They found their sound.

When the song finished, they got a standing ovation. Deana and Mrs. Jarvis' performances would become even better in time as they spent more time working together. It didn't happen overnight, but gradually more people started coming to the church. What Deana and Mrs. Jarvis accomplished was very impressive.

The next day Leon called Mr. Vito. "Is there any way you can give Deana Saturday, March 16th off?" Leon requested.

"Are you nuts, Leon? I can't give my only Irish waitress off any part of St. Patrick's Day weekend; what about the 9th or the 23rd?"

"The 9th would work," Leon replied. "Thank you Mr. Vito."

"This better be important, Leon. I can't have too many Saturday nights without a full staff."

"It is important, sir," Leon responded. "It's about as important as it gets. Let me put it this way: hopefully, you'll be changing the last name on Deana's time card soon."

"Well Leon, if you're saying what I think you're saying, the odds are pretty good she'll say 'yes'. You and the boys are all she ever talks about. If she does say 'yes', you need to make sure you thank God for sending you a special girl like Deana."

"The truth is, Mr. Vito, if Deana was not as special as she

is, I would never even consider re-marrying. Thanks for your help. I'll tell Deana the good news when I get home tonight."

That evening, after the boys were in bed, Deana came into the living room to watch television with Leon.

"I have something to discuss with you Deana." Leon said as Deana approached. "In twelve days, on Saturday March 9th, I want to take you someplace special. The Friday night before, when you are at work, I'll leave the boys with the Johnson's. Early Saturday morning I'd like us to leave for Savannah, which is on the east coast on the Atlantic Ocean. I cleared it with Mr. Vito so that you won't have to work that Saturday night. We can come back Sunday morning for church, and then go get the boys."

"Is there something special about Savannah?" Deana asked.

"Savannah is very romantic," Leon answered. "There are some beautiful sights there, especially as the sun is setting."

At first Deana was a little confused. Then she remembered what she said to Leon a week and a half ago. Her doctor's appointment was next Monday. The time line was fitting. Would Leon propose marriage to her in Savannah?

"I'd love to go to Savannah with you." Deana responded.

That was the first 'yes' Leon was looking for. In twelve nights, hopefully he'd get a second 'yes.'

When Mr. Vito told Delores and Peggy that Deana would

be off the following Saturday, they were curious and wanted to know why. After Mr. Vito let on that it was something important, they were even more inquisitive. Eventually, they wore Mr. Vito down and got it out of him; Leon was going to propose to Deana.

When Deana got to work on Wednesday Delores and Peggy were all smiles. Deana wanted to know what was up.

"We know something you don't know," Peggy teased. "It's about your big Saturday night off in a week and a half."

"What have you heard about my trip to Savannah?" Deana inquired.

"You have no clue why Leon is taking you?" Delores asked.

"I think I may know why." Deana said. "But I'm not positive."

"It seems one of us is about to get a change in status," Peggy proclaimed.

Saturday morning, March 9th, Leon picked Deana up at her place just after 9am. The ride through eastern Georgia was beautiful. Leon had reserved a hotel room a few blocks west of the beach. They enjoyed a quick lunch together.

At the hotel room, Deana went into the bathroom and put on her blue bikini. Up to this point, Luke had been the only one of the Samuels' to have ever seen Deana in a bikini. She wore it only when the weather was warm enough at the little beach in Dothan.

As Deana emerged from the bathroom, Leon was speechless. Deana looked like a fitness model; muscular and toned yet feminine.

"Did you want to go down to the pool and show off your girlfriend?" Deana teased as she spun her hips to the side and shook her butt at Leon. She knew he had watched her the other night in the kitchen.

"I don't think I'm in any condition to go out in public right now," Leon joked. "Why don't we watch a movie and rest up for later?"

"Rest up for later," Deana repeated. "Are we going to a club tonight to dance the night away?"

Deana was enjoying seeing Leon squirm.

"Uh, maybe," Leon responded and added, "I'm not positive exactly how tonight is going to play out."

"Oh, I see," Deana replied. "Would it be a safe to assume you brought me here to Savannah to do more than just watch movies?"

"Yes that would be a safe assumption." Leon finished.

Deana lay down next to Leon and they watched a movie. After it ended, they dozed off and got out of bed just after 5pm. Tonight would be the last early sunset until fall. At 2am Daylight

Savings Time would kick in.

Deana put on a tank top and jean skirt over her bathing suit. She was surprised Leon put on dress slacks and a nice shirt. They jumped in the truck and headed to the beach.

When they found a good parking spot, Leon reached in the back of the truck and grabbed a large cooler and beach blanket.

As they approached the beach, they were treated to a magnificent sunset. The sky was both red and caramel colored. Dusk over the Atlantic Ocean was breathtaking. Leon spread the blanket on a nice flat stretch of sand and placed the cooler in the bottom corner.

"There is something I want to ask you," Leon said kneeling. "Deana Murphy will you marry me?"

Leon removed a small box from his pocket. He pulled out a diamond ring and took her left hand, kissing it. Then he put the band on her left ring finger. Deana wrapped her arms around him and started to cry.

"Deana" Leon interjected after several minutes, "We are one word short here. Please don't leave me hanging."

"Yes, of course I'll marry you Leon," Deana said between sobs.

Leon opened the cooler. He popped the cork on a bottle of champagne and filled two glasses.

They drank the champagne. Deana took off her skirt and tank top. Leon removed his shirt and shoes. Deana and her new fiancé danced and frolicked in the Atlantic Ocean .

CHAPTER 11
WHAT COULD GO WRONG?

"We've had a four month courtship, how would you feel about a four month engagement?" Deana asked Leon after they were fully intimate together for the first time in the hotel room in Savannah. She continued, "I think the 4th of July weekend would be a lot of fun because everyone will already be in celebration mode. The boys will be out of school, so if we do a honeymoon, it will be much easier."

"Deana, you're always so practical," Leon said, complimenting her. "I love that about you."

Unfortunately Leon was not as practical. He was letting his mother, Gracie, put together an engagement party for them for the following Sunday. It would be on St. Patrick's Day weekend, a weekend that Deana would be working long hours.

The following morning, Leon drove Deana to church. She was going to do another new song with Mrs. Jarvis. She wasn't nervous this week. The Savannah trip took her mind off of performing in church, which was a good thing. The song had only three easy chords so she focused on her singing. She would have the words in front of her, so it would be like karaoke. When the time came, Deana sang lead and Mrs. Jarvis backed her up. They sounded even better than the previous week.

After church, Deana and Leon drove to Macon to get the boys. Leon told her about the engagement party.

"You know I'll only be able to stay a couple of hours." Deana said. "If we leave immediately after church it will still be afternoon before we get to Athens. I'll have to leave at three because Mr. Vito wants me at work at four because of St. Patrick's Day. A good portion of the engagement party will be missing half of the happy couple."

"I know it's not ideal." Leon stated. "But to be fair, many people work on Saturdays now, so Sunday was our best option. I guess we'll have to drive separately and you can leave when you need to for work."

"By the way," Deana asked. "What did your brother Lester say about our engagement?"

Leon gave her the blank stare he uses when he doesn't want to answer a question.

"Let me rephrase my question." Deana said. "Have you told your brother you wanted to marry me?"

Deana got another blank stare.

"Leon!!" Deana said; frustrated by the lack of response she was getting. "I hope you're not waiting for your mom to tell him."

More silence.

"I'm so disappointed." Deana stated. "You need to call him later and tell him. Please, it's important to me that you do this."

There was silence the rest of the way to Macon. In four months this was the first rift between Deana and Leon. Deana was concerned. She knew they wouldn't always see eye to eye, but she needed to know Leon had a backbone. She had a feeling Lester was going to try to talk Leon out of getting married. And judging by Leon's silence, she knew Leon was thinking the same thing.

When they got to Macon the Johnson's were very cordial. They congratulated Leon and Deana. Mrs. Johnson even complimented her ring. Deana was happy that all the boys seemed fine with what was going on.

Deana had been considering giving Leon an engagement

gift. She knew he had pretty much spent his last few dollars to buy her the ring. She was very touched.

Deana had one last ace in the hole she hadn't utilized yet. She had come so far with Leon; she didn't want to lose him. She needed a knock-out punch.

Deana was extremely photogenic. She decided on a professionally done photo album with six or seven 8 ½ x 11 photos of herself. She did not want to do sexy pictures; she wanted a book he could show off to everyone. Her new ring would be on display in the pictures.

When she got to work she showed the ring to everyone. She was so proud. It was just over a quarter carat in size, but as far as she was concerned, it was as good as a carat and a half.

The following morning, after Matthew and Mark went to school, Deana went online to find a photographer. The one she liked the best was in Atlanta. She dreaded the long drive with Luke it would require, but she was determined to give Leon a gift he'd never forget.

"What did you have in mind Miss Murphy?" The photographer asked.

"I was thinking something spiritual," Deana replied. "I'd like six or seven photographs for my fiancé. A photo album he can show to everyone. We met at church, so I'd like at least a couple that make me look angelic."

"Do you like animals?" the photographer asked.

"Very much so," Deana answered. "I would love it if you can show my soft side."

"I have the perfect first picture," the photographer told her as he handed her a Labrador puppy. "Hold the puppy's face next to yours. It will make the cutest head shot you've ever seen."

The puppy they gave her was white and the blouse he had her change into was black. This gave an amazing color contrast. The picture was gorgeous.

"I have another idea that will give us three more great pictures. This will require you to do some homework," the photographer said. "You'll need to buy the best denim blue jeans you can find and a green satin blouse as close to your eye color as possible."

"For your two spiritual pictures," the photographer continued "buy an ivory, prom-styled knee length dress. We can alter the shade and design enough to use the same dress in two separate photos. Tomorrow meet me at this address at eleven o'clock."

He handed Deana a piece of paper with an address and a map.

"We can knock out three beautiful pictures in one venue," he concluded. "Wear the jeans and green blouse with boots. It will look amazing."

Deana left the photo studio and immediately took Luke for lunch. She did not want him to fall asleep in his car seat yet. She needed to go to the mall to buy the new clothes. She wanted Luke to sleep on the way back to Dothan.

They ate briskly and then headed to a big department store. She tried on jeans, green tops and ivory dresses. She bought the outfits she liked the best and headed back to her place. She let Luke finish his nap and she called Mrs. Jarvis to discuss this Sunday's song. She downloaded the chords and rehearsed until Luke woke up.

Luke and Deana got to Leon's just as Matthew and Mark were getting home.

"I got an 'A' on my Math test we studied for last week" Mark said proudly.

"I got a 'B+' on my English exam" Matthew boasted. "We've been doing really well."

Deana went in the kitchen and started making dinner. She loved Monday nights. It was the first night of her two nights off.

The following morning, Deana and Luke headed back to Atlanta. The address the photographer gave was to a horse paddock. Deana had on the new blue jeans, green blouse and her brown tassel boots. She had not worn jeans in almost a year.

The photographer wanted to do three photo shots. The first shot would be from the front. Deana would be walking a beautiful mare from her stable to an open area.

The second shot would be of Deana on top of the mare. She was to lean forward with a very small smile. She would be holding onto the reins of the horse with her hands in a position to show off her new ring.

The third photo would be from the back. It would be either the last or second to last photo in the album. The photographer had noticed what an amazing posterior Deana had and wanted to take advantage of this. The picture would be of Deana walking the mare back to the stable.

Tomorrow they would be back at the photo studio. They would shoot the two spiritual pictures. Deana was most excited about these.

Deana and Luke headed back to Dothan. Like last night Deana got to have dinner with the boys and spend the entire evening with Leon. At eleven O'clock she went to bed with Leon.

It was now fourth consecutive night Deana and Leon had been fully intimate together. Leon was pleasantly surprised how assertive and physically aggressive Deana was.

"I said no to quite a few boys in high school and college. I said no to a couple of men after college," Deana stated. "None of them offered me the kind of commitment I needed to be comfortable with them. I wasn't sold they had my best interests in their hearts. That is so important to me."

"I thank God for giving me the strength and discipline to wait for the right man and right time. I realize I am almost twenty-six years old. I understand I am different. I have many years of pent up passions, desires, and emotions built up inside me. I hope you find this to be a positive and not a negative."

Wednesday morning, Deana and Luke headed back to the photographer's studio in Atlanta. Deana was impressed with what an amazing facility it was. He was going to use something called a green screen; which allows you to superimpose an actual image onto any backdrop you want.

Deana was wearing a beautiful, flowing, ivory dress. She was holding both a Bible and a Christian cross. The picture would be of her kneeling and praying. It would be the last picture in the book and the only picture with a caption at the bottom of the page. It read: "I'm praying you love me forever." The green screen backdrop was similar to an old biblical movie set. It was very beautiful.

The next shot would be of Deana releasing two doves, one from each hand. The lens the photographer used was able to shade the ivory dress to make it look light brown. His assistant cut and hemmed the sleeves on the dress which allowed her to extend both arms as she released the doves. The release of the doves was intended to symbolize love and peace.

The photographer, Mr. DeRoberts, suggested the book have seven pictures. He wanted to take a picture of Deana at a local botanical garden. Mr. DeRoberts knew the owner. The backdrop with all the flowers would add a beautiful element to the album.

Like Tuesday, he gave Deana an address and a map and told her to meet him there tomorrow at eleven. He'd then have seven beautiful pictures he'd arrange in the album on Friday; ready for Deana to pick up Saturday morning. It was a great plan. Deana would have the beautiful gift to give to Leon at their engagement party.

Unfortunately, late Wednesday night Mr. DeRoberts' mother was taken ill. His assistant called Deana early Thursday morning to postpone all work. Mr. DeRoberts probably wouldn't be back until Monday morning; Deana was crushed.

She did get a call Friday confirming they would do the last shoot Monday morning and have the album finished Monday night.

Friday night was very busy at work. Mr. Vito was serious about his St. Patrick's Day promotion. He made the waitresses wear ugly green shamrock print bandannas. When Mr. Vito first showed Deana the bandannas she gave him a look of displeasure which Mr. Vito didn't appreciate.

The restaurant did so well they did not close the doors at

9:45 like usual. They kept the doors open until almost eleven. She did not get home until close to midnight. Deana went to her place to shower and change and get clothes for tomorrow. She needed some alone time. She called Leon and told him she needed a little down time. He sounded upset with her.

The week started out so well, and slowly disintegrated. She got out her guitar and turned on the Top 20 countdown on music television. She played five songs. It took her half an hour to unwind.

Deana didn't get to Leon's until after one. Leon apologized to her. He could see how tired she looked. He could see the exhaustion in her eyes.

Early Saturday, Deana and Leon spent most of the day on the couch. They watched the College basketball tournament until Deana had to leave for work.

Deana punched in at 3:55pm and had another busy seven and a half hour shift. She made good money, but she preferred to spend her Saturday nights like she did last weekend, at the beach or doing something fun.

Deana had put her Sunday church clothes in the back of her Stratus so she wouldn't get to Leon's as late as last night. Sunday morning she made breakfast for the boys and they went to church together as a family. Her new song with Mrs. Jarvis went really well. After church, in separate vehicles, they went to their party in Athens.

Deana met friends, relatives and co-workers of Leon's she had never met before. Everyone was cordial to her. She did her best to be polite and friendly to everyone. As three o'clock approached, she excused herself so she could get back to her place to shower and change real quick. Mr. Vito wanted her there at the restaurant again at 3:55.

Around 5pm all of Leon's guests had left. It was just Leon, the boys, Gracie, the Colonel, Claire and Julie.

"Why do you want to get married again so quickly, Leon," Lester asked. "The ink is barely dry on Rebeccah's death certificate. I know Deana seems great now, but you barely know her."

"Women can change when they get married." Claire added. "You see it on television all the time. They put on a big act to get what they want. But over time, their real personality comes out. It can be very scary."

"Honestly," Lester asked. "How much do you really know about Deana? Maybe she left Florida to get away from the cops or an abusive boyfriend. There could be all kinds of skeletons in her closet. Admit it, you really don't know her. Plus, the fourth of July is awful soon. Let's take Deana out of the equation. After all you've been through, do you really want to sprint to the altar again?"

Leon hesitated to answer.

"That's exactly what I thought." Lester stated. "You're not ready. The dirt on Rebeccah's grave is still fresh. Please tell me you'll postpone this mistake at least a little longer than the beginning of July."

Leon nodded affirmatively.

"Good!" Lester and Claire said at the same time. "We agree."

Leon, like he did many Sundays, left his cell phone in his truck on his charger so his battery would be full for work on Monday. His niece Julie knew this and also about her parents' plan to try to stop the July wedding. She snuck into Leon's truck and got his cell phone. She scrolled to his text function. Julie found Deana's number and Leon's texting style.

She sent this text to Deana from Leon's phone: *The July 4th wedding is off. Can we just B friends. L.* After sending the message, Julie erased the text from the cell phone's memory. She then turned Leon's phone off and put it back on the charger in the truck.

Deana had a full station when she heard a text message come into her phone. She had an ominous feeling and was hesitant to pull her cell phone out. She quickly made sure her customers had what they needed. She snuck into the kitchen where only Robert could see her. She opened the text and started to cry. Food came into the window but she was too distraught to serve it.

Delores saw Deana and scooted her into the break room. Deana completely broke down. She couldn't speak; she could barely breathe and couldn't stop crying.

Delores got Deana's cell to call Leon to figure out what happened. The call went straight to voice mail. "Leon, you need to call back right away." Delores commanded.

Delores had to help Peggy take care of three full stations. Deana sat alone at a small table in the break room. She cried for over an hour, leaving a small pool of tears on the table. She finally cleared her eyes so she could see to drive her Stratus back to her place.

Deana did not know Delores had kept her cell phone. Delores wanted to have a little talk with Leon. Leon got her message just after 7pm when he loaded up his truck to come back to Dothan.

"Delores, why do you have Deana's cell phone?" Leon asked.

"Never mind why I have Deana's cell." Delores answered angrily. "What the hell did you say or do to her? I've never seen anyone that upset in my entire life."

"I was considering postponing the wedding a little bit," Leon said. "But how did she know that?"

"You need to get down here; we need to talk," Delores demanded.

Half an hour later Leon's truck pulled up to Vito's. The restaurant had cleared out considerably. There were only a few patrons left. Delores put the boys in her station and sat them at a table. She took their food order and took Leon back into the break room.

"Do you see that puddle on the table, Leon?" Delores asked. "Do you know what that is?"

Leon did not answer.

"That is where Deana was sitting after she found out." She took out her rag and wiped up the big puddle. "These are Deana's tears. You did this to her."

Leon looked stunned.

"Let me tell you something about your ex-girlfriend," Delores started. "For all practical purposes, I should dislike and be jealous of Deana. She is younger, prettier, more popular and quite honestly, a better waitress than I am."

"We have a tip policy here at Vito's amongst the servers; if two waitresses give service to the same table the tip is split 50/50, no matter how much or how little service is given. For years, waitresses before Deana always shorted me. I was lucky to get 30%, even if I did 90% of the work. Your ex-girlfriend gives 75%-80% every time to me and Peggy. Deana says it isn't good for only her to prosper. She says we should all prosper."

"One time when I knew she was looking, I deliberately shorted her. I just wanted to see what she would say or do. Deana didn't bat an eye. She didn't get upset or lose her temper. As a matter of fact, I've never seen her lose her temper. That is why she is such a great waitress. She has an incredible memory and focus to detail. Deana also has amazing composure when handling customers."

"I've never seen her lose her temper either," Leon agreed.

"The truth is, Leon, I don't give a rat's rear end about you. You can die destitute and alone. When you meet your maker, you can explain why you spit in the face of the angel he sent to you. You can burn for all of eternity and you will deserve your fate."

"What I do care about," Delores continued, "Is those three boys sitting at my table. How are you going to explain this to them? Luke sometimes calls Deana 'mommy', even though she doesn't encourage it. Four months ago he spoke so poorly, practically no one could understand him. Now he speaks like a five year old. If you noticed, I gave him a menu. You could see his lips move as he tried to sound out the words. Deana says he will be reading on a second grade level by the end of this year."

"Matthew and Mark's teachers have come into the restaurant. They can't believe what Deana has taught them in just a few months. They look at Deana like she is a miracle worker.

Matthew's worst grade is a "C", and Mark may even make second honors."

"You are a thirty-two year old man, Leon," Delores finished. "You have three beautiful boys. They are your responsibility. Even if Deana was ugly, even if Deana was obnoxious and gross, she is the best thing for your family. You need to get her back. You need to do the right thing!"

Delores went back to her station to check on the boys and one other table. Leon sat in the back room thinking to himself. He knew every word Delores said was true.

Ten minutes later, Leon and the boys were in the truck on their way to Deana's. When they got there Deana was on the porch still in her work uniform. She was sitting on the top step. Her feet were on the second step. Her knees were even with her shoulders with her arms across them and her head resting on top and she was still crying. Before the truck was even in park, the truck doors opened and the three boys ran to her. Luke hugged and embraced her with his entire body. Matthew and Mark stood at each one of her shoulders as if protecting her.

The brunt of what Delores had said to Leon was hitting him. All he could do was sit in the truck and watch the love his boys showed to Deana. Their feelings for her were on full display.

After what seemed like a long time, Leon finally walked over. Deana asked the boys if they would please go inside and watch television while she talked to their father.

"I'm so sorry," Leon began. "I didn't mean to hurt you."

"You used me," Deana said. "You used me and it was very unfair what you did to me. I don't deserve to be treated like this."

"I still love you," Leon said. "Things just seemed to be going too fast. My first marriage wasn't very good and here it is only seven months later and it looks like I'm rushing into a second one. What if we were to live together for a while?"

"What do you think we've been doing the last four and a half months?" Deana replied. "We're closer than just about any married couple I know. I've told you every intimate detail about myself. I've shared every intimate everything with you. Is there something you're expecting to find out about me down the road you don't already know?"

"No," Leon said shaking his head side to side. "You've been nothing but candid and open with me about everything."

"I don't just want to be your friend," Deana continued. "It's not fair to me or the boys. We should be a family. I should be able to do the paperwork if someone has to go to the emergency room. I should be able to sign them up for school or for sports. You shouldn't be able to walk through the front door with some other woman and kick me to the curb."

"I would never do that to you." Leon replied.

"There's only one way I can believe that." Deana stated.

"How's that?" Leon asked.

"There's a special ceremony that takes place in front of God, a preacher, friends and relatives. You promise in sickness and in health you will forsake all others." Deana said. "It's called a wedding."

"I don't know what to say." Leon replied.

"There are only two things you can say." Deana followed. "Let me rephrase that. There are only two things I want to hear you say. If you can't say them, you can take your butt back home without me."

"What would those two things be?" Leon asked, even though he pretty much knew the answer.

"Tell me you love me with all your heart and you'll love me unconditionally forever." Deana answered.

"I do love you with all my heart." Leon started. "And, I probably always will."

Just as he said 'probably' he realized his mistake.

"Probably?" Deana said, trying not to scream at Leon.

Deana turned red and her eyes glared.

"You've got to be kidding me," Deana exploded. "Take your 'probably' home with you!" Deana pointed Leon in the direction of his truck with her right hand. Deana had switched the diamond ring from her left hand to her right hand, signifying the end of the engagement. Leon did not know why this hurt him as badly as it did.

"I'll still pick up Luke after you leave for work and before the boys leave for school." Deana said. "Other than that you are on your own. I'll call you tomorrow when I get home from Atlanta and you can pick up Luke here."

Deana rushed through the front door and quickly into her bedroom. She locked the door and couldn't stop herself from crying again.

Later that night, Leon was home alone in his bed. He knew Deana should be there with him, not at her place alone and crying. How could he have been so stupid? He had to make this right, no matter what Lester and Claire thought.

To this day, neither Leon nor Deana know Julie sent the text to Deana from Leon's cell phone. When Deana saw the '*Can we just B friends*' text, she assumed Leon was breaking up with her like she feared. When Delores referred to Deana as his ex-girlfriend, Leon assumed Deana broke up with him for being spineless.

CHAPTER 12
THE RESOLUTION

Deana did not feel like wasting her entire day off going to and from Atlanta. Nor did she want to write a big check for an engagement gift to Leon under the circumstances. She definitely was not in the mood to pose for any more pictures, even if it was at a botanical garden. Her eyes were red and swollen and her face was drained. Nonetheless, she picked up Luke like she promised and headed to Atlanta to finish the photo album for Leon.

Leon had one of the worst nights of his life. Deana was all he could think about. How could someone so small have such a huge hold on him? Leon had been in love before. He had a two year relationship with a girl named Amber in High School. He had his marriage to Rebeccah. For some reason though, the feelings he had for Deana were different; they were so much stronger and intense. It was becoming obvious to Leon there were different degrees of love that a man could feel for a woman. His love for Deana had grown to the highest level. He hated himself for falling so deeply in love; he did not like feeling this vulnerable. He was actually afraid of losing Deana. What if she packed up her things and moved back home to Tampa?

Deana and Luke got to the botanical garden just before eleven o'clock. Last week Deana had been excited and talkative. Today she was quiet and sullen. Mr. DeRoberts and his associates could see she was upset. Regardless, the plan was to forge forward. Deana wore blue jeans and a pretty white top. She was positioned in front of waves of beautiful flowers. It was a beautiful shot, maybe the most beautiful of the seven. It would become page five in the photo album.

Mr. DeRoberts had what he needed to finish. He told Deana he'd need five hours. At 5pm the photo album would be finished, complete and perfect.

"Miss Murphy," Mr. DeRoberts stated, "You may be the most photogenic customer I've ever worked with. I think you missed your calling as a model."

"Thank you." Deana said somberly.

Deana and Luke went to lunch and a movie to kill the five

hours. At five o'clock they were at the studio picking up the photo album. The seven pictures were stunning with the 'praying you love me forever' photo serving as the grand finale.

Deana and Luke went to dinner; then headed back to Dothan. She called Leon and told him she would be back at seven-thirty. Leon was relieved she was at least still talking to him.

"I'm looking forward to seeing you tonight," Leon said. "There's so much I have to say to you."

There are some choice words I'd like to say to you Deana thought to herself but didn't say out loud.

"Before anything else is said, I still need to give you your gift." Deana replied "I'm hoping it will leave you speechless."

"Hopefully not too speechless, I really do need to talk to you. I'll see you soon, I love you." Leon said as he hung up.

He loves me, probably. How do I even begin to process all this Deana thought. Nine days ago he proposes marriage, gives me a diamond ring, and wants to marry me. Yesterday he just wanted to be friends and shack up with me. Tonight he's back in love. Lord help me, Deana prayed.

Deana and Luke played the radio loud and sang along to the songs they knew. It helped clear Deana's head. One hour later they pulled into Dothan. Leon and the boys had gotten to Deana's and were there waiting. Deana got Luke out of his car seat and like the night before, she asked the three boys to go inside and watch television. She wanted to speak to Leon in private.

She reached into the back seat of the Stratus and pulled out the photo album.

"A picture is worth a thousand words," Deana stated. "There are seven pictures here of me. I put everything I had into these pictures for you. I left nothing out. If there was anything, anyone ever thought I was hiding from you, they were wrong. Everything is in this book for you in living color. Picture five was taken today. You can see the tears in my eyes."

"Whether you love or hate this photo album," Deana continued, "please tell me you love it. Even if you throw it in a dumpster on your way home. It would kill me if you didn't love it because what I put into it is such a big part of me. Like I said earlier, I left nothing on the table."

Deana handed Leon the book. She watched his eyes as he looked at picture after picture. When he got to picture five, she could see the emotion build up in his eyes as he saw the tears in hers. He stared at it for almost ten minutes.

"I was so wrong and stupid," Leon began. "I never should have doubted you. The reason my first marriage was so bad was because we were wrong for each other. We didn't love each other enough and we both failed as spouses. I realize now that my relationship with you is so different. Last night, one night without you, was all it took. After sharing the best nights of my life with you, last night I found out the hard way what my life without you would be like. I hated it."

"I called Lester this morning," Leon continued. "I told him if you would have me back, I would ask you to go to the Justice of the Peace next Tuesday and get married. Kenny can be my best man. We can apply for the licenses tomorrow and we can have everything formalized in one week."

"That is very sweet," Deana said as she switched her ring back to her left hand. "But you have to understand, I've been waiting for my wedding day since I was four years old. I need a little time to enjoy being engaged. I have some money saved. I need time to plan a nice ceremony and party. I know this is your second marriage, but it is my first and only. I also want time to enjoy the process. I agree with one thing you said last night. Fourth of July probably is too soon. I'm willing to compromise. How about Labor Day weekend? It would be August 31st, just after my birthday."

"Labor Day weekend sounds great," Leon said. "This photo album is amazing; you never cease to surprise me. And yes, I do have two very important things to say to you. I love you with all my heart and then some. Also, I'll love you unconditionally forever and ever. Now please come home with me."

Luke was standing at the door. "What did daddy say?" he

asked.

"Daddy said he is going to marry me and we are going to be a family," Deana replied.

"Is it okay for me to call you mommy now?" Luke asked.

"Yes, of course it is, honey." Deana answered with a tear in her eye. Tonight though, it was a happy tear.

Wednesday night, when Deana was at work and Lester was at a church function with Claire and Julie, Leon drove up to his parents' house with the boys. Deana had made a casserole during the day for him to take up to his folks. Gracie, the Colonel, Leon and the three boys had a nice dinner together.

"Deana and I came to a final decision Monday night," Leon said as Gracie was removing the dirty plates from the table after dinner. "We are going to be married at Dothan Christian Church on Saturday August 31st. There will be a short service at 5pm followed by a big party in the park across the street. I say big, because I'm pretty sure Deana will go all out."

"Oh, by the way, dad," Leon continued, "Deana said her foster father, Mr. Wilson, in Tampa has been ill. She asked if you would give her away at the ceremony."

"Of course I will," the Colonel stated. "I'd be honored. You know, Leon, you were a real chicken spit for not standing up to Lester and Claire the other day. Neither one of them knows what's best for you. They both act like they're still in high school."

"Deana gave me something to show you," Leon said as he got up to go to the truck. He came back with the photo album. "These pictures will blow you away."

Gracie and the Colonel slowly went page to page, stopping at page six.

"My lord, look at the butt on that girl," the Colonel remarked. "That is one fine woman."

"Of all her fine qualities, it's her butt that does it for you?" Leon asked.

"It might not be her most important quality," the Colonel explained, "but it sure alleviates any shortcomings she may have."

"That's the point, dad," Leon proclaimed. "We've been together almost five months. She doesn't have a whole lot of shortcomings. She's great with the boys, a great cook, she's smart, likes sports, plays music, and looks like a model. I'm pretty sure I'm getting a decent wife this time. Tell Lester and Claire when we come back for Easter, I don't want any problems from either one of them. Our decision is final."

The day before Easter Deana spent hours in the kitchen working hard on the next day's dinner. She was roasting a ten pound pork loin. Everyone had liked her cheese mashed potatoes and fried okra, so she was making them again. Claire was going to bring a few of her sides.

Deana was not really looking forward to another trip to the elder Samuels', but she wanted to be a team player. If she was going to be part of this family, she had to figure out how to co-exist with Lester, Claire and Julie. The restaurant was closed for Easter so she couldn't leave early to go to work. It could be a long day.

Matthew, Mark, Luke, Leon and Deana arrived in Athens just before one o'clock. Deana's dinner looked phenomenal and everyone was impressed as Leon, Matthew and Mark brought Deana's food into the Samuels' kitchen. Deana was walking with Luke, holding his hand.

Julie and Gracie had the table all set. Claire brought corn and apple sauce. Deana didn't think it was really fair she had ten times the expense and had to do ten times the work, but she didn't say anything.

Dinner was fantastic. It was one benefit of minimizing Claire's participation. Everyone was complimentary towards the meal and everyone seemed happy. There was even an Easter egg hunt put together for the children after dinner.

Later in the afternoon, Lester pulled Deana aside. He asked if he could talk to her. He seemed more polite and subdued than usual.

"I know you are probably mad at me," Lester began. "You

have every right to be upset. I interfered in your affairs and I apologize for that. But, Leon is my little brother, my only sibling. I have always been the one who looked out for him. I wasn't trying to break you two up. He loves you too much for that. I just thought he was going too fast with you."

"To be honest, Lester, I would be disappointed if you weren't concerned about your brother. I know it seems like I came out of nowhere and because of that maybe there is distrust. I wish I was the girl next door from your childhoods. I wish I was someone you were comfortable with. I don't have that luxury. All I can do is promise you this; I won't be just a good wife to Leon, I will be a great wife. I won't be just a good mother to your nephews, I will be a great mother. I don't do things half way or half hearted. I excel at everything I do. That's who I am."

Lester had no response. After a minute or two he just walked away.

The following evening, Deana and Leon were watching television. Leon was watching a fishing show.

"From what I've been learning at the restaurant," Deana said, "an awful lot of Georgians like to fish. Leon, do you like to fish?"

"When I was in my teens, my dad bought a used johnboat. We would take it out on the lake up by our house two or three times a week," Leon reminisced. "I absolutely loved it. Our little fishing excursions were some of the best times of my life. I really miss the relaxing days out on the water dropping a line. It was a great way to get away from the rest of the world for a little while."

This gave Deana an idea. It was Leon's birthday on April, 29th. She had four weeks to put something together for him.

When Deana was fifteen and living at the orphanage, Mr. Wilson took a few of the boys and Deana on a small fishing trip. She had so much fun and always wanted to do it again, but she was never able to.

"Leon, your birthday is on a Monday this year," Deana said. "Is there any way you can get the day off from work? There is something special I would like to do for you."

Leon submitted a request form at work for his birthday off and it got approved. Deana went to work on her computer. She found a resort just northwest of Athens and northeast of Atlanta. It was only half an hour from Leon's parents' house. It had beautiful cottages on a big gorgeous lake that offered private fishing excursions. Deana made a deal with the manager for a one day package. It wasn't too expensive so she booked it.

April 13th, was Matthew's 11th birthday. It was a Saturday. Because Easter and Matthew's birthday were so close every year, Leon and Rebeccah would go to the elder Samuels' for Easter and the Johnson's for Matthew's birthday. There were two boys in the Johnson's neighborhood and they would always come over every year for a little party. Because Deana had to work tonight, they got an early start to Macon.

Deana got up at 7am to start work on Matthew's birthday cake. Matthew loved cherries and he loved chocolate. Deana baked a double layer chocolate cake with two bottles of Maraschino cherries in it, topped with chocolate frosting. It was brilliant. She made chocolate chip pancakes for breakfast. Everyone got cleaned up and dressed and they were off.

During the week, Mrs. Johnson called Deana about Matthew's gift. Matthew had requested a violent combat game. Mrs. Johnson wanted to clear his request with Deana first. Deana explained her feelings to Mrs. Johnson and Mrs. Johnson respected them. Deana suggested the college football video game. The boys had practically worn out the pro football video game.

Deana thought it was very classy and respectful of Mrs. Johnson to call Deana first, instead of buying something Deana would be uncomfortable with and making her have to deal with it.

Leon and Deana bought Matthew a new baseball glove, a baseball bat and a baseball that looks like a hardball. The baseball is foam instead of thread so if it hits you it doesn't hurt. When they got to the Johnson's, the boys wanted to play with the ball, glove and bat right away.

The neighbor boys were named Sam and Elliot. They were eleven and twelve years old respectively. Deana agreed to be the designated pitcher and Luke the designated catcher. The older boys alternated hitting and fielding. They played for over an hour. It had been a long time since Deana had played baseball. It was a lot of fun.

While they were playing, Leon told the Johnson's their unusual engagement, un-engagement and re-engagement story.

It was Sunday, the day before Leon's birthday. Deana was nervous with anticipation. She wanted everything to be perfect. Matthew, Mark, Luke, Leon and Deana went to church. Deana and Mrs. Jarvis had another solid performance. Four weeks ago, Easter Sunday, the church was almost full capacity. Many of the members that only went to service on special occasions were coming more frequently. The improved music gave the service an energy filled vibe. It made service less boring and it appealed to the younger people.

Leon, the boys and Deana left quickly after service finished. They were going to leave the boys off with Leon's parents. If something were to go wrong, Leon and Deana would be only half an hour away. Deana had called the boys' school in advance. It would be all right if the boys missed first period on Monday. As long as they were in school by ten, the absence would be excused. Since November 8th, the boys had perfect attendance.

Deana and Leon got to the resort just before 1pm. They had their own cottage on the lake. Inside the cottage there were rose petals everywhere, especially on the king-sized bed. The attendant said a stocked 16-foot johnboat was ready for them to take out on the lake. The boat contained a large cooler with beverages, sandwiches and fried chicken that Deana special ordered for Leon. They were given high quality fishing poles and the boat had a live well full of shiners. Shiners are little silver fish used for bass fishing.

Leon helped Deana onto the boat and started the engine. The magnitude and beauty of the North Georgia lake was stunning. Being the end of April, all nature was in full bloom. The rolling hills were deep green and lush.

Leon found a quiet, scenic part of the lake he thought would be the best place to "drop a line". The lake they were fishing on was famous for being plentiful with bass. Bass fishing is extremely popular in both Florida and Georgia.

Leon got Deana's hook baited and she got a bite quickly. She was very excited. Leon helped her reel in a very small one and a half pound baby bass. Deana didn't care. She made a catch. At the resort, they had a catch and release policy. Deana had Leon unhook the fish and gladly sent it back into the water.

The next four catches went to Leon. The bass he caught

were adult. They ranged from three to five pounds. Evening was approaching and Deana was getting discouraged. She knew it was getting close to time to bring it in. She looked at Leon and made a face at him. He was feeling bad for her.

Just as Leon was getting ready to put everything up so they could get back to their cottage, Deana got a huge tug on her line. She screamed for Leon to help her. Leon motioned for her to spin the reel. Deana spun her hand and reeled the large bass into the boat. Leon grabbed the bass by the bottom lip to show it to Deana.

"Deana, get out your phone and take a quick picture," Leon instructed.

Deana took her shot at an angle that would show off the bass, the lake and the gorgeous green hills in the back-round. Then Leon put the largest catch of the day back in the lake. Deana was ecstatic.

They got back to the cottage around seven and took showers to get ready for dinner. Deana had another surprise for Leon. During the week she had gone into town and bought a little black dress for this specific occasion. When Leon came out of the shower and bathroom, Deana was already dressed. She looked stunning. Leon was absolutely elated.

Dinner was at a five star restaurant at the resort. It made even her cooking pale in comparison. The food was amazing. The restaurant was open air and the view over the lake and mountains was breathtaking. The waiter had brought a special wine for Deana and Leon to sample. It was a house specialty. It was half strawberry wine and half champagne. The waiter jokingly called it rich redneck's delight. Deana loved it, Leon tolerated it. He didn't want to upset Deana so he played along he loved it too.

After dinner, the engaged couple walked through the beautiful gardens of the resort. Every bush, every shrub was manicured perfectly. The sky was filled with stars. It was a beautiful Georgia night. The smell of the late evening air coming off the lake was wonderful. When Deana and Leon were alone on a hidden path, he kissed her. He kissed her with all the passion he had. He kissed her with all his heart and soul. He thanked God he made the right decision and he thanked God for sending her to him.

Deana and Leon had been fully intimate with each other now for over seven weeks. Every time it had been great, especially the first time. But tonight had been different. Leon was more passionate than ever. He was on fire. He was like a man with something to prove. This time, it was Deana who was pleasantly shocked and amazed.

Early Monday morning, Deana gave Leon one more of his many birthday presents, before they had to go to Athens to pick up the boys. Leon had never had anyone in his life make a big deal about his birthday. This was, without a doubt, his most special one.

CHAPTER 13
FINALLY THE WEDDING

Early Sunday morning, May 12th, 2013, it was Mother's Day. Leon and Deana were awoken by a loud knock on their bedroom door. Deana was exhausted because the restaurant had been very busy the night before. Still, she was overwhelmed by what she saw when she opened the door. Matthew and Mark held trays of breakfast food and orange juice. Luke was carrying a large handmade card.

Deana tried not to cry, but when the boys in unison said "Happy Mother's Day, Deana" she lost it. Her eyes filled with tears. So did Leon's, although he would never admit it.

"I love you boys so much," Deana said "Thank you from

the bottom of my heart."

"We love you too Deana," they each replied.

A few Sundays later it was Father's Day. Deana and the boys made sausage, scrambled eggs and corn potato pancakes. The corn potato pancakes were something new, but she was confident Leon would like them. She needed to have a big talk with Leon that afternoon.

Deana put the food on a big plate. Each of the boys carried handmade cards they'd made for their dad. They woke Leon up and gave him breakfast in bed.

After lunch, Deana sat down with Leon, who was waiting for the baseball game to come on.

"We need to talk," Deana started. "I may be making a big mistake in bringing up this subject, but this is very important to me. The wedding is eleven weeks away. I'm at a point where I need to start putting deposits down for my dress, the band and for the food."

"This is your opportunity to get out of your commitment to the wedding if you so desire," Deana continued. "If you don't want to get married, I need to know now. Are you 100% sure you want to marry me or do you still have any doubts?"

"I'm 110% sure I want to marry you and spend the rest of my life with you," Leon replied with a smile.

"That's the answer I was praying I'd hear," Deana said as

she gave Leon's hand a squeeze. "There is, however, one more issue I need to discuss with you. In a few weeks I'd like to go to the attorney's office to start the paperwork to adopt Matthew, Mark and Luke. Do I have your permission? Also, I'd like to legally change my name from Murphy to Samuels."

"You have my full permission and blessing," Leon said. "On August 31st, we will officially be one big happy family."

As Delores predicted, Matthew and Mark finished the school year with really good grades. Matthew got two A's, two B's and two C's. Mark got three A's and three B's.

As a reward Deana signed them up for soccer. Luke was thrilled but Matthew and Mark really wanted to play football; but they were too late to sign up for football because registration had been back in the spring. Plus, the football league was in Athens which would be a major burden on Leon and Deana. She'd be late to work every Thursday. Football practice was Monday, Tuesday, Thursday, and some Saturdays. Saturdays were either games or practices.

Soccer was much easier. Registration was in the summer. The soccer club was only a town away. The drive was only ten minutes. All three boys could practice at the same time and same night. Practice was only two nights a week; Tuesday night and Thursday night. Most importantly, Mike Richards, a boy up the street would be on Luke's team. Mrs. Richards allowed Deana to take the four boys on Tuesday nights to and from practice. Then Mrs. Richards would drive all the boys Thursday night when Deana had to work. The games were on Saturdays between 8am and 2pm so Deana and Leon would be able to see all the games.

Deana made an agreement with Matthew and Mark. "If you want to play football next year you will have to train hard and be in excellent condition. Nothing is better for conditioning than soccer. If you will play the entire season of soccer and get in shape and keep your grades up I'll coordinate things with your father so you can play football next year."

After finishing up with the boys, Deana looked at her calendar and was disappointed. Like Valentine's Day, her birthday this year was on a Thursday. Last year she spent her birthday in the hospital and the year before she was at a training seminar for her new job at the finance company.

"I'm not going to torture you the way I did Valentine's Day," Leon said on the way to the boys' first soccer game. It was the Saturday before Deana's August 22nd birthday. "I talked to Mr. Vito last night and he said you could have your birthday off. I took the day off also. Luke's birthday is on Friday so I thought we could go to my parents' house. We can have a little party for the two of you. At night my parents can watch the boys for a little bit. We can go back to the restaurant you liked so much that we went to on our first date."

"Can we go back to the lake again?" Deana asked. "Now that the weather is warmer, I have something special in mind."

"How can I say no to that?" Leon said smiling.

Luke's game was first at 8am. He'd played some form of soccer almost every weekday since the previous November. He was really good. He had two goals and two assists. His team won 8-4; Leon was quite impressed.

"It looks like Luke has gotten some pretty good coaching," Leon said complimenting Deana. "He is one of the youngest players yet one of the best."

Matthew and Mark's game was at twelve o'clock. They were on the same team. Deana was surprised both boys won starting positions, even though they had very little soccer experience. Deana had taught them how to defend against an attacking forward from the other team and some other basics. It paid off because the coach put both boys back on defense. Matthew sometimes got subbed out but Mark played the entire game. He was a relentless, physical defender. They won 2-1.

During the past few weeks Deana had been planning the finishing touches for the wedding and party. The guest list was set for 80 people. One day at work she looked stressed out. Robert the cook noticed and asked what was wrong.

"Half the people coming to my wedding are from church and very devout," Deana answered. "If I serve alcohol at my wedding, they will be offended. The other half are expecting a big time party. If there is no alcohol they will be disappointed and may not have a good time."

"Deana, I think I can solve your problem for you." Robert said. "Consider it my wedding gift. Tell your church friends you won't be serving or providing any alcoholic beverages. I'll discretely sneak in a few coolers full of adult beverages on my own for the party crowd. Everyone should be happy."

"Thank you so much," Deana replied. "If my dress alterations go well, the rest should go pretty smoothly."

Deana had found a beautiful designer dress at a consignment shop in Athens. It was an Italian style "Princess" wedding gown. It featured draped satin detail with subtle hints of pearl embroidery. The detachable shrug and draped net pick-up skirt created added elegance. She was so excited about how she looked in it.

Mr. Vito was going to cater the wedding. He was actually closing the restaurant for the night. That way all the employees could attend.

The big surprise of the evening would be the band. Deana put out a feeler for the best band she could get. The resounding answer was the Jacobson Brothers Band; the band that played at the big church near Morrison Georgia. Eli Jacobson played lead guitar; his brother Edwin played rhythm guitar and sang lead vocals. They also had a drummer and bass player in their band.

One afternoon, Deana made an appointment to talk with them. They had burned a four song CD of their music for her which was outstanding.

"I would love to have you play our wedding," Deana said. "Your music is amazing. Do you think I could perform a few songs with you? I'd be very grateful."

"That would be fantastic," Eli exclaimed. "If you could do the first couple of songs with us, it would really get the crowd going."

"I could do two with you in the beginning in my wedding gown," Deana stated. "Right before I leave with Leon, I'll do two more in regular clothes. It will be so much fun. We can practice the Monday and Tuesday before the big weekend."

Mid afternoon, August 22nd, it was off to Athens to Leon's parents' house to celebrate Deana and Luke's birthdays. It was Deana's actual birthday; Luke's birthday was the next day. He didn't mind celebrating a day early. Deana had baked him a banana-coconut custard cake earlier in the day. It was Luke's favorite.

Matthew and Mark both had two wrapped gifts with them. Two were for Luke, two were for Deana. Luke had one for

Deana and Deana and Leon had a gift for Luke.

Deana was going to make cheese-steak sandwiches with Gracie when they got to the Samuels' home. Leon and Deana's reservations were for 6:30. They wanted it to be dusk when dinner was over so they could enjoy watching the sun go down when they went to the lake.

Before she started dinner for the boys, she wanted to exchange gifts and have a talk with Matthew, Mark and Luke.

Matthew gave Deana a handmade soap dish. He gave Luke a little race car Deana helped him pick out. Mark gave Deana a handmade pen and pencil holder. He gave Luke a little fire truck. Luke gave Deana a miniature stuffed soccer ball for her key chain, which Leon had helped him buy. Deana and Leon gave Luke the new lightweight soccer cleats he'd been wanting.

After the gift exchange, Deana told the boys she had a birthday wish she wanted to share with them.

"Two months ago, I had my attorney petition the Circuit Court of the State of Georgia so that I could legally adopt the three of you," Deana explained. "My request was granted. When your father and I marry in nine days we will officially, all five of us, be a family. My name will become Deana Samuels."

"My birthday wish, or should I say request, is for the five of us to go to the courthouse and get sworn in so the judge will sign and finalize my petition. We have a court date this Monday afternoon to do this. I want the three of you to be in the wedding ceremony with your father and me. Your father and I will exchange vows like in all weddings, but after the vow exchange, the three of you will come to the side of the altar and participate in what is called a Unity sand ceremony. We will each get a vase full of colored Unity sand. We each get one color. Leon will go first; he will have black colored Unity sand. He will pour his sand into a heart shaped Unity vase which will serve as the first layer or bottom layer. I will go next with a white Unity sand layer. You boys can pick your own colors. Are you all right with this?" Deana asked.

"That sounds pretty cool," Matthew said. Mark agreed. "Maybe now Matthew and Mark can call you mommy, too." Luke said.

"Matthew and Mark can call me what they are most comfortable with," Deana laughed.

Just after six o'clock, Deana freshened up, then jumped into Leon's truck with him. They had requested the same table they sat at last November. They ordered the same dinners and wine.

"Leon, this has been the most amazing year of my life," Deana reflected. "Twelve months ago I was in a Tampa hospital thanking God I was still alive. Tonight I sit here with my loving fiancé, nine days before my wedding."

"I never dreamed I'd ever remarry," Leon stated.

"The week after our long Thanksgiving weekend I started to get an inkling we might be on our way to a permanent relationship," Deana admitted. "I knew it was going kind of fast, but I kept getting a feeling we belonged together."

"I have a confession to make," Leon stated. "From the very beginning I tried to convince myself I shouldn't fall in love with you; and not just you, any woman. But, the harder I tried to not fall in love with you the deeper I fell. Valentine's Night at the lake you overwhelmed me. I reached the point of no return."

"Everything you did was so amazing," Leon continued. "I loved your cooking, your parenting, the photo book, and your financial advice. When we dated we both seemed proud to be out with one another. Spending the Holidays together was a blast. Kenny's birthday was so cool. But the thing you did that so impressed me was the night I went to get water at the kitchen sink and I could hear you putting the boys to bed. The way they respond to you is amazing. Your temperament and tolerance is so impressive. Rebeccah would lose patience with the boys. Before anyone knew it, she would be yelling at the boys and I had a hard time dealing with that."

"Another great thing was your timing," Leon continued. "That first week of November, when we met, I had pretty much hit rock bottom. You entered the picture and provided the change that was needed. The Sunday you took me fishing at the resort didn't hurt either. I really am very much in love with you."

"How about we go to the lake now so I can show you how much I'm in love with you?" Deana asked. "The sun should be starting to go down right about now."

Deana was right. It was a sensational summer sunset. Leon drove to where the black top ended; to the clearing overlooking the lake. Leon and Deana kissed as their favorite song played on the radio. As the sun went down and the stars filled the sky, Deana and Leon took their clothes off and things got hot as they played in the cool Georgia water. It was a wonderful birthday for Deana.

It was finally Saturday, August 31st, 2013. The big day was upon Dothan. This celebration was going to be more than two people getting married. It was a big event and party the town desperately needed. Deana spared no expense. Even the floral arrangement on the altar was extravagant. The cake was spectacular. She wanted everything to be perfect. Deana put her heart and soul into this wedding and making it a day to truly remember.

Deana had chosen Delores to be her Maid of Honor. Leon had chosen his brother Lester to be his Best Man. It surprised Deana when earlier in the week Leon told her he wanted to write his own vows. She thought it sounded romantic, so she agreed. She was happy to see Leon starting to open up more.

In the morning Deana had her hair and nails done. She bought a brand new special perfume. She did her own make-up at home. Next, she met with Delores inside the church. Delores helped Deana into her Italian Princess wedding dress and cowgirl boots. Leon had a matching pair of cowboy boots. Deana looked radiant; she was an absolute vision.

Following the Processional, Pastor Beckmann opened the ceremony with a heartfelt welcome and introduction. He then nodded to Leon to recite his vows.

"I, Leon Samuels, take this woman, Deana, to have and to hold, in good times and in bad, in sickness and in health. I promise to be faithful and forsake all others. If asked if I understand the sanctity of these vows, I do. If you ask me if I love this woman with all my heart, I do. If you ask me if I take Deana to be my lawfully wedded wife, I absolutely do."

Deana started to cry. She was so overwhelmed she didn't know how she was going to make it through her vows. "I, Deana," she said in between sobs, "love this man with all my heart. I love when he holds me in his arms and makes me feel safe. I love when he watches me dance to the radio when I clean the kitchen. I love every minute we spend together. I will love, honor and cherish this man until death do us part. Will I, Deana, take Leon to be my lawfully wedded husband? Yes I Do!!!!"

Following their vows, Leon and Deana exchanged wedding rings.

Pastor Beckmann then declared: "By the authority vested in me by the State of Georgia, witnessed by your friends and family, I have the pleasure to pronounce you husband and wife. You may now seal your vows with a kiss."

On cue, Leon and Deana shared their first kiss as husband and wife.

Next the boys came up to the altar for the Unity Sand ceremony. There was a big heart shaped vase that was positioned in the middle of the five Samuels. Leon, Deana, Matthew, Mark and Luke had smaller vases filled with sand. Leon went first. He poured black sand from his small vase into the big vase creating its first layer. This would be the foundation. Deana went second adding a layer of white sand. Matthew went next adding blue colored sand. Mark went fourth using orange sand. Luke finished by adding a green layer from his little vase.

Pastor Beckmann explained to those in attendance the significance of the sand and how the layers represent the unique members of this family coming together as one. The center Unity vase would be sealed with wax to keep the sand safe and secure. In a few days it would permanently rest on the mantle at the Samuels' home.

After the Unity Sand ceremony, the Recessional music began playing and Leon and Deana lead the wedding party back down the aisle and out of the sanctuary.

During the ceremony, Mr. Vito got the food ready while the Jacobson brothers set up the stage for their performance. Since Edwin Jacobson played rhythm guitar, all Deana would have to do is sing. They opened with the song "My Kinda Party." The crowd loved it. Deana then sang the ballad "Lost in the Moment." It's a fantastic wedding song and Deana dedicated it to Leon.

When the second song was over, Deana with microphone still in hand, talked to the crowd. "When I went to a wedding a few years ago in Florida, people had to pay to dance with the bride. I feel I should have to pay to dance with you. Y'all have been so wonderful to me the past year. I could not have been made to feel more comfortable and welcome."

"Since most of us are on a budget," Deana joked, "how about we skip the money exchange and I'll dance with every one of you for one minute. Whether you are male or female, young or old, let's share a dance together." Of the eighty people there, Deana danced with seventy-eight people. She even danced with Lester; he was one of the first in line. Unfortunately, Claire and Julie had run off, nowhere to be found.

Over an hour later, Deana finally got to sit down with

Leon at the Bride and Groom's table to have dinner. The sun was starting to set. It was a beautiful evening.

"I can't believe you were able to dance for over an hour straight without a break," Leon said to Deana.

"It's one of the perks of all the training I do," Deana explained.

By now Deana was starving. She filled her plate and sat back to soak in the celebration. The Jacobson's had some elaborate lighting so the party could go on pretty late. Everyone seemed to be having a great time.

After Deana ate, she went back into the church to change into the tassel vest, skirt and boots she wore for Leon at Kenny's birthday party back in January. She waited for her cue to sing two more songs before she left with Leon. They were going on a two day honeymoon to Hilton Head Island, South Carolina. While she sang, she looked into the crowd. She saw people she thought didn't even like each other dancing together or at least socializing together. The party seemed to bring the people of Dothan closer together.

When she was done singing, Leon brought the truck around just as Deana yelled into the microphone, "God Bless you and thank you so much. I love each and every one of you!" She ran off the stage and hopped into Leon's truck.

"I wore this outfit for you to let you know even though we

are married, I will still dance for you and party with you just like when we were courting. If anything, things will be even better."

Leon looked out the window. What an incredible day and celebration it was. The tone and feel of the day was so festive, a complete contrast from his first marriage.

"Deana, I had the most amazing day," Leon reflected. "It was a blast. It was so much fun. You throw a heck of a party. You are, without a doubt, the most remarkable person I have ever met. I'm very proud you are my wife."

"Leon, thank you from the bottom of my heart. Your love for me made all this possible."

CHAPTER 14
DEANA SAMUELS

After Deana and Leon left for Hilton Head Island for their honeymoon the Johnson's took the boys back to Macon to celebrate the remainder of the Labor Day weekend. They would all meet back at the newlyweds' house Monday night. Matthew and Mark had school Tuesday and Leon had to work. Deana would start to move out of Mr. McGee's and fully into Leon's.

Hilton Head Island is a perfect place for a honeymoon; famous for its pristine beauty. Its South Carolina beachfront is one of the most beautiful on the Eastern Seaboard. The view from Leon and Deana's hotel room was breathtaking. It was a wonderful beginning they would cherish forever.

Sunday afternoon the happy couple explored the backwaters and salt marshes of Hilton Head aboard a Skimmer Nature Charter. A Skimmer is a twenty foot boat with a canopy over it. The Captain knew where dolphins frequently swam and realized his passengers would be interested in this encounter. Deana and Leon were able to watch and enjoy the dolphins and other wildlife at relatively close range.

Deana and Leon got back in time for an early dinner. The restaurant featured outdoor dining overlooking the Atlantic Ocean. As they enjoyed their meal and each other's company, they were treated to a magnificent sunset.

"Leon, why don't we go down and build a sandcastle together. I have never done that before. I saw some children building one earlier and it looked like so much fun."

Three hours later, an impressive sand structure was erected. It was two and a half feet tall with a molded, tiered roof. It featured a large moat.

"Not bad for our first time," Deana boasted. "Leon, what do you think?"

"I think we make a pretty good team," Leon stated. Then he scooped Deana up and carried her into the ocean. The stars were bright and the water was warm. The newlyweds were off to a good start.

Monday was the day Deana was excited about. She hadn't

been able to go fishing with Leon since his birthday in April. One reason they chose Hilton Head Island for their honeymoon was because they would have the opportunity to go fishing together again. They booked an Egret 18'9" flats boat. Its engine was incredibly quiet and lightning fast. They could get to any fishing spot in no time at all.

They decided to fish inshore on the flats. They wanted to catch redfish. During September, the redfish were in tailing mode with their heads down and tail up. It's a beautiful act of nature. Leon easily caught a twelve pound redfish. He then helped Deana pull in a ten and a half pound red. She was thrilled.

Unfortunately, the honeymoon had to be cut short because they had to get back to Dothan before eight o'clock to meet the Johnson's. Despite its brevity, they had the time of their lives.

On the way home Leon had a little surprise for Deana. One of the drivers Leon worked with and was good friends with had come to the wedding two days ago. While Deana was doing her thank you dances during dinner, the young driver told Leon he desperately wanted to get Leon and Deana a wedding gift but he had no money. Leon gave him twenty dollars and told the young man what he could do.

On the way back, Leon parked his truck in front of the big water tower everybody passes on their way into town. In big red letters painted on the water tower were the words: LEON LOVES DEANA 4EVER AND EVER. Deana almost started to cry. But, before she could Leon asked her to get out of the truck and for her to sit on the roof of the cab. He positioned the truck so he could photograph Deana and the water tower and the sun going down all at the same time. It was a remarkable photograph.

Tuesday morning, Deana got Matthew and Mark off to school. She and Luke did a quick workout. Then they went into town. Using the money she got as wedding gifts and some of her savings, she bought a brand new bedroom set. She had made sure it was all right with Leon first. Then she proceeded to buy a new larger dresser. She bought two new end tables and a bigger bed with a brand new mattress. The old mattress had always made her feel uncomfortable.

She cleaned Rebeccah's belongings out of the closet. In a show of respect, she never threw any of Rebeccah's belongings out. Deana put Rebeccah's things in storage with her own belongings. In time she would try to sell most of the things she owned that she had kept at the duplex she'd been renting from Mr. McGee. Financially things would be better for Deana and Leon. Deana would no longer have to pay rent, cable or electric. The storage unit was inexpensive so they'd have more disposable income.

Later, Deana went to the bank. Leon had been doing

pretty well keeping the mortgage between twenty days past due and current. She direct wired $712 to General Mortgage. She wanted the mortgage paid current all the time from now on. Now that they were going to have joint credit she wanted their score to be as high as possible.

After dinner, Deana joined Leon on the couch. She wrapped her arms around him and exclaimed: "I finally have a family and a home!" Later that night when she made love to her husband, it was truly special. Physically, nothing was different. Emotionally, everything was different. She was with her own husband, in their own home, and in their own bed.

That Saturday, Luke's team won its third straight game. Mark got a red card in his game and was very upset. A boy from the other team and Mark went for the ball at the same time. Mark was much bigger and stronger than the other boy; he flattened the kid. They had to carry him off the field. Mark was ejected from the game and his team had to play the entire game down a man. They lost the game and Mark got a mandatory one game suspension. The referee sent Mark away from the field.

Deana caught up to Mark in the parking lot. She wanted to calm him down.

"I can't believe that stupid kid and that idiot referee," Mark griped. "The kid ran into me more than I ran into him. My coach didn't even say anything to defend me. What's up with that?"

"Mark, red and yellow cards are part of the game, other players will deliberately try to draw fouls. Sometimes they'll exaggerate the foul to draw a card against you. That's why your coach didn't say anything. It's all part of the game."

"Well, it's a stupid game."

"If you still feel this way next spring, I'll honor our agreement and you can play football. You just have to finish this soccer season and keep your grades up."

"Done," Mark responded emphatically.

Deana smiled. She had to agree with Mark that he was more suited for football. Mark was a natural hitter. Watching him play football was going to be exciting.

When Deana lived at the orphanage in Tampa, something cool Mr. Wilson did for the children was called "Special Day." One day a year, not a birthday or holiday, each child had a day to pick something fun to do away from the orphanage. Usually it would be dinner and a concert or a sporting event; Deana preferred concerts.

Since the boys birthdays were in the spring and summer, fall would be perfect for "Special Day." She asked the boys to pick an upcoming concert they wanted to see. It could not be on a Friday or Saturday. She would take them to dinner at the restaurant of their choice, even if the restaurant and concert was in Atlanta.

Deana asked them to pick an event between the end of September and mid December. Matthew picked a country concert. Deana helped Luke pick out a country concert too. Mark wanted to go to a rock concert. The good news was that Mark's concert was on a Tuesday night. She wouldn't have to miss work. Mark's event came up first. On Tuesday, October 1st, at five o'clock Deana and Mark jumped in the Stratus and headed to Atlanta.

Mark wanted to eat at a pizza restaurant with a huge video game arcade. After eating, Mark got in a solid half hour of video games. At the concert, Mark ran into one of his friends from school.

"Wow, Mark, is that your new step-mom you were talking about?" the boy asked.

"Yes," Mark said laughing. "This is my step-mother Deana."

"Man, how do I get me a step-mom like that?" the boy continued. "That's so crazy."

Deana looked embarrassed but Mark was smiling. After the concert, Deana asked Mark if going out with his step-mom was uncomfortable. "No way," Mark replied. "I like seeing my friend's responses when they meet you."

"Oh," Deana replied and continued: "I always pray that you boys accept me as your step-mother and that we become a happy family."

"You don't have to worry. Before you came to us, I used to get teased by some of the kids at school. My first mom didn't always get us decent haircuts or clothes like the other kids wore. She really didn't care how we looked. Many times our clothes weren't even cleaned. The one night when you and my dad broke up, we thought you might not come back. We were all scared and crying."

Deana was surprised but did not respond. There was a long pause, and then she told Mark what a nice time she had. "I really loved the concert. It was a great show."

Three and a half weeks later it was Matthew's turn. It was a Thursday night. Mr. Vito said it was all right to take off. Mark had told Matthew how cool the pizza and arcade restaurant was, so he chose that restaurant also. The concert was fantastic. It featured three of the most popular artists, all in one show. Matthew and Deana danced in the aisles together and sang along to all the popular songs. They had a great time. On the way home, she had a similar talk with Matthew to the one she'd had with Mark.

"I've been praying," Deana began, "that you boys will

think it's a good thing having me as your step-mom."

"So far, it's been great," Matthew explained. "Our first mother wasn't always there for us. When she was there, she'd often yell at us or get upset about something. She was also intimidating. She was almost as tall as our dad; and sometimes she'd scare us."

"When I was growing up, I never saw being shorter as an asset," Deana replied, "but I'm glad it helps you feel comfortable with me."

"I think the most important thing is you are consistent," Matthew continued. "You tell us what you expect and if we have trouble you are there to help, not criticize. You make the difficult things easier for us. You also helped us be a family again. Thanks!"

Deana was touched. It was more than just a fun evening. It was also a bonding experience.

"You're welcome Matthew," Deana replied. "I can't wait for next year."

Luke's turn was next. It was mid-November. He chose to see Deana's favorite band in concert. Also, it was a Monday night so she didn't have to miss work. Luke never really cared where they went, if he was with Deana, it was fun.

Deana took Luke to the same restaurant as his brothers. All three boys loved it there. This concert was the best of the three. Luke and Deana laughed, danced and sang the whole night.

When Deana and Luke were out together, they looked and acted like mother and son. Deana was twenty-six, Luke was four. The time line fit. Deana and Luke even shared many physical features.

On the way home, Luke fell asleep. It was fine; Deana didn't feel she needed to have the same talk with Luke she'd had with Matthew and Mark.

As far as Luke was concerned, he was the one who chose Deana last November in church when he went over to Deana and sat on her knee. Deana was Luke's choice to be his mommy. As long as Deana was there every morning to take care of him, he couldn't care less about DNA or who his father was dating.

As Thanksgiving approached, Deana figured out a way to make the most of the few days off she'd have with Leon while the boys were at the Johnson's. Like last year, she'd have the Friday after Thanksgiving off. She would have one-on-one time with Leon until her Saturday night shift began.

For a few extra bucks a month, she upgraded her storage facility. She found a man in Morrison who was selling his fourteen foot johnboat, trailer and hitch at a great price. She even got the man to deliver it to her new storage facility for no extra cost. She couldn't wait for next Friday.

Thanksgiving went smoothly. Lester, Claire and even Julie were starting to accept Deana. Deana assumed the biggest reason they were being nice to her was because she was the only person in the family who could cook well. Also, Claire wasn't so jealous of Deana anymore because she was now five months pregnant and she'd found out Deana couldn't have children.

Deana wanted to wait until the boys were dropped off at the Johnson's before she told Leon her plan.

As Deana and Leon left Macon, she told Leon about the johnboat. "I want to use the Christmas present I bought for the four of you this weekend," Deana explained. "Because you and I have so few days alone together, I want to fish with you as much as we can this weekend. Before the boys get back, we can put the boat in storage until Christmas. Then I will officially give it to you guys as a gift."

Friday was a beautiful day and they had a wonderful time on the lake trying out their new boat. It rained Saturday so they had to recreate inside back at their home.

On Christmas day Leon went to the storage facility and brought home the boat to the boys. They were thrilled. The Samuels' family spent most of Christmas break "dropping a line" in a beautiful Georgia lake. The time they spent together was a wonderful family experience.

As 2014 rolled in, Matthew and Mark studied for mid-term exams. Their grades so far had been excellent. They completed their soccer season without further incident, so Deana would be signing them up for football soon. She was really looking forward to it. She loved watching the boys excel. Luke was one of the best players in his soccer league and Deana had a feeling Matthew and especially Mark, were going to be really good football players.

One spring Sunday morning, before church, Deana made an extra big breakfast with eggs, sausage, grits and her chocolate chip pancakes. Leon anticipated there was going to be some kind of discussion with Deana later that afternoon. He had now figured out some of Deana's tricks.

"All right, Deana," Leon asked. "When is the part coming that you tell me we need to have a talk this afternoon?"

"Am I that obvious?" Deana asked laughing. "Yes, we need to talk."

When they got back from church, Leon and Deana sat in the living room and talked.

"Matthew and Mark would rather play football than soccer," Deana began. "Their grades are good and they certainly seem to have the aptitude especially Mark. Luke, however, wants to keep playing soccer. He is a really good soccer player and he loves the game. To make all three boys happy will require a lot of work and driving for both of us. I came up with a plan, I need to make sure you're all right with it."

"Matthew and Mark will have practice Monday, Tuesday and Thursday nights," Deana continued. "They will have practice or games Saturday afternoon. Luke's practices will be Tuesday and Thursday nights with most games Saturday morning."

"Mondays won't be a problem," Deana concluded. "I can drive the boys to Athens and stay with them from beginning of practice at 6pm to the end of practice a couple of hours later. Tuesdays will be more difficult. I will have to bring the boys to you in Athens. You'll have to take them to practice and drive them home. I will leave Athens with Luke and take him to practice in Claybon. I will bring him home when he's done. Thursday will be even tougher. You'll have to do the same as Tuesday. For Matthew and Mark, I'll drive them to you again. You'll have to take them to and from practice. I will have to take Luke to Mrs. Richard's house and Luke will have to go with Mike to practice at six on Thursdays. I will have to ask if I can be a little late on Thursdays. Dinners will be ready for you when you get home. On Saturdays, it should work out that we will be able to go to everyone's games."

"It sounds like you have it all planned out," Leon said. "It should work."

Deana talked to Mr. Vito and he was okay with her being a little late on Thursdays. She talked with Mrs. Richards; she was fine with helping on Thursdays. She then got sat down with Matthew and Mark and gave them the good news.

"For me to do all this for you, though, I'm going to ask something in return." Deana stated.

"Anything," Matthew and Mark agreed.

"My first request is obvious," Deana began. "You have to keep your grades up. My second request is you have to respect your coaches. Football coaches can be very hard on you. There's a lot of conditioning and discipline involved. My third request may sound strange, but it's very important to me. I want to do a small version of Special Night once a week."

"I loved doing a large version of Special Night last fall and we will do that again this year," Deana continued. "But as you boys get older you will spend more time with your friends and away from home. I want a way to stay close to you. I'd like each of you to pick one of my nights off and spend two hours with me. We can play board games or walk to the little beach up at the park. For Matthew's birthday in April, I'm going to buy a weight set we can put up in the carport. If you want, we can hang out and lift weights and talk. I want a way for us to stay connected and to stay part of your lives."

"One night a week sounds good," Mark replied. "I'll take Monday night as long as we don't have practice."

"Yeah, that should work out," Matthew followed. I'll take

Tuesday night. Maybe you can spend Sunday afternoon with Luke."

"There's no need to rush this," Deana finished. "We don't have to begin until football season is over; but either late November or early December I want two hours a week with you. Also, after football registration and the end of school, we need to have a few weeks to train together before practices start. Some of the boys out there have been playing since they were seven years old. I don't want you to be behind. I'll get you ready like we did for school last year."

"How are you going to train us Deana?" Mark asked. "I thought you only played soccer growing up?"

"There was a man that came to our orphanage every once in a while named Regan Upshaw. He played professional football in Tampa. He was a first round draft pick and really knew the game. He was a defensive end, but he also knew about all of the other positions. He'd come to the orphanage to help my foster brothers who played youth football," Deana said. "Mr. Upshaw would coach my foster brothers and teach them all of the pass rush moves."

"Mr. Wilson asked me to take notes so that in between Mr. Upshaw's visits we could work on all the things he taught the boys. I still have all my notes and I can go online to refresh my memory. I will help you like we did for my foster brothers."

The boys agreed to all of Deana's conditions. She then registered them to play football.

CHAPTER 15
ARE YOU READY FOR SOME FOOTBALL?

The Samuels' were enjoying the new johnboat and going out on the lake as often as possible. Valentine's Day was a Friday this year and the restaurant was very busy. It wasn't until 11pm that Deana got off from work. Leon still took her to the lake again and gave her flowers. Being newlyweds, they enjoyed even more physicality and romance than the year before.

On March 16th, Claire gave birth to a baby boy; she and Lester were thrilled. It seemed to make them easier to deal with.

Matthew's birthday party in Macon was fun, but Leon's was even more fun. His birthday was on a Tuesday. He took off work like the previous year. This year, however, Matthew and

Mark had exams so they couldn't miss any school and needed to be home Monday night to study. Deana, Leon and Luke took the johnboat out during the day and fished until they had to be home to meet the boys when they got back from school.

Deana was learning how to filet fish. It was something she'd never learned growing up in Tampa. Leon was patient with Deana and soon she was making some pretty amazing fish dinners.

Deana and the boys enjoyed their first "official" Mother's Day together as the school year was finishing. This would be the last few weeks of Deana and Luke being alone together during the day. Soon, Matthew and Mark would be off for the summer. At the end of August, Luke would start Kindergarten. Luke and Deana had grown extremely attached to each other; it was going to be a tough transition.

As promised, Deana and Leon bought a weight set for Matthew for his birthday. Deana, Matthew, and Mark would lift weights together weekend afternoons, Monday nights and most Tuesday nights.

When school ended, Deana took out the lawnmower and mowed as deep into the brush in the backyard as possible. Their lot was not very big. Deana, however, tried to maximize it. She even cut into the next door neighbor's yard a little to help create extra space to train the boys.

Practice was going to start in a few weeks so they went and got fitted for their practice uniforms. They were both given used shoulder pads, used helmets, used pants with built in pads and used jerseys. The new uniforms and helmets were saved for game days only.

"I don't want you to get discouraged with football like you did with soccer. I want you to know how to play well by the time practice starts in a few weeks," Deana said. "The two most important parts of football are blocking and tackling. I can help you with both, especially tackling."

She gave Mark the football. He had all his pads on. She told him to run in the same direction as the property line and she would show him how to tackle. Mark easily jogged with the ball in his hands as Deana came across the lawn at him with no pads on. She got low by bending her knees like Mr. Upshaw had shown. She hit Mark sideways and low. Mark's helmet went one way, the ball went another way and Mark went straight down hard.

"Deana, what the heck are you doing?" Mark asked.

Matthew was laughing hysterically.

"That's how you have to tackle, Mark," Deana said. If your technique is proper, you won't get hurt, even without pads. I got lower than you did by bending my knees. When I tackled you I used my body, arms, hands and fingers. You have to use everything to do it right."

Over the next few weeks, Deana continued to teach Matthew and Mark how to tackle, block and rush the passer.

She taught them the 'Club' move, the 'Rip' move, the 'Hump' move and the 'Spin' move; all are effective pass rush techniques. The best move of all is called 'Tex.' Tex Stands for 'T'ackle and 'E'nd crossing. The crossing or stunt is the 'X'. Basically, one defensive lineman is picking off one of the offensive lineman and the second defensive lineman shoots through a now open gap. Quarterbacks and running backs hate this.

Teaching blocking is mostly about teaching positioning. 'Mirror and Slide' and 'Walling Off' are the best pass blocking techniques. Deana brushed up online and then spent the next day instructing the boys. Matthew and Mark worked hard and were motivated to learn from Deana. The Samuels' Brothers demolition crew would soon be unleashed on the football field.

One hot, Wednesday night in the middle of summer, a neighbor that lived on the same street as Deana and Leon came into the restaurant and sat in Deana's station.

"Deana, I'm not sure what you did to Leon, but it really is amazing," Mrs. Brantley stated.

"Ma'am, what do you mean?" Deana asked.

"I moved to Dothan with my husband three years ago,"

Mrs. Brantley said. "When we first moved in I would always wave or nod to Leon and most times he never even responded. His eyes would be toward the ground and he would just drive past us."

"I know he was going through a rough stretch back then," Deana tried to explain."

"Well that rough stretch is obviously over," Mrs. Brantley continued. "He's a different person. He waves to us, he smiles and most importantly he looks happy."

"I pray every day he is happy," Deana stated.

"It looks like your prayers are answered," Mrs. Brantley replied. "I know you two are still newlyweds and things are probably a lot of fun in the romance department right now, but there must be more to it than that."

"Absolutely, Mrs. Brantley," Deana answered. "The physical aspect of the relationship is extremely important. Sex is the glue that keeps a man and a woman together during their marriage. But, there are other very important elements to factor in."

"I think spirituality has to be very high on the list, Leon and I go to church together every Sunday. We pray together during the week. I always remind Leon how grateful I am to God for finding him. I know Leon thanks God for finding me."

"The very most important thing is raising the children," Deana stated. "Leon has the peace of mind we are bringing up the boys in a competent, caring, and Christian manner. Each of our boys is really doing well."

"Little things are very important also," Deana concluded. "Providing a clean house and clean clothes. Preparing good dinners and weekend breakfasts can't be overlooked. Leon knows if he has a problem I will stand shoulder to shoulder with him with my sleeves rolled up ready to jump in."

"Pretty much any woman can be a wife and mother. It is very difficult to be a great wife and great mother. I hope Leon is now so happy because he found a great wife and great mother to his children."

Mrs. Brantley adamantly agreed.

Just before Mark's birthday in July, football practice began. The boys were put on the same team. In youth football weight is more important than age when they group the boys into teams, divisions and classes. Fortunately, even though Matthew was older and taller, Mark weighed the same as he did.

Deana had the boys prepared. They were in shape, football savvy, disciplined and good at all of the techniques. After practice, the coach pulled Matthew and Mark aside.

"Aren't you Lester Samuels' nephews?" the coach asked.

The boys were surprised at the question, "he did a bang up job teaching you boys to play football. You boys really looked good out there today."

"Our Uncle Lester has never taught us anything," Mark replied. "We barely speak to him."

"Y'all are trying to tell me you're kin to a Parade All American football player, come here as polished as you are and won't give him any credit?" the coach asked.

"Why should he get credit, sir," Matthew answered. "He never taught us a thing. Our step-mom helped us learn the moves and techniques."

"Are you really gonna stand there and tell me your 90 pound waitress step-mom taught you to play football this well?" the coach asked as he spit a huge wad of tobacco on the ground and walked away.

"What a jerk," Mark said.

"I wonder what he has against waitress step-moms?" Matthew asked. "Deana said we gotta respect this guy but it's gonna be tough.

Mark's birthday was on a Saturday this year. Deana took Luke to soccer in Claybon and Leon took the boys to football in Athens. Matthew and Mark had a scrimmage game. Leon said they did very well. They all met at the lake at two o'clock and took the boat out for a little while until Deana had to go to work.

Leon took the boys for pizza and a movie that night to further celebrate. Mark got to do most of his favorite things in one big day.

The next big day in the Samuels' household would be Deana's birthday. "Having my birthday only nine days away from my anniversary probably is not ideal," Deana lamented to Delores one August evening at work. It's like having your birthday nine days away from a big holiday. I'd rather have two of my favorite days spread out a little more."

Sunday August 17th, things were a little tense at the Samuels' household. It was the last day of summer break. Tomorrow would be back to school for Matthew and Mark and the first day of Kindergarten for Luke. Deana was on the verge of tears the entire day. She wanted to be strong for Luke, but almost every day for two years Deana and Luke had been inseparable. She dreaded the thought of being all alone.

The next morning, her eyes were red and puffy; she hadn't slept well. At 8:40am Deana buckled Luke's seat belt as he sat in the passenger seat of her car. They drove to the schoolyard and Deana helped Luke get out of his seat. Luke grabbed onto her and told Deana he didn't want to go.

Deana's lower lip quivered. "Remember the talk we had two years ago when we first met? You are now at an age where you have to go to school like your brothers. I promise I'll be right here at three o'clock to pick you up. I won't be late."

Luke started to cry which caused Deana to cry. They were quite a sight standing together balling their eyes out. The teacher had to come out of the classroom and take Luke by the hand into the schoolroom. Deana knew she looked foolish just standing on the sidewalk and waving. But that was her baby, her pride and joy walking away and growing up.

Friday August 22nd, was Deana's twenty-seventh birthday. Leon had taken off work to celebrate with her. Peggy had sprained her ankle earlier in the week so Mr. Vito couldn't give her the night off. It was all right. She and Leon had plenty of time to go to the lake while the boys were in school and enjoy a beautiful day together.

"I think I have news that will make you happy," Leon said, as they drove home from the lake. "Our anniversary is on a Sunday and the next day is Labor Day Monday. Mr. Vito said to make up for you having to work your birthday tonight you can take off that Sunday night. The Johnson's said they will watch the boys Saturday through late Monday night. I made reservations for a two day second honeymoon back at Hilton Head Island."

Deana's eyes lit up. "Leon, I love you so much. You just made my birthday perfect. What a wonderful gift that will be."

Of all the good times Deana and Leon had shared over the

last two years, their honeymoon at Hilton Head Island had been her favorite. She loved the dolphin sightseeing excursion, the red fishing off the Skinner/pontoon boat, the sand castle building and the great restaurants.

This year they even went midnight miniature golfing. Over time, Leon was starting to gain wisdom. He was a much better golfer than Deana, but he knew she was extremely competitive. If Leon were to beat her on the scorecard she would not be happy.

"Is it all right if we don't keep score and just play for fun?" Leon asked.

"Sure, anything for my hubby."

Leon and Deana did trick shots and made fools of themselves. You could hear their laughter all the way in the parking lot. The warm breeze was coming in off the Atlantic Ocean and the stars were shining brightly. Round two was even more fun than round one.

An interesting thing happened to Deana and Leon over the last twenty-two months. Yes, they fell in love and got married and were raising children together. They also became best friends.

The next Saturday was a big one for Matthew and Mark. It would be one of the toughest games of the year against a heated rival from the other side of Athens. The boys' coach wanted to win this game in the worst way.

Their opponent dominated the game for the first three quarters. However, Matthew and Mark's team trailed by only one touchdown; the score was 14-7.

As the fourth quarter started, the other team had the ball at midfield. Most coaches would have run the ball to kill off much of the remaining time. For some reason, the other coach wanted more than a close victory; he wanted one more touchdown. He had his quarterback take a deep drop and look downfield for an open receiver. As he was looking downfield, Mark executed a perfect inside spin move against their right tackle and crushed the quarterback. The hit caused the ball to pop straight up in the air.

A heavy set defensive tackle caught the ball. He wobbled as he ran but no player on the other team wanted to get in his way. It had been a long game and it was brutally hot. Fifteen seconds after the interception he rumbled into the end zone.

Down by a point, Matthew and Mark's coach made a gutsy call and signaled in a trick play on the extra point. The holder jogged into the end zone untouched executing a two point conversion. They won the game 15-14. They celebrated like they just won the Super Bowl.

Luke's soccer team was doing very well. They were undefeated. It was the last game of the season and they were playing a team with only one loss. Luke scored three goals and had one assist. They won 5-1. The parents threw the boys a party and made a big deal over Luke. He loved the lime light.

Matthew and Mark's football team had five wins and four losses. They were down to their last game as Thanksgiving approached. The team had gone 5-5 the past season, so they were hoping for a win today to finish this season with a better record.

The right tackle Mark was going up against was easily the worst tackle in the division. The coach had Matthew playing right outside linebacker and Mark playing left outside linebacker. Matthew was having a solid season. He had six sacks and over twenty tackles for a loss. He was a good pass rusher and even stronger against the run.

Mark, however, was a beast. He had eleven sacks going into today's game and led all players in tackles for a loss with thirty-eight. Mark was big, strong and relentless. Even when the other team thought they had him blocked, he still stayed in the play. Today would be no different.

Matthew and Mark's team scored the first touchdown right before halftime. The second half started with them having a 7-0 lead. The other team would have to try to pass the ball to try to catch up. On third and seven the other quarterback dropped back to pass, Mark used a club move on the right tackle and at full speed leveled the quarterback. A club move is when you punch an offensive lineman's hands down so he can't use his hands to grab or block you. The opposition's most important player had to be carried off the field. Instead of getting a red card or yelled at, Mark was the game's MVP. He sacked the back-up quarterback three times. They won 21-10 and Mark finished his first season with fifteen sacks. It wasn't too bad of a rookie campaign.

The sports seasons were over now for the boys. As was agreed to, Special Night for Mark and Matthew were about to kick in. Mark went first that Monday night. Mark and Deana took a slow walk to the park and back. They talked about football, friends and a cute girl Mark liked. Deana talked as little as possible because she wanted to do her best to just listen. Mark seemed to enjoy the two hours with Deana.

The next night with Matthew was similar. Matthew asked when they could go to another concert like last year. Deana said any weeknight except Friday. She told Matthew it would be easier if they could go after the holidays. He agreed. Matthew, like his dad, was easy to talk to. The two hours went very fast.

The following Sunday afternoon with Luke was completely different. Luke asked Deana the most difficult questions Deana had ever been asked.

"Why did God take my first mommy? Why was she even my mommy? Why weren't you my first mommy?"

"Luke, honey, these are very difficult questions. Only God knows for sure. But, if you want I'll give you my opinion.

However, I can't promise you my opinion is the right answer."

"That's all right," Luke said. "Just do your best, please."

"Wow, Luke, this is a tough one," Deana replied. "As you know, I lost my mother at the same age as you were when you lost your first mother. The difference is, your father was still there for you. I lost my father before I lost my mother. When my mother died, I had no parents and I had no home."

"I became the property of the State of Florida. That was a bad thing. I ended up being raised by foster parents. Foster parents can be great. Foster parents can be really bad. My foster father did things so bad to me he ended up in jail and I ended up not being able to have biological children."

"I don't understand," Luke replied politely.

"It's a very complicated adult subject matter, honey," Deana tried to explain. "My foster father hurt me in a way that caused me a lot of problems. For many, many years I asked God why such bad things happened to me. Then, one Sunday in early November two years ago at Dothan Christian Church, a little boy came and sat on my lap during service. I realized why God put me on the road he put me on. Walking to the park with my beautiful son Luke, I am very grateful to God now."

CHAPTER 16
PROSPERITY

"10-9-8-7-6-5-4-3-2-1, Happy New Year." Matthew, Mark, Leon and Deana said simultaneously as they watched the ball drop on television. It was now the year 2015. The boys were almost teenagers and allowed to stay up late for special occasions.

Leon had rebuilt the burn pit and they had fun roasting hot dogs and marshmallows all night. New Year's Eve was Wednesday night so Deana got four days off in a row like she did the week before for Christmas. Days off from work were a fun thing. The boys were off from school and she enjoyed being with them.

New Year's Day would be spent watching college football

Bowl Games and doing some fishing and picnicking at the lake. January was cold, but if they went around noon and finished by 3pm, it wouldn't be too bad.

The following Monday night, Mark and Deana went for a walk.

"Have you decided what you want for your annual Special Night, Mark?"

"Yes, once the pro baseball season starts in April, I want to go to Turner field in Atlanta to watch the Braves. Atlanta is going to be a really good team this year."

"If you can find a game on a Monday or Tuesday night I'll be glad to take you."

"Thanks. There's one more thing I wanted to ask you about. You said I can ask you anything, right? It will just be between you and me?"

"Absolutely. I'll never tell anyone what you and I talk about; not even your father. I promise."

"Sometimes when I'm with my girlfriend and we kiss she looks at me like she's expecting me to go further; to do more than kiss. How do I know what she's expecting?"

"First of all, Mark, you two are only eleven. Kissing should be as far as it goes. If she wants to go further at eleven, she'll be pregnant by fifteen. I don't want to preach to you, but the answer to your question is communication. She has to tell you. You need her permission. It may seem unfair, but you can get in a lot of trouble if you touch a girl inappropriately without her consent."

"Thanks Deana, I'm glad I have you to talk with."

The following Tuesday, Matthew informed Deana there was a concert in Atlanta he wanted to see. It was a new band that had crossed over on the charts. The band was popular on both the Top 40 and country stations. Deana was more than happy to oblige. Two weeks later, Matthew and Deana enjoyed a show full of good music, state of the art lighting, lasers and pyrotechnics. It was an awesome show and great time.

Mr. Vito's restaurant was getting busier and busier. It was looking like this would be his best year ever. Having worked with Deana for over two years, it was as if Delores and Peggy were learning to be more like Deana with her attentiveness, attention to detail, and affable style. The restaurant had a pleasant atmosphere and was getting very popular.

A new church member, an older man named Gary, joined Dothan Christian Church. He was a guitar player also. However, he played a solid body electric guitar in contrast to Deana's hollowed body acoustic. Gary didn't like to sing, but his guitar playing really complemented Deana and Mrs. Jarvis' sound.

The next big Special Night was Luke's. It was a big, three band country concert in Atlanta. Deana was really excited about this show. It was three of her and Luke's favorite bands.

"School is all right, but I miss going to the beach and the park with you and playing soccer every day. I wish I didn't have to go to school." Luke wrinkled his nose in distaste.

"I miss you like crazy, too, Luke. But, it's part of life. I know going to school is not your favorite thing in the world. The secret is to have fun when you're not at school, like now. I hope you're having a fun night."

"This is a great night, mommy. But it's almost over and I still don't want to go back to school."

"That pretty much sums up life. In a couple of days it will be the weekend and we'll have fun. Monday and Tuesday I'll be off from work and I'll get to go on walks with your brothers and spend extra time with you at night. Some of the things we have to do in life are not fun, so we have to make up for it on nights like tonight."

Luke smiled and nodded his head.

Tuesday night, Matthew was excited to share a story with Deana. "Do you know old man McCarthy from the other side of town?"

"Yes, he comes in the restaurant with his wife and runs up

a big bill but we're lucky if he leaves a dollar tip. Usually, it's only fifty cents."

"Well the other day he got into it with my friend Tommy Thompson. I think he got mad at Tommy for cutting through his property on his bike. He started yelling at Tommy and Tommy got mad. Tommy has two really big pit bulls he keeps in his back yard. He filled a brown paper bag with dog poop. That night he put the bag on old man McCarthy's doormat. He put a little lighter fluid on the outside of the bag and set it on fire. He rang the door bell and pedaled his bike out of there as fast as he could. Old man McCarthy sees the fire on his doorstep so, of course, he starts to stomp it out. Dog crap goes flying everywhere: all over the porch; McCarthy's pants and shoes. He called the cops but fortunately most of the evidence got destroyed when he stomped out the fire."

Deana could not help but laugh, "Absolutely classic."

In April, the week before Matthews's birthday, Mark wanted Deana to take him to a professional baseball game in Atlanta for his special night. The game was to be played at the historic Ted Turner Field. The field was built in 1997. Turner field combines the nostalgia and atmosphere of old time baseball with a state of the art environment unlike any other park.

Deana had been to a pro baseball game one time when she was a teenager. It was played in a dome in south St. Petersburg

Florida. Both games were fun to attend, but Turner Field had a lot better atmosphere. There were over 30,000 people in attendance and there was a feeling of electricity in the air. Atlanta won the game 5-3 and the home fans went home happy.

"We definitely have to do this again," Mark exclaimed.

Deana agreed. It was a great experience.

Monday April 13th, 2015 was Matthew's 13th birthday. Two weeks before, Deana had signed Matthew and Mark up for football again so one of his birthday wishes was already granted. They all went out for pizza and a movie together. Deana and Leon bought Matthew the new college football video game which made Matthew very happy.

Leon's birthday was on a Wednesday. Leon could not get the day off from work but Deana got the night off. When Leon got home, the five of them went fishing at the lake. Deana had made a picnic basket full of butter basted fried chicken, corn bread, and fried okra. Deana had also baked a cosmopolitan cake. It was a two layer cake; the bottom layer was chocolate, the top was strawberry. She also made her own vanilla icing. It was a beautiful night and everyone had fun.

On Mother's Day, Deana was treated to breakfast in bed again. After church, Leon and the boys took her out to lunch at one of her favorite restaurants in the area. Unfortunately, she had to be at work early for what would be a very busy shift.

School was finishing up for the boys. Both Matthew and Mark made the Honor Roll. Luke's teachers were impressed with how well he could read. He also had an excellent vocabulary and was surprisingly articulate for being only five years old.

Deana was happy to have the boys at home with her during the day over their summer vacation. She'd missed having Luke with her once he'd started Kindergarten.

Deana trained Matthew and Mark for the upcoming football season. She also helped Luke prepare for his upcoming soccer season. Each boy worked out diligently every morning and afternoon.

When football season came around this year, things were a little different. At the level the boys were playing on, most of the quarterbacks were the sons of the head coaches. Mark's pass rushing skills and prowess had not gone unnoticed. Coaches were concerned when they saw or heard what Mark was capable of. His vicious hits made other teams try to maximize their pass protection schemes toward Mark's side. Many teams were leaving a tight end and running back to the side of the offensive tackle that was trying to block Mark.

This strategy was effective in stopping Mark most of the time, but it really made life easy for Matthew who was pass rushing from the other side. He saw exclusive, one on one, man blocking. He was notching one to two sacks every game. He had twelve sacks in nine games. Mark only had eight sacks, but even with all the triple teaming it was almost impossible to run the ball at Mark's side.

The last game of the season was a big one. Matthew and Mark's team was now 7-2. The East Atlanta team they were playing was 8-1. If they could beat East Atlanta they would win the division. Even though both teams would have the same record, the tie breaker would be head to head competition. In essence, this game would also be the tie breaker.

The East Atlanta team had very good offensive tackles on the outside, but were not very strong inside at offensive guard or center. Matthew and Mark's coach changed defenses to capitalize on this. He kept Matthew at right outside linebacker/rush end but brought Mark over to right defensive tackle next to his brother.

At the end of three quarters, the game was tied 7-7. They knew East Atlanta would now try to open up the offense in the fourth quarter by using their passing game more. On one East Atlanta offensive series the offensive guard jumped off sides. East Atlanta ended up with a third down still needing nine yards to get a first down. It was a definite passing down. Matthew and Mark decided to use the TEX maneuver they had learned from Deana. Matthew ran in fast and occupied East Atlanta's left guard and center. Mark went uncontested through the gap. Mark hit the quarterback so hard he fumbled the ball. Matthew picked up the ball and ran it in for a touchdown.

East Atlanta got the ball back but could not convert on a key fourth down. Matthew and Mark's team ran out the clock and won 14-7.

After the game, Mark expressed his disappointment that he didn't have big statistics like the year before. Deana made him feel better when she told him stats did not always indicate a player's value to the team. She also brought up the fact that the other team's coaches respected him because they were coming up with special game plans to use against him.

During the football season Matthew had started eighth grade, Mark had started seventh grade and Luke began first grade.

Matthew was excited about the upcoming eighth grade dance. It was a celebration of their last year of middle school. He was going to take a girl named Cherie Hopkins to the dance. Matthew was very fond of Cherie. They had known each other since the first grade. She was one of the prettiest and most popular girls in Matthew's class.

As Matthew looked through his closet, he complained to Deana. "I don't have anything nice enough to wear to a dance like this."

"Don't worry, on Sunday afternoon we can go shopping

and buy a suit for you. If you don't want to wear the jacket, you can just wear the slacks, dress shirt and shoes."

The suit was expensive, but it looked very sharp on Matthew and Deana wanted him to look nice. Matthew was very grateful for the new addition to his wardrobe.

The Tuesday night after the weekend of the dance, Deana and Matthew discussed all that had happened on his big night. Cherie and Matthew really hit it off. Matthew was confident Cherie liked him enough to continue going out on an exclusive basis. Deana was thrilled to see how well Matthew was maturing.

Luke's Under Six soccer team went undefeated again. Next year though, he would have to play in the U8 league, which means every player has to be under eight years old to play. It was going to be a big step up in competition.

One Saturday night at Vito's, a couple came in and sat in Deana's station. The boy looked 21 years old; the girl looked about 17. Vito's served beer and wine, but no hard alcohol. The boy and girl both wanted beer so Deana carded them. The boy had a Georgia driver's license which indicated he was 21. The girl had a West Virginia license showing her age to be 22. Deana knew the girl lived in Dothan and was almost positive she was still in high school.

"I'll gladly get your boyfriend a beer," Deana told the girl. "But I will not get you one. I won't tell anyone, but I believe your license is fake. I'll get you any non-alcoholic drink you want and I'll even pay for it. You don't even have to leave me a tip. If I were to give you alcohol and something bad happened, I'd never forgive myself."

The girl glared at Deana. "Fine, just get me an iced tea."

"My pleasure," Deana replied with a smile.

This year, Deana's birthday fell on a Saturday. Saturday morning they all went to Luke's soccer game. In the afternoon they went to Matthew and Mark's football game. Mr. Vito asked Deana if he could please give her off Sunday night instead of Saturday night. Saturday nights had been extremely busy at the restaurant lately. Luke and the boys threw Deana a big party and picnic at the lake after church on Sunday. It was also Luke's birthday so the day was even more special.

Deana and Leon's anniversary was on a Monday. Usually the Monday closest to their anniversary was Labor Day and everyone was off from school and work. This year Labor Day was the following Monday, September 7th. Deana was disappointed; they'd only have Sunday to celebrate. Mr. Vito gave her Sunday night off so it wasn't too bad. They had a wonderful picnic lunch at the lake, got a little fishing in, and went home to get cleaned up. At night, all five of them went to the movies and had a late dinner at a nice restaurant. It was a great time had by all.

Leon promised Thanksgiving weekend they would do something extra special to make up for the abbreviated anniversary celebration. September, October and most of November flew by quickly. The next thing Deana knew she was preparing Thanksgiving dinner. This year there would be eleven Samuels' gathering together. Claire had recently given birth to a baby boy; they named him Lester Jr.

After dinner, Leon drove the boys to the Johnson's as Deana slept. From the Johnson's Leon drove Deana to Gatlinburg, Tennessee, to spend a day and a half in a cabin in the woods. The cabin Leon rented had a fireplace with chopped wood inside. All Leon had to do was light a match and they were soon sitting in front of a roaring fire. It was absolutely beautiful. They stayed up late into the evening and enjoyed a romantic night together.

The cabin had its own kitchenette. Leon had put some of the Thanksgiving leftovers in a cooler. Friday they went into town and bought more groceries. Gatlinburg, Tennessee, is deep in the Smoky Mountains. These mountain ranges are visually stunning, especially in the fall. Autumn in Tennessee is a gorgeous time of year.

The cabin they were staying in had a hot tub inside a screened in porch overlooking the mountains. Deana and Leon enjoyed the hot tub, each other's company and a breathtaking view.

After the hot tub, they spent the rest of Friday in front of the fireplace. Deana was sad she had to get back to Dothan on Saturday for work. It was a short, but memorable time with her husband.

Monday, December 7th, 2015, was a rainy, dreary day. The next day, however, was forecast to be nice, especially at night.

"Mark, would you mind moving our night together to tomorrow night?" Deana asked. "I'd like to talk about something very important with you and your brother."

Mark replied that it would not be a problem.

Deana asked Matthew the same question and got the same answer.

Tuesday night, 7pm, Deana, Matthew and Mark started their walk.

"There is something very important I need to talk to both of you about," Deana said. "I don't want to preach to you, but I do want us to discuss the topic of drugs. Matthew you are already a teenager and Mark you are about to become one."

Both boys swore to Deana that they'd never do drugs.

"That's great," Deana replied. "But there has to be a deep

seeded reason why you won't. It needs to be more than *they're bad for you* or *drugs are anti-life.*"

"What exactly do you mean?" Matthew asked.

"I want to ask you boys a favor, this is something you don't have to do tomorrow. It's something I want you to do over time. I want you to compare the lives of a few young adults you suspect did drugs when they were in high school to a few young adults you know avoided them."

"Why?" The boys asked.

"Mr. Wilson had me do this exercise when I was starting high school. This is what I found; the kids who did drugs, sometimes did not finish high school. Very rarely did they finish college. Some of them ended up in jail. If they weren't in jail they were living with their parents or leaching off friends. Some of them ended up homeless or they'd have to stay on the couches of family members. One of my subjects even died."

"The non-drug users," Deana continued, "almost always finished high school and many went to and finished college. Most of them ended up with good jobs. They had better relationships with their families and better lives."

"That's kind of the way it is in Dothan," Mark replied. "The kids that did drugs a few years ago are losers now. They are always in trouble and looking to get high."

"What about the kids that steered clear of the drugs?"

Deana asked.

"Most of them went to college," Matthew answered, "or they got decent jobs or both."

"Are you kind of getting a feel for the point I'm making?"

Both boys nodded their heads.

"Over the next couple of years, I'm going to ask you to continue doing this observation for me. I'll follow up with you again in the future."

CHAPTER 17
DEANA AND LEON GO TO NASHVILLE

With Christmas and New Year's Day falling on Fridays this year, Deana's schedule was really chopped up. She'd be off Monday and Tuesday; she'd work Wednesday and be off Thursday and Friday. She would then have to work both Saturdays and Sundays. She'd also have two church services to practice for. The first would be the Christmas service on Friday morning; the second would be the regular Sunday service.

Nonetheless, she wanted to have fun with the boys over Christmas break and spend time with them. Together they enjoyed fishing at the lake; Christmas shopping and watching some new movies at the theater. Like Deana had told Luke, you have to make the most of your time off.

The following Monday night, Deana and Mark went for a walk and a chat session. Deana told Mark about Matthew sharing the old man McCarthy story. Mark replied that his friends had pulled an even bigger prank at school three and a half weeks ago.

"There's a 7th grader named Myron who is in three of my classes. He's a real goober. Very few of my friends can stand him. For some reason, he always puts his cell phone in his locker during classes. We figure his mother tells him to do this so he won't be tempted to text during class and get his phone taken away."

"Mark, I hope you never pick on this boy."

"I always ignore him, but two boys who really dislike Myron played the ultimate prank on him and our Math teacher. One boy looked over Myron's shoulder when he was opening his lock on his locker. They got his combination code and got into his locker after he had walked away to his next class. They took his cell phone and lock, and then went to an old part of the building where no one goes anymore. There were a couple of lockers in this abandoned room. They activated the record function on the cell phone and utilized a twenty five minute stagger. They banged on the lockers and yelled, "Help me, let me out. You've got to help me. I'm stuck in here and I can't get out. Please! I'm claustrophobic!"

Mark glanced at Deana to make sure he had her attention before continuing his story.

"They took the cell phone to Math class. The one boy distracted the teacher while the second boy put Myron's cell phone into an empty locker and put Myron's lock on the locker. About twenty minutes into the class everyone hears a banging from the back lockers. Then they heard: "Help me, let me out. You've got to help me. I'm stuck in here and I can't get out. Please! I'm claustrophobic!"

"The teacher went to get the maintenance man while all the students laughed hysterically. He brought big bolt cutters and busted Myron's lock. The Math teacher was furious and confiscated Myron's cell phone."

Mark grinned triumphantly as tears of laughter streamed down Deana's face.

"I told you my prank story was funnier than Matthew's."

After completing their Holiday musical performances at church, Mrs. Jarvis, Deana and Gary all admitted they didn't sound as good as they would have liked. They hadn't practiced enough. The three agreed, as a New Year's resolution, to work harder during the new year.

Every Monday and Tuesday at 10am they'd meet at church to rehearse. Both Gary and Mrs. Jarvis were retired; and, with all three boys in school Deana now had the time to practice with them. Gary loved Classic Rock and Blues music and he taught Deana some intricate guitar licks. Deana enjoyed expanding her musical horizons. Gary joked she would be less of a yahoo now.

Deana did the extra Special Night again with the boys in the spring. Like last year Deana attended concerts with Matthew and Luke. She then went to Turner Field again with Mark to see another pro baseball game. On Mother's Day, Leon and the boys had a surprise for Deana. Leon purchased five tickets to a Memorial Day bash featuring four of the most popular country bands on tour. Deana was ecstatic. It ended up being her favorite concert. It was also the first concert she ever attended with Leon.

It was now the end of another school year and Matthew was graduating from Middle School. Next fall he would start High School. The boys' summer vacation was Deana's favorite three months of the year. She enjoyed helping Matthew and Mark with their football training and getting Luke ready for soccer season. She loved having the boys at home and not being alone during the day.

Tuesday June 7th, 2016 Matthew was looking forward to talking with Deana on their walk. They left the house earlier than they usually did.

"Matthew, what's wrong?"

"Cherie told me she wants to go in a different direction; she wants some kind of change. I have no idea what she's talking about, I was hoping you might know."

"I have a feeling I may know what she's thinking, but I'd hate myself if I gave you my opinion and then found out I was wrong."

"Deana, even if you're wrong, I'd still like to know what you think."

"OK, here it goes. You and Cherie will both be starting High School next fall. Lots of guys will probably be interested in going out with her. She may feel if she comes into High School with a boyfriend she'll be limiting her options. I hope I'm wrong."

"To be honest, I kind of get the feeling you're right."

"Will you still be talking to each other over the summer, even if it's just over the phone? The best way to find out the answer to your question is to ask her."

"That sounds like a good idea, thanks. I really like taking these walks with you."

Matthew did a really mature thing that greatly impressed Deana. There was no way Deana and Leon, even with the help of Mrs. Richards, could get all three boys to separate practices.

Matthew had one more year of eligibility to play city league football again with Mark; but playing High School football was more prestigious. However, High School football practice was 4 to 6pm every week day. To make matters worse, the games were Friday nights when Deana was working. Plus, there would be no one to pick Matthew up Thursday nights unless Deana missed work.

On top of that, Leon would have to drive extra every day of the week instead of the usual three days like last year if Matthew played school ball. After Leon spent all day driving at work, it was asking a lot for him to shuttle the boys back and forth to practice each day.

Being a team player, Matthew skipped his freshman year of High School football and played one more year of city ball with Mark.

With the boys' busy schedules, it was getting harder and harder for Deana and Leon to get away. But, they did the best they could. Leon's birthday in April was on a Friday and he took off from work to celebrate it with Deana at the lake.

Deana's birthday, August 22nd, was a Monday. Leon took the day off from work to celebrate with her. Their anniversary was on a Wednesday. They both took off from work. On both of their birthdays and their anniversary, Deana packed an extra special picnic lunch and she and Leon celebrated at the lake together, just the two of them. They were three of the most fun and wonderful days of Deana's life.

Luke was now turning seven and playing U8 soccer. He was bigger and taller than most of the other boys and had more experience playing soccer. Because of Luke, his team was very good. The coaching director at Luke's soccer club wanted Luke's team to play in a competitive tournament. He signed Luke's team up to play in a Columbus Day Weekend tournament October 8-10. The tournament would be held in Atlanta. Luke and Deana were excited about the opportunity to go up against some very high quality teams.

September 12th, 2016, was a sad day at Vito's restaurant. Robert the cook was leaving Dothan to move to Columbus, Georgia. He'd met a young lady who owned a graphics design company in Columbus and they were going to get married. Since it would be easy to get a job as a cook in Columbus and too difficult for his fiancée to move her business to Dothan, Robert was moving to Columbus. Columbus is about a two hour drive from Dothan.

Deana had mixed feelings. She was thrilled for Robert, but good cooks were hard to find. Plus, she considered Robert a close friend and hated to see him leave. Robert had treated Deana with respect from day one. He looked after her like he would his own sister. She also appreciated his help at her wedding.

"Robert, I'll never forget all of the wonderful things you've done for me." Deana wiped a few tears from her eyes as she spoke. "Thank you so much for saving my wedding and being such a good friend and co-worker." She gave Robert a big hug and then went into the break room to compose herself. She was really going to miss him.

Luke's soccer team had won seven games, lost only one and had two ties during the regular season. The tournament in Atlanta was a bonus for doing so well. It would give them a chance to see how they measured up to top level competition.

Luke's team lost the first game 3-1. They seemed surprised by how good the other team was. His team played much better the second game and it ended in a 2-2 tie. Luke, however, was frustrated because he hadn't scored a goal yet.

In the third game, Luke did score, as did two of his teammates. They won the game 3-2. The win and the tie qualified them to advance to the semi-finals. Luke's team lost 2-0, but it was a very well played game by both teams. Deana was pleased to see Luke play so well against such good opponents.

In Athens, Matthew and Mark's city league football team

had a rough season. Their starting quarterback was hurt in game five and had to miss the rest of the season. The offense, with a new quarterback, struggled mightily. The defense, however, was the best in the league. Mark had sixteen sacks, Matthew had eleven. The run defense allowed the least amount of rushing yards in the league. The fact they finished with a winning record, six wins, four losses, was a huge statement of how well their defense actually played.

Mr. Vito hired a new cook. He was a man in his mid-forties named Leo. Leo really had his hands full trying to replace Robert. Mr. Vito would sometimes have to go into the kitchen and help Leo when the restaurant got really busy. Weekends, in particular, were very chaotic.

Delores and Peggy frequently complained to Mr. Vito about Leo. Deana never did. She knew Leo was doing his best and it was only a matter of time before he'd settle in. Leo was grateful for Deana's patience. Slowly, but surely, Leo did improve. He never forgot which server showed him compassion.

By the time Thanksgiving arrived, Deana definitely needed a few days off. Leon had been promising her something extra special this year. Deana awoke just before 6am Thanksgiving morning. Leon slept until 10am so he would be nice and rested for all of the driving he would be doing over the course of the day and night. Deana cooked a beautiful 16lb turkey. As she did every year, she made her bread, celery and onion stuffing. She boiled and mashed real potatoes. Deana put the mashed potatoes in a very large casserole dish then proceeded to bake cheese into the potatoes. She finished her part of the meal by boiling three pounds of green beans which she flavored with butter.

Claire made another pitiful Thanksgiving turkey. This time it just sat on the table. No one even tried to eat it.

Leon, Deana and the boys left for the Johnson's even earlier than usual. Deana slept in the truck as Leon drove to Macon. After they dropped off the boys, Leon headed the truck north toward Tennessee. The happy couple was heading back to Gatlinburg like last year. This year, however, Leon had something special planned for Deana.

When they arrived at their cabin in Gatlinburg, Leon prepared the living room fireplace. Soon, the firewood became golden embers emitting heat. Deana and Leon fell asleep in front of the fireplace wrapped together in blankets.

Friday morning, Deana and Leon woke up to a gorgeous Smoky Mountain sunrise. It was breathtaking; but also very cold. Over the years Deana had tried to adapt to a colder climate than what she'd grown up in. But the truth was, she still had a lot of cracker in her.

Leon's big surprise was that they were taking a three and a half hour jaunt to Nashville, Tennessee. Deana was overjoyed. She'd wanted to visit Nashville since she was a teenager. Nashville is the home of country music. Leon told her they were going to Music Row. Music Square East and Music Square West combine to make Music Row. Leon was going to take Deana on a studio tour so she could see where some of her favorite music was made.

The drive through north central Tennessee was stunning. Leon and Deana drove through the Appalachian Mountains, Cumberland Plateau, the Eastern Highland Rim and finally the Nashville Basin. Their directions led them to 16th and 17th Avenue South and Division Street. This section of Music Row serves as the headquarters of America's Country Music industry.

Deana was thrilled at the thought of visiting RCA's famed Studio B, where hundreds of famous musicians, including Elvis Presley, have recorded.

The Music City Walk of Fame on Demonbreun Street is across the street from the Country Music Hall of Fame. It pays tribute to Nashville's legendary musicians. Leon and Deana had a blast taking in all of the sights and sounds. The music made in Nashville played a very important role in Deana and Leon's lives and their relationship.

Deana did not care how much Gary at church teased her, she was proud to be a yahoo!

CHAPTER 18
DEANA TURNS THIRTY AND OTHER MILESTONES

Christmas and New Year's were on perfect days this year. Christmas Eve was Saturday, so Deana was off Saturday night. Christmas was on Sunday, so she had only one church service to prepare for. Most importantly, she wouldn't have to be back to work until Wednesday night.

Christmas day was another interesting event at the elder Samuel's house. As agreed to, Claire would bake and bring the ham and Deana would make the sides. Deana baked a beautiful macaroni and cheese casserole along with a broccoli and cheese casserole. She fried four pounds of okra. She concluded by baking an extra large, out of this world, peach pie.

Claire showed up with a pork shoulder that looked and tasted like a big piece of Spam. Even Lester and Julie seemed embarrassed by Claire's lack of effort.

"Deana honey, may I ask a favor of you?" the Colonel asked in a very polite way.

"Yes sir."

"Will you please make the Christmas ham from now on? Claire's ham really sucks."

As a family Christmas gift, Leon bought tickets for himself, Deana, and the boys to a huge theme park in Atlanta. Leon would take them Monday, the day after Christmas, because he got it off work as a vacation day.

The Atlanta theme park is one of the largest in the world. It features a towering roller coaster that appears to defy gravity. Leon stayed on the ground with Luke because Luke was not tall enough or quite ready to ride something quite that imposing. However, Matthew, Mark and Deana were willing to give it a try.

As the ride began, it actually felt like they were soaring like birds to the top of the park. Two seconds later, following an enormous drop, it seemed like they were underneath the park. They were suspended from the rails one second, then falling on a straight drop the next. It was literally the ride of their lives.

During the day Matthew and Mark ran into some

teammates from their football team. They asked Leon and Deana if they could spend a couple of hours at the park with their friends. Deana was all right with the idea because it would give her a chance to go on some family rides with Luke and Leon.

Luke asked his parents to take him on the Scary Mansion ride. The theme music was very cool and eerie and the ride featured playful monster animatronics. It was like the car you were riding in was driving into the middle of a 3D movie.

As they got off the ride, Luke had a huge smile on his face. "That was the most amazing ride ever; those were the coolest special effects."

"It was incredible," Deana agreed.

Later, Luke, Deana and Leon went on the Wild River Rapids Raft ride. The raft ride was one of the featured attractions at the park. White water and rolling, roaring rapids created a rafting adventure the three of them would always remember. Luke liked the fact they got real wet on the ride. Deana was happy she wore a dark colored tank top.

"Mom and Dad, this was the best Christmas gift ever," Luke said as the day started to come to an end.

Next weekend would be almost as fun. New Year's Eve was Saturday night; New Year's Day was Sunday. Deana had another four day weekend. Most of Saturday and Sunday were spent out on the lake in the johnboat fishing and picnicking.

Leon had to be back to work on Monday, so Deana took the boys to the movies. They went to a matinee so Deana could be home in time to make dinner and have it ready for Leon.

Tuesday, early afternoon, she took the boys bowling. Deana wanted to spend time with the boys, especially Matthew and Mark. They were at an age where they'd want to start spending more time with their friends, like at the theme park. More time with friends meant less time with Deana; it was inevitable.

April 13th, 2017, Matthew turned 15 years old and Deana took him to a really big concert in Atlanta that month to celebrate. Matthew spent most of the concert texting his friends. He was getting close to six feet tall. Soon, he'd be an adult; Deana was not quite ready for this.

Sixteen days later, it was Leon's birthday. It was on a Saturday. The weather forecast called for beautiful weather. They decided it would be a perfect day to go to the lake; they had not been there together in a while. The fish were biting. It was an incredible spring day and all of nature was in bloom. The smell of wild flowers was in the air. It was spectacular.

That Tuesday, Matthew had a funny story from his High School. Apparently a couple of boys did not have time to study for a biology exam. Before the teacher got to class, the boys pulled the hinge pins out of the classroom's entrance door. When the teacher arrived to the classroom he went to open the door. It fell forward when he pushed the door and the glass part in the middle shattered into a million pieces. The maintenance man had to come to the classroom to clean the mess and try to fix the door. Needless to say, the test got postponed. There were some very happy biology students that day.

What happened at Vito's restaurant one night was even funnier. It was close to nine o'clock one weeknight and towards the end of Deana's shift. Mr. Cullen, a Vito's regular, came in and sat in Deana's station. Mr. Cullen liked to drink.

She brought Mr. Cullen three beers within forty-five minutes. Mr. Cullen rapidly downed all three and wanted more.

Deana was not sure that was a good idea. "Mr. Cullen, I know you drove here and I don't want to see you get yourself into any trouble. I'm going to have to cut you off."

"Your new cook, Leo, lives on my street. He can drive me home."

"Let me go ask him if it's all right. If so, you can keep on drinking."

Deana went back into the kitchen to check with Leo. "Leo, can you drive Mr. Cullen home tonight? He's had a lot to drink and he wants to keep on drinking."

"Sure, it won't be a problem. He lives close to me."

Deana brought Mr. Cullen number four. Then he asked for a fifth beer. He quickly drank it. When he finished the fifth beer he looked into his jacket pocket at a picture of a woman.

"I need one more beer," Mr. Cullen informed Deana.

Deana told Mr. Cullen it would have to be his last one. Leo was almost ready to leave.

Mr. Cullen guzzled his sixth beer and then looked at the picture of the woman again. Deana saw a slight smile on his face.

Deana prepared his bill. As she brought back his change, she asked, "What's the story with you and the woman in the picture?"

"That is no woman; it's a picture of my wife. When I look at her picture and she starts to look good to me, I know I've had enough to drink."

"That is absolutely terrible, Mr. Cullen," Deana chided as she put his change on his table. "You ought to be ashamed of yourself!"

"You lift weights like a man, Deana," Mark said one early June day. It was Deana's favorite time of the year. The weather was warm and she had her boys home from school for the entire summer.

Deana smiled at Mark. "Is that meant as an insult or a

compliment?"

"It's just that Matthew and I outweigh you by about sixty pounds and you lift almost as much as we do."

"I've been training hard since I was thirteen years old and I'll be thirty in a couple of months. I'd better be strong."

"Deana, you bench close to double your body weight. That's pretty impressive."

"Like I said, I've been training hard a very long time. I've never used drugs, never smoked cigarettes or pot and drink very, very little alcohol." Deana paused for a moment. "Since we're kind of on the subject, do you see a lot of drug use at your school Matthew?"

"Some, but not a huge amount. I mean there are potheads, a few pill users and a couple of hardcore druggies, but it's not like it's out of control."

"Are any of them in your circle of friends?"

"No, most of my friends are on the football or basketball teams. If you're an athlete and you get caught with anything, you can't play sports anymore. I think they call it zero tolerance."

"That's good. Mark, I hope you take the same path as your brother when you start High School next August."

The second to last week August, 2017, had two huge events. Tuesday, August 22nd was Deana's 30th birthday. Friday, August 25th was Matthew and Mark's first High School football game.

Mr. Vito threw a big party at the restaurant on Tuesday night to celebrate Deana's big milestone; she was very popular. It was probably the most crowded it had ever been on a Tuesday night.

Similar to Deana and Leon's wedding, there was a big group from church. She also had a lot of friends, mostly customers she'd served and befriended working at Vito's. It was hard to imagine she'd been there for almost five years.

In a way, her 30th birthday was a five year anniversary of a lot of things related to her arrival in Dothan. Deana had belonged to Dothan Christian Church five years. She'd worked at Vito's five years. Most importantly, she had been the woman who took care of the Samuels boys, Leon included, for the last five years. Matthew, Mark and Luke were each about a foot taller than when she first started "using their stove."

The Jacobson Brothers set up a stage in the corner of Vito's. The music was loud and energetic. Mrs. Jarvis couldn't attend, but Gary and Deana performed with the brothers on quite a few songs.

The non-church people drank, danced and partied. The church people mingled and socialized. Everyone had a great time.

Leon gave Deana a past, present and forever diamond necklace as her birthday gift. It sparkled brilliantly around her neck as she tried it on. She had to sneak into the break room so no one would see her cry.

The Morrison High School football team was coming off a 2-8 season. They were definitely no football powerhouse. Deana made a deal with Mr. Vito. She agreed to come in Fridays and Saturdays at 3:55pm, if she could leave Fridays at 7:30 on the nights of Morrison's home games. Because so many people in town went to the High School football games, the restaurant was never very busy when a game was being played.

Deana would not be able to attend the away games with Luke and Leon, but she wanted to see as many of the home games as she could.

Tonight was a home game. The restaurant was busy early with people trying to eat before the football game. Around seven o'clock, it started to empty out. Deana jumped into her Status and sped to Morrison High School. She wore a red jacket which was the color of Morrison's home jerseys. Deana was still wearing her Vito's uniform under the jacket.

When she got to the stadium she found where Leon and Luke were sitting and sat down between them. The first quarter had just begun as she entered the stadium. Leon explained to Deana the coach only planned to play Matthew and Mark on passing downs, to best utilize their pass rush skills. Unfortunately, the other team got a big lead and predominantly ran the football.

By halftime, the boys had been in on only a handful of plays.

"Matthew and Mark are just as good against the run as they are at rushing the passer," Deana said passionately. "I bet they could help slow down their running game."

Toward the end of the third quarter the visitors scored another touchdown. The score was now 28-3. As the 4th quarter started, Morrison turned the ball over again. This time the coach put Matthew and Mark in at the same time. Matthew lined up at right outside linebacker and Mark played left outside linebacker.

On first down, the opposition did a pitch toss to the strong side. The running back streaked toward the sideline expecting to make a big gain like he'd done all night long.

Mark honed in on him before he even got to full stride. Mark hit him hard and solid for a five yard loss. The running back looked like he didn't know what hit him. The opposition's coach thought he would teach Morrison a lesson. On the next play he ran a lead pitch toss to the same side. They brought an extra tight end to the strong side. They ran the same play except this time they had their fullback leading the play.

Mark split the fullback and extra tight end and dropped the running back for a six yard loss. The stadium erupted as the formerly quiet Morrison crowd finally had something to cheer about. The cheerleaders got louder; even the mascot looked more enthused.

On third down the opposing offense needed twenty-one yards to make a first down. They decided to go with a passing play. One of their wide receivers was wide open on the play. As their quarterback went to pass the ball, Matthew hit him from the blind side and the ball fell harmlessly to the ground. It was ruled an incomplete pass.

On 4th down, Morrison's special team's players sensed the momentum was changing. The punter kicked the ball well but Morrison's punt returner played it perfectly. He caught the ball in full stride and ran the ball sixty yards for a touchdown. The other coach spent the rest of the game keeping the ball as far away from the Samuels' as possible.

Morrison got a late last minute touchdown, so the game ended 28-17. Now they had something to build on for the rest of the season.

The following Thursday, was Leon and Deana's 4th wedding anniversary. They both had to work and the boys all had school and practices. Leon asked Deana if they could wait until Monday to celebrate. Monday was Labor Day and everyone in the family would have the day off. Leon wanted to get up early Monday morning and drive the family to Savannah to show the boys where he had proposed to Deana. The boys had never seen the Atlantic Ocean in person.

Deana loved the idea. Even though there'd be a great amount of traffic and a lot of time sitting in the truck, Deana loved being with the boys and doing family things together.

As expected, there was a lot of traffic and parking was almost impossible to find. Nonetheless, the Samuels' family persevered and by 2pm they were all swimming in the Atlantic Ocean near the spot Leon proposed to Deana. Everyone in the family had a fantastic time.

On the way back home to Dothan, Leon had an unusual request for Deana.

"The last time we drove home from Savannah, you had your feet up on the dashboard like you do now and you left toe prints on the glass. I really liked that."

"Leon, the last time we drove home from Savannah I was very nervous. I didn't do it intentionally."

"I know you didn't, that's what made it so sexy and cute. Your toe prints on the glass reminded me of you even when I was alone driving to and from work."

"You are so sweet." Deana smiled and pushed the bottom of her feet onto the inside glass of Leon's windshield.

Luke was now in third grade. His teachers and coaches adored him. If you ever needed anything from Luke it was always "Yes sir," or "Yes ma'am." Luke had all of the tools to be a really great soccer player; he was tall, fast and very smart. He was also a great teammate. He was just as happy getting an assist as he was scoring a goal.

Luke had an even temperament. He never got too excited when they won or too upset when they lost. He was, however, very competitive. He made the other players around him much better by being a leader on and off the field. He always hustled and played hard but never dirty. Luke's teams didn't lose very often.

The third week of Morrison's High School foot ball season was a home game against Billings High School. Matthew and Mark were both in the starting line-up this week. Morrison's offense had trouble moving the ball but so did Billings. Mark spent most of the night in the opposition's backfield chasing down play after play. Matthew was very solid on his right side, he just wasn't quite as dominant as Mark. Morrison lost by only three points. The final score was 6-3.

As Deana got ready to leave Vito's for Morrison's fifth game of the season, she hoped tonight would be the night for their first victory. Morrison High School was 0-4. Richmond High School was 1-3. Richmond was one of the two teams they had beaten last season.

Deana got to the game in the middle of the first quarter. There was no score yet. The stadium was pretty full considering this was not really a marquee match-up. Richmond was running a very conservative offense. Most of their plays were dives and traps up the middle. This was keeping Matthew and Mark from making a lot of plays.

The Morrison coach decided to take advantage of this. He blitzed his two inside linebackers and strong safety all at the same time. The Richmond running back got pummeled. He fumbled the football and Morrison had the ball inside the twenty. Morrison ran a half-back option pass on first down and scored a touchdown off of the play. Morrison later added a field goal in the second half and it was all the scoring they would need. Morrison won the game 10-0.

The following week Morrison had an away game. They lost 13-3. The next week the game was in Morrison and Deana was in the stands with Luke and Leon.

The beginning of the game was slow. At the end of the second quarter there was no score. It was 0-0 at the half. There was a pretty big crowd in attendance and they were getting frustrated with Morrison's lack of offense.

In the middle of the third quarter, Morrison had already punted the ball ten times. Compton was about to punt their tenth time. Compton's left tackle completely missed his block and Matthew came around the corner untouched. He blocked the punt and the ball started rolling toward the Morrison end zone. Johnny Rollins, the right defensive end, picked up the football and ran it into the end zone for the score.

It was the only score the entire game. Compton tried a couple of pass plays in the fourth quarter but Mark sacked the quarterback on both plays. An elated crowd left the Morrison field overjoyed with a hard fought 7-0 victory.

Morrison had a freshman quarterback. He struggled most of the season but continued to improve. With the Morrison defense as good as it was, the offense was getting lots of opportunities.

Morrison's defense continued to excel, led by the Samuels brothers. As the season progressed, the offense was starting to feed off of the momentum and good field position the defense was providing.

Morrison lost their sixth game to one of the best teams in the state. However, they played extremely well in both of their last two games. Morrison won both games and they finished with a somewhat respectable record of 4-6. They doubled their win total from the season before.

By the time Thanksgiving came and passed, Deana was exhausted. She really could have used more than a day and a half relaxing in the cabin in the woods in Gatlinburg; it was so wonderful. The cold winter weather was starting to creep in. Having a cabin with a hot tub and a fireplace was a perfect setting for a romantic getaway with the one that you love. The happy couple made the most of their time together.

CHAPTER 19
THE POWER OF ONE - THE HUGE
DIFFERENCE ONE PERSON CAN MAKE

This year, Christmas was on a Monday. This did not work out anywhere near as well as last year. Deana had to work Saturday night. She also had to prepare for two performances at church. One would be for the regular Sunday service; the second one would be for Christmas service the next day. She was always off Mondays anyway, so the only bonus was she did not have to go to work Sunday night.

The really good news was that Leon had a surprise for the family, Deana in particular. As a Christmas gift for the family he bought five tickets to the Georgia Aquarium in Atlanta. Leon got Tuesday, the day after Christmas off so he would be able to spend the entire day at the attraction with his family.

The Georgia Aquarium's biggest show and gallery is "Dolphin Tales." This exhibit allows guests to better understand the lovable bottle-nosed dolphin. Leon remembered how much Deana enjoyed the dolphin watching excursion at Hilton Head Island. He knew she would love this. Also, it would be a fun trip with the boys. For Deana, it was the perfect Christmas gift.

Christmas morning was spent at church and with the Johnsons. The Johnsons had really grown fond of Deana. They respected the nurturing abilities she had displayed toward the boys over the last five years. Deana was always extremely gracious towards the Johnsons.

Christmas afternoon was spent in Athens with Leon and Lester's parents. Deana prepared a sixteen pound honey baked ham and made a macaroni and cheese casserole. However, she insisted Claire make all of the other sides. Deana did not appreciate Claire taking advantage of her.

Tuesday morning, Leon, Deana and the boys jumped in Leon's truck and headed to Atlanta. The aquarium was a little over an hour away. When they arrived at the gallery section of the aquarium, they were amazed at the entrance lobby that featured an expansive underwater dolphin viewing window.

"What do you think of that, Deana?" Matthew asked her. "You can see their entire habitat through that big glass window."

"I think that's pretty amazing," Deana answered. "I can't wait to see the huge theatre and its show; it's supposed to be really something."

Dolphin Tales theatre is a State of the Art enclosed facility. It's both a spectacular theatrical and musical production. It features humans interacting with dolphins, dramatic costumes and amazing special effects.

"The actual story is a mysterious, seafaring adventure," Leon explained. "The main character gets help from the dolphins and other aquatic mammals to defeat the villain of the ocean."

Deana liked the fact the show stressed the importance of caring for and about aquatic creatures.

The show did not disappoint. The show utilized video, strobe and flash lighting, special effects and amazing audio pieces. It took place in a five level theatre. The theatre overlooked a thirty foot show pool.

"This show is unbelievable," Mark said. It's like there's a bond between the humans and animals."

"Dolphin Tales is the best show I've ever seen. Everything is so huge. Maybe we can come back for my extra Special Day. Would that be all right, mom?" Luke asked.

"I would love to, Luke," Deana happily agreed. "I had so much fun. Leon, Thank you. What a wonderful gift. I love you so much."

"I love you too, Deana," Leon said appreciating her gratitude.

New Year's Eve and New Year's Day were extremely cold this year. Deana and Luke wanted to go fishing anyway but got outvoted. Leon, Matthew, and Mark wanted to watch football. Pro football was on Sunday and college was on Monday, New Year's Day.

Leon rebuilt the burn pit for New Year's Eve. Everyone enjoyed the warmth the burn pit provided and roasting hot dogs and marshmallows around it. Leon fired it up both Sunday and Monday nights. It was an enjoyable yearly tradition.

Tuesday afternoon, Deana took the boys to the movies like last year. It was something they all enjoyed doing together. That night was Matthew's night with Deana. They went on a long walk and talked about his new girlfriend.

"Sandy is way cooler than Cherie," Matthew said with a smile. "She's more fun, has a better personality and is easier to talk to."

"Those three things are definitely important; it's part of what they call chemistry between two people. Without chemistry the relationship will struggle to endure."

Matthew agreed with Deana.

The following Monday night, Mark had a funny story for

Deana.

"My English teacher loves to burn television shows and clips off of the internet and play the DVD in class instead of lecturing. At first it was cool because it was different. But it got old pretty quickly. Most of us think he's really lazy. He sits on his butt, uses a remote control and says and does as little as possible. My friend, Joey Horton, came up with a great idea. He got his hands on a very small universal remote. It was so small he could keep it in his pocket, so no one could see it. Every time the teacher would cue up the part he wanted to use to teach the class, Joey could cause the DVD to go forwards or backwards. Sometimes Joey would mute the teacher's DVD or sometimes he would freeze the DVD. It was flat out funny."

Mark paused to catch his breath before continuing.

"The teacher spent weeks trying to figure out the problem. He never found out it was Joey messing with him. He had to go back to teaching the way we were used to and liked better."

Deana really enjoyed her walks with the boys. It was a great bonding experience.

Matthew, on the night of his birthday, wanted to spend the evening at the movies with his girlfriend. It was a Friday and Deana had to work, so Leon got to drive the young couple around.

Leon's birthday was on a Sunday. Deana asked for the

night off from the restaurant and Mr. Vito said it was all right, after clearing it with Delores and Peggy. After church, Deana butter basted six pounds of fried chicken, made a big loaf of corn bread and fried up some okra. She put it in a big picnic basket. She added a gallon of her home made sweet iced tea and she and the boys threw Leon a birthday party at the lake.

They enjoyed a delicious meal, sang "Happy Birthday" to Leon and got in some quality fishing time. Deana had bought Leon an ice cream cake during the week. The boys devoured that when they got home that evening.

Ever since Deana's birthday last August, Mr. Vito had been trying to figure out ways to recapture the festive, packed house excitement he witnessed at her party. His restaurant did very well on the weekends, but he was looking for a way to increase business during the week.

Mr. Vito discussed it with Peggy.

"One weeknight, we should run some kind of special event. Something that could help fill the restaurant during the week."

Peggy smiled as she thought of a great idea. "You do realize you have one of the best singers in all of Dothan on your wait staff? What if you had karaoke night on a Tuesday or Wednesday night? Deana has a voice worth paying to listen to."

"True, and if the customers don't want to sing Deana can go up and perform. I could hire a KJ one Wednesday night and give it a test run. It wouldn't hurt to try."

KJ is a karaoke jockey. He or she runs the karaoke "sing fest." Karaoke is a form of interactive entertainment in which amateur singers sing along with recorded music. The lyrics can be displayed on a video screen if so desired. KJ's can "rip" entire libraries of songs onto their laptop computers and play those songs and lyrics in a bar, restaurant or someone's living room.

When Deana arrived at work, Mr. Vito informed her of his desire to try having a Wednesday evening karaoke night.

"Oh my," Deana exclaimed. "That would be so much fun. I'd love to participate."

Two Wednesdays later, after some advertising and finding a good KJ, Karaoke night was on at Vito's. They decided to start at 7:30pm. This was usually when the restaurant started slowing down on Wednesdays. But tonight, quite a few people were coming in to check out Dothan's new Wednesday night entertainment spot. Mr. Vito ran specials on all his appetizers and even printed out a special menu just for this event.

The KJ sang the first song. It was a good way to check all the equipment and get the show started. Deana sang the second song. She got a lot of applause and everyone seemed into it, but no one wanted to go third.

There was a little girl sitting close to the small portable stage who seemed fascinated with Deana's singing. Deana asked the girl if she would come up and do a duet with her. The little girl agreed. Deana patiently taught the girl how to time the lyrics as they were displayed on the KJ's video screen.

Deana and the little girl sang a very popular song and it sounded great. The crowd enjoyed it so much they were cheering and hollering

Next, a four year old boy wanted to sing with Deana. Then an eight year old boy sang with her. Next, Deana got the first little girl who sang the duet with Deana to try singing by herself. She did fine.

The mother of the four year old boy went up and sang and then the adults started going up to sing. Vito's was rocking until 11:30. Mr. Vito was thrilled; Karaoke night was a success.

Many people came to hear Deana sing at Vito's. They would tell Deana she had a beautiful voice and they enjoyed listening to her.

In response, Deana told everyone the same thing. "If you like what you hear at Vito's, you should check out the music I perform at Dothan Christian Church every Sunday morning. I play with two other very talented musicians and we have a wonderful sound together."

Deana lived out her faith. She loved her church and

enjoyed helping Pastor Beckmann increase the size of the congregation. If someone saw her sing Karaoke and it inspired them to come to church, Deana was happy.

As the month of May came to an end, the boys finished another school year. All three had very good grades. Matthew was hoping Deana and Leon would buy him a used car or truck. He was now sixteen and Leon had helped him learn to drive and get his license.

Deana did not want Matthew to get a job over the summer; she wanted to be with him and train him for the upcoming football season. Over the years, she and Leon had maintained respectable balances in their bank accounts. As a reward for getting good grades, training hard for football and being a respectful son, they bought Matthew a truck. It was a used 2008 Dodge Dakota quad cab. Deana shopped around and got a really good deal on it.

The boys were getting too old to ride the bus and it would make it far easier when their football practices started. Matthew agreed to help take Luke to his soccer practices when Deana couldn't.

The September after Deana and Leon married, Deana asked Leon's permission to combine all of their individual bank accounts into joint accounts. She explained it would be much simpler for her when she needed to pay the bills. Leon agreed. One September day in the year 2013, Leon deposited his work check and was in for a surprise when he saw the new account balance. There was over fifteen thousand dollars in their new joint account after Deana transferred her money over.

Leon never ceased to be amazed by Deana's generosity. He vowed to himself from that day forward he'd never waste one dime of that money. Deana trusted Leon and he did not want to let her down. Almost five years later, the truck would be the first big expenditure since the opening of their joint accounts.

July 26, 2018, was Mark's fifteenth birthday. The one thing Mark wanted the most was his learner's permit. Mark was ready to start driving. Deana took Mark to get his restricted driver's license and Leon and Matthew taught him how to drive their trucks.

All summer long, Deana, Matthew and Mark lifted weights, ran and trained for the upcoming football season. Even though Morrison was not yet quite a powerhouse, every one was looking forward to the upcoming season.

Luke's soccer season was also about to start. When Deana finished training Matthew and Mark for football, she would help Luke with his soccer. Luke was moving up this season to U10.

This would be his most difficult challenge yet. The U10 soccer fields were much bigger; the goalkeepers were better; the defensive players were more physical and aggressive. Deana was glad Luke enjoyed running with her to the park and to the little beach. Conditioning would be key to having success at this next level on the bigger fields.

In his first game, Luke struggled in the first half. He didn't even get any shots on goal. Luke had some nice passes but that was about it. His team was losing 2-0. As the second half wore on, his high fitness level paid off. He faked out a defender and then shot the ball as hard as he could. The goalie tipped the ball but it still went into the back of the net.

The score was now 2-1. With about seven minutes left in the game, Luke received the ball close to the goal. Two defensemen and a midfielder went to stop him. It left one of his teammates wide open. Luke passed him the ball and he scored. The game ended in a 2-2 tie.

Wednesday August 22nd, Deana turned thirty-one years old. Deana had to do Karaoke at Vito's so Leon took Deana out to dinner at her favorite restaurant in Athens on Tuesday night. Matthew took Luke to and from soccer practice, so Deana and Leon had the entire night to themselves. Leon had taken Wednesday off so he and Deana could stay out as late as they wanted. Leon and Deana went to the big lake in Athens for a romantic evening after dinner.

They went fishing in the smaller local lake by their house Wednesday. They played, fished, picnicked, and partied from late morning until mid afternoon. Leon and Deana had a great time until it was time for them to leave to meet Luke's school bus so they could drive him home.

Luke's birthday was the next day. He'd be nine years old. After his soccer game on Saturday, Deana and Leon took Luke for pizza and a movie before Deana had to go to work.

Friday, August31st, was Deana and Leon's fifth Wedding Anniversary. Leon had gotten the day off from work. Mr. Vito told Deana she had to work; he could not let her off. Deana was furious but it was not in her nature to complain. However, she did not speak to or even look at Mr. Vito for the entire week.

Mr. Vito, Leon and Deana's friends were planning a surprise party for her at the restaurant. Because Deana is so sentimental and sensitive, the ploy worked to perfection. Deana and Leon had gone fishing earlier in the day and Deana was fuming the entire time. She called Mr. Vito every name in the book without expletives. Well actually, there were a couple of expletives.

When Deana walked in the restaurant at 3:55pm and heard a loud "SURPRISE!!!," she started to cry. Balloons, party favors and friends were everywhere.

One of the first gifts Deana received was a new guitar from Leon. Over the past few weeks Gary had started getting donations from some of the wealthier members of Dothan Christian Church. Gary had received close to two hundred dollars. He'd given the money to Leon and suggested buying a new guitar for Deana with the money. The guitar he recommended was an Ibanez AEL20E Acoustic-Electric Guitar. Ibanez makes their own shape shifter pre-amp with an onboard tuner. The sound that guitar produces really is heavenly. Deana's own guitar was close to seventeen years old and the frets were about run down into the neck. Deana's old guitar would be a perfect starter guitar for Luke; he was starting to show interest in playing music like Deana.

Since Deana was now playing to large crowds, the new Ibanez was the perfect gift. Leon found one in a beautiful space blue color. Gary amped it up for her so everyone could hear Deana lay down her new sound. The new guitar truly was an amazing piece of art; Deana was overwhelmed with the gift.

Every one had food, fun and a really good time. Mr. Vito let her leave at 7:15 with Leon and Luke. They were on their way to Morrison High School to watch Matthew and Mark play their first home game of the season.

Deana had been impressed with how hard Matthew and Mark trained during the summer. They, in turn, were impressed with how hard Deana worked out. They seemed to feed off of each other, especially when they were lifting weights.

Morrison's defense again was very strong. They allowed only three first downs in the first half of the game tonight. Morrison had won the field position battle and capitalized on this. They were able to set up for a short field goal before halftime and went up 3-0.

In the third quarter, Burrington tried to open up their passing game. Their right tackle had been struggling to block Mark all game. On a third and ten play, Mark started the play lined up wide of the tackle. When the ball was snapped, Mark cut in front of him making him lose his balance. Mark smashed the quarterback and caused him to fumble the ball. Matthew had worked in from the other side and recovered it

Morrison had the ball inside the Burrington twenty-five. They took advantage of the short field and scored the only touchdown of the game. Morrison got in field goal range one more time in the fourth quarter; they made the kick and continued to play good defense. They won 13-0. Deana and Leon were very proud parents.

The biggest game of the year would be homecoming. Morrison would be playing Claybon, who was their biggest rival. It was such a big rivalry because of how near the schools were to each other. Most players and many parents knew each other very well. Claybon had won the last five meetings, but Claybon won by only one point last year in Claybon. Tonight's game was in Morrison.

Deana got to work early at 3:55, as per her arrangement with Mr. Vito, and was able to leave just after 7:30. She had a feeling Morrison was going to win tonight. Morrison's defense had not given up more than ten points to any team they'd played. Their defense was ranked third in the entire state.

"Tonight's game will be the biggest game we've ever played in," Matthew told Deana earlier that day at breakfast. "A victory tonight will guarantee us of a winning record for the season and mean a real turnaround for our football program."

Deana had never seen the laid-back Matthew that animated before. "It will probably make your homecoming dance tomorrow night a little more festive. I'm willing to bet if you guys win tonight, the dance will really be quite an event."

"I know Sandy is real excited and tomorrow will be our first double date." Matthew glanced at Mark as he spoke.

"Mark, how come you didn't tell me you had a date for the dance? I need to go buy you a suit tomorrow morning."

Matthew answered Deana's question before Mark had a chance to speak.

"Actually, Mark and I both need new suits. The one you bought me before is now too small for either one of us."

Apparently, one of Sandy's girlfriends had broken up with her boyfriend on Thursday. So at the last minute, she needed a date for homecoming. Sandy asked Matthew to check with Mark to see if he'd go with her. Mark said 'yes,' so it looked like Deana would be doing some power shopping early Saturday morning before Luke's noon soccer game.

The game against Claybon wasn't as close as the score would indicate. Morrison won 14-0. Claybon couldn't run or pass the ball. Matthew had three sacks and Mark had two. Claybon was forced to punt twelve times during the game. They were held to only three first downs the entire game. Morrison finished the season with seven wins and only three losses.

Everyone said this Homecoming weekend was the best in many, many years for Morrison. The boys had a great time at the dance. It was looking like both Samuels brothers had girlfriends now.

Luke's soccer team ended up with six wins, only one loss and three ties. It was good enough for first place in the division. Luke's coach wanted them to play in a Veteran's day tournament in Atlanta.

This time, Luke's team did much better. Playing better competition during the season paid off. They won three of their first four games. They qualified to play in the Championship game. They lost 2-1 but it was probably their best played game of the season. Luke had seven goals and four assists during the tournament. Everyone associated with the team was excited by their dramatic improvement.

Thanksgiving night, Leon and Deana arrived in Gatlinburg Tennessee. They rented their favorite cabin in the woods again. The mountains were as beautiful as Deana had ever seen them. Once inside, Leon ignited the fireplace. "What an amazing year it's been. It really is unbelievable the difference you've made in everyone's lives since you came to us from Tampa."

Michael Haden

Michael Haden

CHAPTER 20
THE END IS GETTING NEAR

Deana was upset. Christmas and New Year's Day were both on Tuesdays. There would be no extra days off this year. Matthew and Mark spent most of their Christmas break with their girlfriends. Deana understood and tried to make the best of it. She and Luke went Christmas shopping, to the movies and to the little beach at the park. At least he still enjoyed spending time with Mom.

On Monday December 31st, Leon, Deana and Luke shared a picnic lunch and fished. At night they fired up the burn pit and watched the end of the year countdown on television. They welcomed in the New Year and enjoyed each other's company.

New Year's Day they watched College Bowl games on television. All day long everyone talked about it being 2019. For the first time, Deana realized how close it was to 2020. Over six years had flown by; the extra time God had given her was almost up. When you are 25 years old, eight years seems like forever. Deana would turn 32 this summer.

Deana did everything in her power to not dwell on what may happen in 2020. Unfortunately, one night the harsh reality caught up to her. On a Tuesday night, she'd just returned from her walk and talk with Matthew. After the boys went to bed, Deana sat on the couch to the left of Leon. She rested the side of her body against the side of his body. She tucked her legs up and in with the flare of her skirt pinned between her knees. He put his left arm around her and Deana held his left hand with her right hand. She kissed the back of his hand. Then it all hit her like a ton of bricks.

Deana's deal with God was not to lead a long, prosperous life in Dothan, Georgia. It was to prevent something really bad from happening at Morrison High School on April 20, 2020. It would all be over very soon; Deana broke down and cried profusely.

Leon was worried. This was not like Deana. Yes, Deana was a very sensitive woman, but she had seemed like she was very happy. Leon thought things were going extremely well.

"Deana, sweetheart, what in the world is wrong?"

Deana was afraid to say anything. Part of her deal with God was for her to say nothing about the deal. Leon was her best friend and she desperately needed a friend right now. However, she had to be careful what she said. She looked Leon in the eyes. "I'm scared."

"I don't understand, what are you afraid of?"

"My time is almost up." Tears rolled down Deana's face. She wished she hadn't just said what she did, but it was too late.

"Now you've really got me confused. You're young; you're in perfect physical condition. When God takes you, he takes you; but what makes you think it's your time? If anyone should be nervous it should be me."

Deana stopped crying and tried to laugh. She knew she should not be having this conversation with Leon. Nothing positive could come from it.

Deana changed the subject. She told Leon that Karaoke Wednesday made going back to work after two days off not so bad. She was almost starting to enjoy Wednesday night.

Dothan Christian Church was full to capacity almost every Sunday now. Gary, Deana and Mrs. Jarvis had really perfected their sound. Some people initially came to the service just to hear them play; but they also got to hear a powerful spiritual message from Pastor Beckmann. It was a winning combination.

One Tuesday, Matthew asked Deana if Sandy could go on their walk with them. Deana was taken a little off guard, but said 'yes.' Since Deana had their undivided attention for a while, she told Sandy about the observation question she had posed to Matthew and Mark a couple of years back.

"Matthew, what did you notice about people you've known a long time who do drugs versus friends you know who stayed clean?"

"I really understand the point you were making. The kids that got into weed and other drugs almost all tanked by their early twenties. They almost all had criminal records and couldn't get or hold onto jobs. Most ended up living back home or in the State or County Condo.

Sandy laughed when Matthew used State or County Condo as slang for jail.

"What about the kids you know that stayed clean?"

"Most of them finished high school and went to college. They have good jobs and some of them have already started their own families."

Sandy understood the point Deana was making to Matthew. "I never would have thought to break it down that way," she exclaimed. "It's so true. I'm never going to do drugs or be with someone that does."

"Now we need to move on to something more complicated," Deana said. "Drinking alcohol is off limits until you turn 21. There will be temptations for you to start drinking before then, however. If you do drink, regardless of your age, please, please, please don't drink and drive. Call me, call your father or call your brother. Even if you're 30 years old, we will drive you home, no questions asked."

Sandy looked at Matthew and smiled. "You're lucky. Your step-mom really seems concerned about you. My parents never have talks like this with me."

Over two hours had flown by and they could see their house two blocks down the road. As they finished the last small part of their walk, Deana had one last request.

"You can tell me to mind my own business or tell me I am being unrealistic," Deana added. "If there is any way you can wait to consummate your relationship until after you are married, I would be so happy!"

The next Monday, Deana asked Mark to bring his girlfriend with them on their walk. There were a few things Deana wanted to talk to them about.

Valentine's Day this year was on a Thursday. It didn't deter Leon. He showed up at the restaurant just before 10pm. He brought Deana a bouquet of flowers and a little dolphin ankle bracelet in a cute gift box. Deana jumped up in his arms and gave him a big hug.

They walked to his truck with their arms around each other; they drove down to the lake and seriously celebrated Valentine's Day together. Leon and Deana made sparks fly as they warmed up a cold February night. Things got hotter and more intense than ever before.

On Sunday April 20th, 2019 Deana realized this was it. The final year was upon her. Deana refused to get down or be depressed. Life's a blessing and a gift; she wanted to embrace and enjoy her final year. She wanted to make it the best year ever.

When Deana played at church earlier that morning, she threw herself into the performance. Sunday dinner was even more elaborate than usual. She baked an amazing cherry cobbler she'd never made before. She was even more upbeat and friendlier to the customers at Vito's. Leon got even more attention from Deana, especially when the boys weren't around.

Monday, April 29th was Leon's 39th birthday. Deana got up extra early. She started cooking and baking for their day at the lake. She made butter basted fried chicken and all the fixings. Everyone had loved her cherry cobbler so much she thought she'd fix an apple cobbler for Leon's big day. All she had to do was fry up some okra and her picnic basket would be complete.

She had bought a new, white bikini just for today. It was even smaller than the blue one Leon liked so much. She was pretty sure he would like this one even better. She was right. She kissed Leon good morning even more passionately than usual. When he saw the new bikini, the picnic basket and the sparkle in Deana's green eyes, he knew he was going to have a very happy birthday.

Matthew, Mark, Sandy and Ashley had a great time at the Junior Prom. Even though Mark was only a sophomore, his girlfriend Ashley was a junior. Deana liked the double date concept. One brother would always be looking out for the other.

As May was ending another school year was coming to an end. All three boys made the Honor Roll. Deana and Leon were very proud.

The first week of June, training began. Running, lifting weights and skipping rope constituted most of the work out. The running gave the boys fitness and endurance. Lifting weights was for building power and strength. Skipping rope was also for endurance and to build and strengthen twitch muscles. Obviously, the training Deana did with the boys was paying off. The rumor was that a scout for Georgia Tech University was coming this fall to watch Mark play. Mark could get a scholarship to a Division 1 college.

If you are a football fan, watching Mark Samuels play linebacker is a thing of beauty. He is nasty, relentless and has a motor that does not stop. When he tackles an opposing player it's almost always a punishing blow. Offensive tackles and tight ends hate trying to block him. He never stops coming and never loses his intensity.

One poor offensive tackle on one of the weaker high school teams actually benched himself. Mark had beaten the kid all night long. In the second half, in the middle of an offensive series the kid takes off his helmet and hip pads and walks off the field. He tells the coach he's done and walks over to the bench to sit down. His coach had to use a time out to figure out who was going to play right tackle.

A dad of one of the Morrison football players came up to Deana and Leon during a home game and said jokingly, "Your son Mark goes after the other teams quarterback and then he goes after the rest of his family. He is one ferocious football player."

Deana was proud that Mark played with intensity but he never got one single unsportsmanlike conduct penalty. Also, he very rarely jumped off-sides. He played disciplined football.

Morrison went 7-3 in 2019 just like they did in 2018. A seven win season for Morrison was considered an extremely successful campaign. They were a small high school in comparison to the other schools they played. Morrison did not have many winning seasons in the history of the school.

On Thursday August 22nd, 2019 Deana turned 32 years old. If this was going to be her last birthday, she wanted to do something she loved. Leon and Deana took off from work and got Luke out of school for the day. They went back to the Georgia Aquarium. Deana and Luke absolutely loved the "Dolphin Tales" show. Friday would be Luke's birthday and she'd promised to bring him back, so this seemed like the perfect opportunity.

This year's show was even better than the show they'd seen a year and a half ago. The man sitting behind her said, "It's basically a dolphin Cirque du Soleil." Deana had heard Cirque du Soleil shows were very good. She was thrilled with all the cool new things she was learning. They had an early dinner at a nice restaurant then picked up something for Matthew and Mark. They rushed home to get Luke to soccer practice and be there for Matthew and Mark when they got home from football practice.

Saturday August 31st, was Leon and Deana's sixth Wedding Anniversary. There were two places Deana wanted to see one more time; Hilton Head Island and the beautiful resort just northwest of Athens.

Mr. Vito needed her to work Saturday night, but gave her Sunday off. It worked out well because Monday was Labor Day. Leon, Deana and all three boys were all off from work, school and practices. Luke had a soccer game Saturday at noon and she had to perform at church Sunday morning.

The most feasible option was to go to the resort. Deana and Leon could leave the boys off with Leon's parents and if an emergency arose they'd only be half an hour away. They could get to the resort early Sunday afternoon like they had done the first time they went there. The boys were happy to spend the holiday with their grandparents.

Deana and Leon got to the resort just after 1pm. Like six years before, they rented a beautiful cottage on the lake. The rose petals Deana loved so much covered the floor and bed. This time, she took a handful of the rose petals and threw them in the air and enjoyed their texture and fragrance.

Next, they went fishing on a lake that was three times the size of their little lake just outside of Dothan. Deana took extra time to enjoy its magnitude and beauty. As autumn approached, Deana was able to appreciate the splendor of the changing of the seasons.

Leon caught five fish and Deana caught three. With all the practice they had gotten over the past few years, both were improving as anglers.

Leon and Deana got back to their cabin just after 7:30pm and took showers to get ready for dinner. During the week Deana had gone into town and bought a little red dress. It was slightly more revealing than the black dress she'd worn six and a half years ago.

If you looked at Deana from the neck up, you definitely knew she was in her thirties. She had deep age and frown lines. She spent way too much time in the sun during her lifetime for a person with such a fair complexion. If you looked at Deana from the neck down, you would think she was in her early to mid twenties. She was just as tone as she was when she moved to Georgia in 2012.

The most amazing part of the resort was the five star restaurant it had on its premises. Not only was the food to die for, the seating was open air and the view of the lake and surrounding mountains was spectacular.

After dinner, the happily married couple walked through the beautiful gardens of the resort. This time Deana lingered over the natural beauty of the manicured paths. She noticed the star filled sky and enjoyed the wonderful smell of the late evening air coming off the lake. When Deana and Leon were alone on a hidden path, she kissed Leon with all the love and passion she had. She never wanted the moment to end…

The following morning, Deana and Leon didn't have to

rush to leave the resort like last time. Today was a holiday and Deana wanted to enjoy the cabin, the view and the sixth and final year of her marriage to her loving husband.

When Deana got to the restaurant on Wednesday, Delores was waiting for her.

"Do you remember Jerod Quinn from church? He asked you out when you first moved to Georgia."

"Of course, I haven't seen him in over a year. Whatever happened to him?"

"Jerod is now 30 years old. He got Lisa Hayes pregnant; she's only 17. He led Lisa to believe he would marry her; he then took off for Ohio to live with his cousin. Mr. Hayes is ready to shoot him."

"It seems God led me down the right path," Deana said. "It was very tempting to choose Jerod over Leon way back then. I just had a gut feeling God wanted me to choose Leon."

"It's because you didn't judge the book by the cover. You knew Leon was more mature and grounded. You knew he could give you a family. Deep down God let you know how to make the right decision."

Deana smiled. "I give God thanks and praise every day for allowing me to make the right decision. I have been truly blessed."

True to her word, Deana said another prayer of thanks as she got ready for Karaoke Wednesday. The restaurant was already starting to fill up.

Luke's soccer team went 8-1-1 and took first place again. They went to Atlanta for the Veteran's Day tournament again. This year they won the tournament. Luke added three new trophies to his wall. One for the division championship, a second for the tournament championship and a third for Most Valuable Player. Only God knew how much Deana was going to miss Luke.

On Friday December 20th, Deana got the email she'd been expecting for some time now. Mr. Wilson was on his death bed and would be passing away very soon. Mrs. Wilson asked Deana to come back to Tampa to say goodbye to him. Deana explained the situation to Leon and the boys and Mr. Vito. She packed a large suitcase and drove six and a half hours to Tampa.

When she got to the Wilsons' big house it was no longer an orphanage. It was for the most part a large vacant structure. What was once a vibrant home for many children was now a big, empty building with a for sale sign in the front yard.

It had been over seven years since Deana walked out of Tampa Hospital. Now she was walking back in to say goodbye to the man that turned her life around. Mr. Wilson was her mentor and dear friend.

"Deana Murphy, please come here and let me look at you. You are as beautiful now as you were as a young girl, maybe even more so," Mr. Wilson exclaimed.

"Thanks for the compliment." Deana did her best to hold back the tears; it was difficult seeing Mr. Wilson in the condition he was in. "I'm sorry for not coming back to Tampa to visit. My seven years in Georgia have been wonderful and amazing, but I really have missed you. I just wish you would have had a chance to meet my husband and our three boys."

"I understand," Mr. Wilson said. "Your calling from God was not in Tampa. Obviously He needed you to go to Georgia; I'm just glad you listened to Him."

Deana squeezed his hand as she replied. "Believe me, I heard God loud and clear."

Mr. Wilson fell asleep. Deana took a chair and put it next to his bed. She held his hand and started to cry. It was heartbreaking to see him like this.

Mrs. Wilson walked in and tried to console her. "Always remember Deana, death is not the end it's really only a new beginning."

Two days later Mr. Wilson passed away. Deana tried to comprehend what Mrs. Wilson told her. All she knew was that a new beginning scared her. She hated that Mr. Wilson had to die and the ramifications dying had on the ones you leave behind.

Mrs. Wilson waited until after Christmas to have the funeral. This would be the first Christmas in seven years that Deana would be away from Leon and the boys. Deana had a lot of time to think, cry and pray.

Deana was riding an emotional roller coaster. Mr. Wilson's death was hard to accept. The wake and funeral were emotionally draining; and she was really struggling trying to understand God's ways.

She went with Mrs. Wilson to the worship service at her Tampa church one last time. It helped to see so many old friends and acquaintances. But when Deana left Tampa on December 29th, 2019 she had a heavy heart. As she crossed the state line, she started to shake and cry. She pulled into a rest stop and found an area where she could take a walk and think.

Deana prayed and reminisced about the good times. She had four more months; she was going to make each one count.

CHAPTER 21
GETTING READY FOR 4-20-2020

Deana got home just before 6:30pm. The sun had already set. Luke was waiting by the door, eager to welcome her home. Leon rushed out to help her with her large suitcase. Matthew and Mark were on their way home after spending the day with their girlfriends.

Deana was tired; her eyes were red and puffy. She'd lost weight. Nonetheless, she marched herself into the kitchen and made one of the best Lasagna dinners she'd ever made. Later that night she enjoyed sitting by the burn pit with Leon and the boys. Leon rebuilt the burn pit for the New Year's Eve countdown Tuesday night. The five of them roasted marshmallows together.

Her smiles and laughter were a bit forced, but she smiled and laughed anyway.

The following Monday night, as she started her walk with Mark, Deana was wondering how she was going to figure out who was going to hurt Mark at school and why.

Mark could sense Deana's anxiety. "Deana, you look stressed. Is there something wrong?"

"I heard something kind of strange at work Friday night. I don't quite know what to make of it."

"What did you hear?"

"Policemen come to Vito's all the time. Friday two of them sat in my station. They were talking about one of your classmates. They said his name but I could not hear. The restaurant is very loud on the weekends. They said he was having trouble or some kind of dispute with his parents. For some reason they are monitoring the situation. Do you know anything about this boy?"

"I'm not sure who they were talking about. Are you sure you didn't hear part of a name?"

"No, I wish I did. Please keep your head up and your eyes open for me. The police made it sound very serious."

The truth was, Deana made up the story about the policemen and their conversation. She was trying to get any kind of clue or information from Mark. She knew the 'when' and 'where.' She knew part of the 'who' was Mark. She needed to know the rest of the 'who,' the 'what' and the 'why.' Deana also wanted to alert Mark that something was going on.

All Deana could do is pray and wait. Hopefully, in time, more clues and information would present itself. If it didn't she was in big trouble.

This year, more than in the past, Deana strictly enforced Special Night for Matthew and Mark. Every Sunday afternoon Luke and Deana spent two hours together. Deana loved spending time with the boys and they enjoyed talking to her. It was a great experience for all four of them. Most importantly though, it helped her keep an open dialogue with Mark.

"The boy Ashley dated before you, is he upset at you for taking his girlfriend?" Deana asked Mark one Monday night on their walk.

"I don't know why he would be. When I started dating Ashley, he started dating Jennifer Allen. Jenny is smoking hot and they're still dating each other."

On another Monday night toward the end of February, Deana asked Mark," Do any of your friends or any of the other boys have really bad tempers. Have you ever noticed a mean streak in any of them?"

"The only kid I know that remotely fits that description is Randy Mullins. I've known him since second grade. He likes me, but he is one of those 'I hate the world' kind of kids."

"Is he violent? Have you ever seen him go off the deep end?"

"No, never. He just talks a lot of crap. He hates the baseball coach for cutting him. He hates the teachers for giving him bad grades and he hates the principal. He's said on occasions he would love to cap all of them. Randy is just talk."

Deana quickly changed the subject. She asked Mark if he would go back to Turner field with her this April. Mark said he'd love to. Deana praised God; she may have gotten the lead she needed.

"Delores, what do you know about Randy Mullins?" Deana inquired two days after her talk with Mark.

"I know a lot about the Mullins. They live on the street behind me. I know I'd never want to get them mad at me."

"Why is that?"

"Gerald Mullins was in Special Operations in the military. He was given some kind of unusual discharge. Rumor has it he beat the heck out of quite a few Iraqi police officers. He was training the policemen and he heard they backed down from a fight. I guess Gerald wanted to toughen them up. When he got home, he was in a bad mood. Now his disposition is even worse. I've heard him beat his dogs and I pray he doesn't beat Randy or his wife Nadine."

There was a good chance Deana may have found the 'who' and possibly even some of the 'why.' She was thankful for the progress.

It broke Deana's heart when she thought about what her death would do to Luke. Imagine being under twelve years old and being told you have to bury your second mother.

Deana was everything to Luke. She was his cheerleader. She never missed a soccer game. Deana cooked and prepared all of Luke's meals. She was his best friend and confidant. If Luke ever had a problem, he had a rock solid woman who had his back. Deana was the source of his confidence.

When Leon was at work and the boys were at school, Deana would rigorously train. She lifted weights, ran 3-5 miles per day or skipped rope. She spent hours on her music; she rehearsed alone or with Gary and Mrs. Jarvis. Often, when no one was around, she broke down and cried. She loved her life and didn't want it to end.

As March was coming to an end, Deana stayed committed to enjoying the last weeks of her life. Her cooking skills were better than ever and she took the time to enjoy every meal. Her Sunday performances at church were awe-inspiring. She made love to Leon every single night. They shared more passion and more depth than any other time in their relationship, which was already extremely good. The kisses were even sweeter and Leon was late to work quite a few times.

Even work was more enjoyable. The job she hated seven and half years ago, and all the way through college, no longer seemed that bad. In hindsight, if Deana was not a waitress, it would have been almost impossible to raise three boys the way she did. Working only 25 hours per week from 5 to 10pm, and making what most people make working full time, gave her time to be a homemaker. She could cook, clean and invest time in the boys. She was now grateful for the opportunity she had been given.

Monday March 30th, 2020 would be one of the last times Deana would be able to talk to Mark before the big event happened.

About 15 minutes into their walk Deana turned to Mark. "How is your friend Randy doing?"

"Randy is a strange guy. He's real upset at our English teacher Mr. McAfee. He gave Randy an 'F' on his term paper. It's 1/3rd of our grade. If Randy fails English and one other subject he will not have enough credits to graduate next year no matter what he does over the summer or how good a senior year he has. Randy is livid; he says if he fails, Mr. McAfee will pay dearly."

"What do you think he means when he says he'll make McAfee pay dearly?"

"He keeps talking about wanting to bust a cap in the guy."

Deana acted as if she was surprised. "Do you think Randy would actually bring a gun to school and shoot a teacher?"

"A while back I would have said 'no,' but the way he's been acting lately, I'm not so sure. He definitely talks a big game."

"Hey Mark, while we're on the subject of big games, how about we hit Turner Field next week?"

Mark nodded his head enthusiastically, giving Deana the answer she was hoping for.

It was now Sunday April 12th, 2020. Like every Friday, Saturday and Sunday evening Darla Robertson went to Vito's and drank a lot of wine with and after her dinner. Mrs. Robertson was a widow in her late 50's. She would drink until Deana, Delores or Peggy cut her off. Tonight, Mrs. Robertson was in Deana's station; she liked Deana the best.

That night Deana tried a different approach. She did not cut Mrs. Robertson off, she let her keep on drinking. At 9:45pm Deana approached Mrs. Robertson's table.

"Last call Mrs. Robertson." Mrs. Robertson was too drunk to get her debit card out of her purse.

Deana assisted the older widow. "Let me help you with that." Deana pulled Mrs. Robertson's debit card out of her purse and took care of the transaction for her. "I'm going to have to drive you home, Mrs. Robertson; you can come get your car tomorrow morning."

"You are such a dear, Deana." Mrs. Robertson held onto Deana for support as she walked with assistance to Deana's car. Fortunately, Mrs. Robertson was small like Deana and Deana was extremely strong.

Monday, April 13th was Matthew's birthday. At breakfast he mentioned to Deana that he wanted to take Sandy to dinner and a movie after school. Deana was glad to treat; she gave Matthew sixty dollars and told him to have a good and safe evening.

"Oh Matthew, by the way, I need a favor, make sure Luke gets to his bus stop all right. I need to run into town for about an hour."

Deana hurried to her car and drove quickly to Morrison High School. She needed to know the morning routine for the school janitor. She got out of her car and walked around the school campus. The janitor was in the furthest left of the four buildings; he proceeded to go left to right. Deana got in her car and drove away before Matthew and Mark arrived at school. They always got to school at the very last minute.

That night, Deana and Mark went for their walk. It was mid-April and the weather was getting warmer every day.

"How's your friend Randy doing?"

"Not so good. It's almost certain McAfee is going to fail him and Randy is also failing Math. Randy keeps saying he is going to make McAfee pay. Apparently, Randy, Randy's dad, McAfee and the principal are going to have some kind of talk on Friday. Maybe something will get worked out."

Maybe something will happen Friday that will push Randy over the edge, Deana thought to herself. Maybe this meeting going badly will make Randy lose control.

Tuesday morning, bright and early, Deana went back to Morrison High School. The janitor kept the same pattern as the previous. He would start at the left, which was building 1A and finish in building 4D. Deana left Morrison High School before Matthew and Mark arrived. She then headed to Athens to find a good costume shop.

Deana bought a black colored men's hair wig with curls in it. It looked quite realistic and was very expensive. She also purchased a matching mustache. Deana also bought a woman's wig that looked like Mrs. Robertson's hair. Her final purchase was a janitor's one piece jump suit. It was very similar to the one worn by Morrison High School's actual janitor.

Deana had borrowed Mark's baseball cap and Matthew's sunglasses. She had worn these and a baggy blue jacket into the store. She made sure to pay cash for her purchases.

Next, Deana drove to the biggest retail store in Athens. She bought a big yellow mop cart and mop like the actual janitor had. She also bought a pair of ladies dress gloves and a box of clear skin-tight latex cleaning gloves. Her final item was a medium sized air-tight container.

Finally, she went to a chemical supply store one of her customers owned. Deana obtained a pint of pre-mix ether.

On her way home she drove past the Mullin's house. It was after 3pm so she was hoping Randy would be there so she could get a good look at him. Deana only knew what he looked like from a yearbook picture; she wanted to see what he looked like in person.

Sure enough, he was in front of his house working on his truck. He was very big. He was almost as large as Matthew and Mark. Randy was well over six feet tall and close to 200 pounds. Deana got a nervous feeling as she drove past him; Randy glared at her with a look of disdain.

Deana drove home to meet the boys and to start dinner.

She now had a plan; she also had a lot of praying to do.

Friday's meeting at the school did not go very well for Randy Mullins. In front of Randy's father and the principal, Mr. McAfee reported that Randy was extremely lazy and had a bad attitude. He said Randy deserved a failing grade. Randy became enraged while Gerald Mullins mainly glared at his son. When they got home later, Gerald Mullins gave Randy the beating of his life. Gerald showed no mercy.

Randy vowed vengeance against Mr. McAfee in order to teach all instructors like him a lesson. Not only did he want to annihilate his teacher, he also wanted to vent his rage on as many of the "kiss ass" students as possible. Monday morning it would be Randy showing no mercy.

Sunday April 19th, 2020 would probably be Deana's last performance at Dothan Christian Church. She made sure it was her best effort. That week, Gary, Deana and Mrs. Jarvis had rehearsed for two and a half hours. The hard work paid off. They performed for over twenty minutes during the service and received a standing ovation.

After the service, Deana went to talk to Mrs. Robertson. "If you come to Vito's tonight and sit in my station, I'll get you a free drink or two."

"I will definitely take you up on your offer." Mrs.

Robertson smiled. "I always have such a nice time when I come to Vito's."

Sunday afternoon during lunch, Deana told the boys she had to go to her doctor in Atlanta on Monday morning. Her appointment was at 8am so she'd be leaving early that morning to get there on time. She told the boys the doctor always made her turn her cell phone off during the visit. If they needed her, they'd have to text her and she'd get back to them as soon as possible.

Later that night, Mrs. Robertson went to Vito's and sat in Deana's station. Deana knew she had a high tolerance for wine and it would probably take over six glasses to get Mrs. Robertson tipsy. Deana gave Mrs. Robertson the two free glasses she promised her, and then Mrs. Robertson ordered five more on her own. She was sloshed. When Deana's shift was over, she went into Mrs. Robertson's purse and took out her debit card, automobile insurance card, and driver's license. She carried Mrs. Robertson to her Stratus and drove her home.

When Deana got home, the boys were just going to bed. She kissed all three of them good night. She made a mental note where Matthew put his truck keys before the lights went off. She then took a quick shower and snuggled up next to Leon. Because their time together was drawing to an end, she did everything she could to make it extra special.

In the middle of the night, Deana snuck into the boys' room. She brought two pair of pliers with her; one pair was needle-nosed and the second pair was regular. She proceeded to break Matthew's ignition key in half beyond repair. She wanted the boys nowhere near Morrison High School tomorrow morning. Deana took the broken bottom half and put it on Matthew's floor mat under his ignition. She wanted it to look like it had broken the last time Matthew pulled the key out. She hid the top part of the key still attached to his keychain under his bed.

On the other side of town, Randy Mullins was also making preparations. Randy broke into his father's gun collection. He stole his father's pride and joy, an AK47 Gerald had taken off of an Al Qaeda insurgent that had illegally snuck into Iraq when Gerald was on patrol. An AK47 is an assault rifle; it can put an end to a lot of lives in a few seconds.

Randy also stole his father's hammerless snub nosed handgun. It is one of the premier concealed weapons in its class. Last, but not least, Randy stole a 22 revolver. The two handguns were small, discreet and easy to carry. His plan was to give the two handguns to his friends for back-up while he did the heavy damage with the AK47.

Randy's two friends were Larry Jones and Mark Samuels. He sent text messages to his two friends saying he needed a little help Monday morning. Neither boy returned Randy's message which angered him even more.

He put the three weapons inside a big duffle bag and locked the bag inside the cab of his truck. Monday morning he would wreak havoc at Morrison High School. In Randy's mind, it would all be Mr. McAfee's fault.

Just after 7am, April 20, 2020 Deana parked her car on the other side of the shopping mall where the car rental business was located. Last Friday, Deana had verbally reserved a minivan over the phone using Darla Robertson's name. Deana made an excuse saying she left her credit card at her office and the dealer allowed her to make a verbal reservation.

Deana put on the wig to make herself look like Darla Robertson's driver's license picture. She had put on the dress gloves to not leave any fingerprints. She used Mrs. Robertson's driver's license, credit card and proof of car insurance to procure the minivan. Deana asked the dealer to not run the credit card because she was paying cash when she brought the van back in a few hours. Deana then left a large cash deposit.

"I should be back before lunchtime. I'm just running up the street for a little while to help my daughter move to a bigger apartment."

Deana didn't believe she would be back in a couple of hours. She didn't think she would be back at all. Nonetheless, she had to be prepared for anything. Deana was confident she had planned well and had every base covered.

Deana drove the minivan to the other side of the mall where the Stratus was parked. She transferred the janitor's big cleaning pail on wheels, a mop, the airtight container with the ether soaked rag, one gallon of water, dish detergent, the jumpsuit, other wig, mustache, and a second pair of see-through tight latex gloves to the van.

She was wearing a pair of see through gloves now underneath the dress gloves, to not leave fingerprints. Deana wanted extra protection in case she'd have to handle the ether soaked rag later so she took off the dress gloves and put on the second pair of clear latex protective cleaning gloves. She wanted two layers of latex to keep the ether away from her skin. She was confident the fact she wore dress gloves at the car rental business did not send up any red flags.

When Deana had gotten into her car earlier she had prepared a stamp addressed envelope to Mrs. Robertson. If Deana made it back later today, she'd slip the driver's license, the proof of car insurance and the debit card in the envelope so she could mail them back to Mrs. Robertson. Deana would pay cash so Mrs. Robertson would not be billed.

Deana switched wigs. She put on the mustache and jumpsuit. She had worn her hair in a ponytail so she could put it inside the back of the jumpsuit so no one could see her hair. She had done this earlier at the car rental store. She had worn a high neck blouse and she tucked her hair down the back, inside of the blouse.

It was after eight o'clock when Deana drove the rented van into the parking lot of Morrison High School. Both days last week, the janitor started at 7am in building 1A. At 7:30 he moved to building 2B. At 8am he worked in 3C and finished 4D between 8:30 and 9am. First period started at 9am.

Matthew was a senior; Deana knew his locker was in 4D. Mark was a junior; his locker was in 3C. Randy Mullin's locker had to be in 3C. Just before 8:30, Deana watched the janitor leave building 3C and enter 4D.

Deana got out of the van. She took out the big cleaning pail on wheels, the mop and the container with the ether soaked rag. She put a gallon of water in the pail with dish detergent. Only one gallon of water made the pail light in weight, a lot of dish detergent made the pail look full due to all the bubbles.

She rolled the big cleaning pail into building 3C and pretended to clean very close to where Mark's locker was. Deana's anticipated that Randy would wait until as close to 9am as possible. That would allow him to maximize the damage because more students would be at school at 8:55 versus 8:25.

If Randy had gotten to school early, Deana would have

seen his truck. It was now 8:40am; there was no sign of Randy or his truck.

Deana pretended to clean as time dragged on. If the real janitor doubled back or someone in administration realized there was a janitor at school that didn't belong, she would be unable to stop Randy.

At 8:49 Deana saw Randy Mullin walk through the doors of building 3C and walk right past her. She moved the mop pail out of his way. Randy looked very aggravated. He went to what was obviously his locker and opened it.

Deana got out her container with the ether soaked rag in it. Randy unzipped the duffle bag. Deana saw the outline of the rifle as he started to pull the AK47 out of his bag.

Deana had practiced all weekend holding her breath as long as she could. She could easily hold her breath fifty seconds. She might have to go longer than that right now. Deana quickly took the ether drenched rag out of the container with her right hand. She bolted up behind Randy and forced her right hand and rag into Randy's face as she used her left hand to pin the back of his head down so the rag would temporarily stay affixed to Randy's mouth and nose.

Deana's strength, a huge surge from her adrenal gland and a very strong ether mix dropped Randy to the floor as the AK47 escaped the duffel bag and fell to the floor in plain view of every one present.

A boy had gone to pull Deana off of Randy. He had Deana in his grasp. When he saw a teacher grabbing the rifle off the floor during all the commotion he was temporarily distracted. Deana elbowed him hard in the ribs. The boy let go of Deana as she pulled away with all her might. She spun loose and ran as fast as she could to the parking lot.

Deana jumped in the minivan and drove off of the Morrison High School grounds as fast as she could. She took off the gloves, mustache and wig as her van entered the main road. The police were coming in as she was going out.

Deana bee-lined to the car rental company. She was utterly shocked she made it out alive. She was proud of herself for taking down a young man as large as Randy Mullins. He had hit the floor like a ton of bricks and was knocked out cold by the ether. He would never, ever hurt anyone at Morrison High School. If he ever had the urge to hurt anyone again, it would be at the State or Federal Condo!

CHAPTER 22
A SECOND SURPRISE ENDING

Deana drove the minivan back to the mall to where her Stratus was parked. She put the janitor uniform, black wig and mustache, empty gallon jug, detergent, and used gloves into her Stratus with the stamped addressed envelope to Mrs. Robertson. She put the Mrs. Robertson wig and dress gloves back on.

Deana settled up with the car rental office and walked back to her Stratus. She put Mrs. Robertson's license, insurance card, and debit card into the pre stamped and addressed envelope. Deana drove to the Post Office, mailed back the items, and drove home.

Last Friday, when no one was around, Deana had buried a

large metal box in the backyard. When she got home from the post office the boys truck was still in the driveway. They must have gotten a ride to school because no one was around. Deana quickly got a shovel and unburied the box. She put the jumpsuit at the bottom of the box with all three pair of gloves. She put the two wigs and the mustache on top of the jumpsuit and gloves. She took two pounds of hamburger and put that on top. She drenched the inside of the box and all its contents with lighter fluid. Then Deana lit a match and ignited the contents of the box.

Minutes later, it was impossible to tell what had been in the box. The fire ruined everything except the hamburger and some of the wig and mustache fibers. The hamburger would draw maggots. If anyone in the future were to discover the box, it would look like the remains of a dead animal or pet.

Deana covered the box and the hole. As she put the shovel back in the carport, she heard Mr. Vito's car driving up the road. When Matthew and Mark couldn't get the truck started, they called him to take them to school.

Mark ran up to Deana. "Why haven't you answered your cell phone? You'll never believe what happened at school today. Some mystery janitor stopped Randy Mullins from smoking half the school."

"Crap, I forgot to turn my cell back on after my doctor's appointment." Deana acted surprised at the news. "That is incredible! I want to hear all about it. I guess you boys are getting the day off from school today."

"Yes ma'am," Matthew replied. "It's a good thing because we need to go into town to get a new key made for the truck. The original key was a piece of garbage."

Later that evening, Deana went to the restaurant and talked to Mr. Vito.

"Mr. Vito, first of all, thank you for taking the boys to school today. It was very sweet of you. Second, I have some sad news I need to share with you. I've worked here close to eight years and except for the passing of Mr. Wilson, I've never had more than four days off in a row. I'm tired and I feel stressed out. I have to…"

Mr. Vito cut Deana off in mid sentence. "What did the doctor say this morning?"

Deana had temporarily forgotten about her fictional visit to the doctor's office, but she recovered quickly. "He said I'm run down and need to retire."

It was not the answer Mr. Vito wanted to hear. "Are you saying I need to replace you?"

"Yes sir. It breaks my heart to leave you, but my time is up."

Mr. Vito was stunned.

Deana thanked Mr. Vito and gave him a hug. She quickly walked out of the restaurant. If she would have stayed any longer she would have broken down and cried.

Deana went home and relaxed on the couch with Leon. She told Leon her decision about work. He was surprised, but not upset. Deana had a queasy feeling in her stomach she was hoping was caused by nerves. She prayed it would get better, but she was not very optimistic.

The next morning, on her way to church to practice for Sunday, Deana still felt sick to her stomach. She felt bad about missing practice yesterday, so she worked extra hard today. The song she chose was a slow sad song in contrast to the upbeat, fast tempo songs they usually played.

Deana got back home just after lunch. She went into the bedroom and got on her knees in front of the bed as she stared at a large cross mounted on the wall. Deana began to pray. As she did, tears filled her eyes. Then she began to talk to God.

"Oh Lord, I realize when I first came to Dothan I was unhappy here. When I first met Leon I thought he looked like a hillbilly and I misjudged him. I am so, so sorry. I love Dothan; the people here are wonderful friends and family. I love Leon and I love our boys. I don't want to leave them. I know I've asked a lot from you over the years. This is my final request. I know we had a deal. But I'm begging you, once again, to let me stay."

Tears streamed down her face. She repeated this prayer three more times. At the end she finished with, "Lord I'm begging you to let me stay. There's more good I can do."

Deana climbed onto her bed and meditated. When she was about to start dinner, she kneeled in the kitchen and prayed more until she heard the boys come home.

Every morning and afternoon, Deana prayed. She prayed for Luke. She apologized profusely for disliking Leon when she first met him. She admitted those terrible feelings were wrong. She swore she was madly in love with Leon because, in fact, she really was. She pleaded for God to show her mercy one last time.

Over the weekend, Deana and Leon discussed plans for Leon's 40th birthday which would be on Wednesday. Leon told Deana he was having trouble getting the day off from work.

Deana asked Leon if next weekend they could go to Hilton Head Island to celebrate his birthday. Deana desperately wanted to go back to Hilton Head Island one last time. Since she wasn't working, going over the weekend would be perfect.

Leon agreed. "I'll get off work early on Friday and we can leave Dothan before rush hour. We can have a fun couple of days."

Monday morning Deana got to church early. She wanted to have time to pray before Gary and Mrs. Jarvis arrived. She asked God for forgiveness and for mercy. Tears streamed down her face as she put her entire heart and soul into her prayers.

Unfortunately, every day that went by, Deana felt worse and worse. She felt sicker and sicker. Deana spent even more time in prayer; some days praying for five or six hours.

By the time Friday came around it was May 1st. Deana was nauseous and throwing up all day. However, she was not going to allow her sickness to ruin her opportunity to go to Hilton Head Island.

When Leon got home, Deana had her things packed for the weekend. Matthew was now an adult and he agreed to take care of Luke and keep an eye on Mark.

Deana took some medicine to try and settle her stomach. She was determined to tough the vacation out. The entire ride she was sick and felt awful.

When Deana and Leon got to their hotel room, they enjoyed the magnificent view of the Atlantic Ocean. Then Deana got sick again. She alternated between going to the bathroom and resting on the bed.

Saturday morning was the worst. She could not keep any food down and had a splitting headache. All she could do was rest in bed or sit in a big chair. Deana and Leon tried to watch a movie, but Deana spent most of the time in the bathroom.

Upon Deana's fourth return to the bed, Leon asked an

unusual question.

"Deana, honey, when was the last time you got your period?"

"It was between the first and second weeks of March." Deana looked surprised at Leon's question. "I've had an inconsistent cycle my entire life. I've been later than this before. It's nothing to worry about."

Leon tried not to laugh and Deana did not see his quick smile.

"Deana, I need to run to the store real quick. Is there anything you'd like for me to get you at the store?"

"Maybe some ginger ale, sometimes that helps settle my stomach."

Leon went to the store to buy Deana a home pregnancy test. Leon had seen Rebeccah go through what Deana was experiencing.

Thirty five minutes later Leon walked back into their hotel room. Leon took the home pregnancy kit out of the box with the directions and told Deana to go in the bathroom and do the test.

"You've got to be nuts. Five different reproductive specialists all told me I can't have children."

Leon reached out and held Deana's hand. "Please, just humor me; if I'm wrong, I'm wrong. This will only take a couple of minutes."

Deana went into the bathroom and followed the test instructions. A few minutes later, Leon heard: "OH MY GOSH!!! I CAN'T BELIEVE IT!!! Leon, We're pregnant!"

It was the first time Deana ever saw Leon cry. He had a huge smile on his face. As tears flowed from his eyes, they embraced each other. The joyful news of Deana's pregnancy was the perfect birthday gift.

Deana found a wonderful OB/GYN in Athens that specialized in high risk pregnancies. She took fantastic care of Deana the entire pregnancy. Toward the end of June, Deana went for her first ultra-sound. She was having a baby girl. In the almost eight years Deana had known Leon, it was the happiest she'd ever seen him.

"Leon, I have the perfect name for our daughter. At the hospital, when I give birth, I will tell you the name."

Over the summer, Matthew graduated high school with honors. He rented an apartment in Athens with a friend. It was located only three blocks away from the University of Georgia where he would be attending in the fall.

Leon and Deana hired a contractor to expand the rear of their home where the boys' bedrooms were. The contractor enlarged the rooms and created a cute bedroom and bathroom for a little girl.

On Friday December 25th, 2020, Deana, Leon, Matthew, Mark, and Luke welcomed baby Johnna into their family.

Deana's doctor was incredulous. "Mrs. Samuels, the odds of you conceiving and giving birth to a healthy baby were probably about a half million to one."

Deana smiled. "Maybe the odds get better when there's Divine intervention."

Later that night, after Leon and the boys went home and baby Johnna was back in the hospital nursery, Deana fell into a deep sleep. God spoke verbally to her one last time.

"Deana Samuels, the baby is your reward. Enjoy a long life. I am very proud of you, my daughter."

Deana pressed her hands together in prayer. "Lord, I'm so grateful, thank you so much."

Matthew, Mark, Luke, and Johnna
with
Mama Deana and Big Papa Leon

Michael Haden

ABOUT THE AUTHOR

Dean Michael Polizzi A.K.A. Michael Haden is a successful Tampa business man and volunteer girls Division 1 competitive soccer coach. His inspiration for this book came from the girls he's coached. He currently coaches for FC Tampa and has coached some of the most amazing and fascinating young women to ever play sports in West Central Florida. Dean has coached well over two hundred young women and each one has their own amazing story.

Please visit: www.ADealWithGodBook.com.

Made in the USA
Lexington, KY
21 February 2016